OUT OF
THE FIRE

by

Deborah Froese

SUMACH
PRESS

To my mother and father,
who planted seeds for
the character of Gram.

NATIONAL LIBRARY OF CANADA CATALOGUING IN PUBLICATION DATA

Froese, Deborah, 1957-

Out of the fire: a young adult novel
ISBN 1-894549-09-0
I. Title.
PS8561.R5908 2001   C813'.6   C2001-902018-X
PR9199.3.F77508 2001

Edited by Rhea Tregebov
Cover & Book Design by Liz Martin
Cover portrait by Jen Duncan

Printed in Canada

Published by

SUMACH PRESS

1415 Bathurst Street, Suite 202
Toronto ON Canada M5R 3H8
sumachpress@on.aibn.com

www.sumachpress.com

ACKNOWLEDGEMENTS

This story exists because some incredible people were willing to share their time and personal experiences. My good friend Barbara-Ann Hodge, an occupational therapist specializing in burn injury at Winnipeg's Health Sciences Centre, provided me with research material and answered countless questions about the medical aspects of burn recovery. She shared her professional and personal insights and lent a guiding hand as I shaped all of that information into a story. Barb, I could not have written this book without you.

Barb also introduced me to Jane, a young woman who shared with me the pain and triumphs of her own burn recovery. I was in such awe of what she had gone through that I could not write for weeks after meeting her. Thank you, Jane, for your generosity. I was — and am — deeply moved.

I would also like to thank George Nytepchuk for demonstrating physical therapy for burn injuries; Linda Sparrow, RN, for reading one of my early drafts; and friends and fellow writers Melissa Kajpust, Linda Holeman and Patti Grayson for all of their support, reading and otherwise.

When this project was in its early stages of development, the Manitoba Arts Council was kind enough to award me a grant. I'm very grateful to them, not only for the financial benefits of that grant but also for the accompanying morale boost.

Thanks also to Lois Pike, Beth McAuley and Liz Martin — the women of Sumach Press — for taking on this project with such enthusiasm. My editor, Rhea Tregebov, saw clearly what I could only sense. She was a delight to work with, generous with her criticism and praise — keys, I believe, to a polished work. Thanks, Rhea! I'll never look at commas the same way again.

Last, but certainly not least, I'd like to thank "the boys," all four of them, for letting me leave the laundry for another day.

* * *

The following materials were of great assistance in writing this novel: Patricia N. Watkins, MD, et al., "Psychological Stages in Adaptation Following Burn Injury: A Method for Facilitating Psychological Recovery of Burn Victims," *Burn Care Commentary: A Forum for Burn Care Issues,* Augusta Regional Medical Center, Winter 1989; and Stacy Robberson, RN, BSN, *An Introduction to a Pictorial Book for Burn Patients and Their Families,* Sherwood Medical Company, 1992. The brief quotations from Tennyson are from Alfred Lord Tennyson, "In Memoriam A.H.H." (1850), and "Come Not, When I Am Dead" (1850), both of which are found in *The Oxford Dictionary of Quotations,* Revised Fourth Edition, Oxford University Press, 1996. The references to the Mockingbird song are taken from "Hush Little Baby," a Southern lullaby whose author is unkown.

PROLOGUE

For weeks after it happened, images of that night came to me in fragments, like scraps of shredded paper or parts of a jumbled puzzle. Some days I wanted to put the pieces together; most days I just wanted to bury them in the past with the person I used to be. But the memories refused to rest.

Of everything that happened, it's the light I remember most clearly, a light that gave me hope when nothing seemed hopeful and courage to go on when I knew that nothing would ever be the same again.

The light stays with me even now, shining through clouds, illuminating shadows. It reminds me that there's more to life than flesh and blood and the distorted reflections of mirrors.

Some fires flare up with a lit match, others simmer slowly below the surface where you can't tell what fuels them. Those are the worst kind. They gather heat and momentum, and when you least expect it, explode with a gluttonous rage.

— OLIVIA BROWN

CHAPTER ONE

Friday, May 16

AMY SAT UNDER AN OLD ELM TREE, tangled in the grey shadows of its branches. She clutched her knees to her chest and stared down the grassy slope to the river. Bud whimpered and licked her fingers.

I crossed my legs and leaned into the rough bark of the tree next to hers, peeling back the tab on my soft drink can. I held it out to her, hoping she would say something, anything — even "yes" or "no." But she shook her head.

A thin veil of pewter clouds slipped over the sun and Amy squeezed her eyes closed, as if to ignore the changing weather, the awakening breeze that flicked feathery strands of hair into her face. Her bottom lip quivered.

A squirrel's chatter split the silence and Amy jerked to attention. She plucked threads of hair from her mouth and licked her lips. Then finally, she sucked in a deep breath and spoke. "Someone broke into our house last night, Dayle."

"What?" I bolted upright, splashing cola on my jeans.

"We were robbed."

"Robbed?"

Amy's eyes flickered open, tears pooling around her lower lashes. Bud nuzzled her cheek; she gently pushed him away. "Somebody smashed the back door window and got inside and ripped through everything." Her voice cracked. "Everything."

I crept across the grass and sat in front of her. "Oh, God. That's awful. Were you home when it happened?"

Amy shook her head and blinked furiously. Tears streamed down her cheeks. "No. Dad was at work and Bud and I were out for a walk."

"Why didn't you tell me? Sooner, I mean?"

"I tried calling last night, but you were out. I left a message ..." Amy's shoulders quivered. Thin raspy sounds rose from her chest.

I chewed my bottom lip. I had noticed the red throb of the answering machine's message light when I got home last night, but I'd left it for Mom or Denise to worry about. I had wanted to float into bed without breaking the enchantment of another evening with Keith. How could I have been so selfish? I grabbed Amy's hand. "You should have told me this morning."

"In school?" She pulled her hand away and wiped her eyes with the back of her fist. Mascara smudged the parchment skin below her eyes. "So I could cry and look like a total idiot?"

I swallowed hard. Something, some weird thing, like the faint echo of a familiar voice, had nagged me from the moment I'd climbed out of bed that morning. It told me I should walk to school with Amy instead of riding with Keith. But I'd ignored that nagging feeling, just as I'd ignored the answering machine. I should have clued in sooner; Amy had barely spoken to me all day, and when we met in front of our lockers, her eyes wouldn't meet mine.

"Did the police come?"

Amy nodded. "Two cars. Without lights or sirens. Guess they thought it was no big deal. They took fingerprints and photographs, though, just like on TV. They think two guys broke in."

"I can't believe this. What did they take?"

"All kinds of stuff. The stereo. The TV. My computer." Her voice fell to a whisper. "Mom's jewellery."

"Oh no." I could feel Amy's dismay. Her mother had died from some mysterious virus when Amy was only three, long before I met the Frosts. All Amy had of her mother was the photograph on her dresser — a long-necked woman in denim and pearls — and a pink plastic box full of costume jewellery.

"Why would they want all that stuff? The computer and TV ... they're so old ... and the pearls ..." Amy stumbled, then caught her breath. "The pearls weren't even real."

I just shook my head.

"And I'll probably never see any of it again. That's what the police told me." Amy clutched her knees to her chest. "Oh, Dayle. That's not even the worst part. The worst part is the way the thieves —" her voice broke. She shook her head and gulped. "The way they ravaged everything. They threw dishes on the floor, pulled books off shelves, smashed walls. And they went through all the stuff in my bedroom. My diary. My clothes. Even my underwear."

"Your underwear?"

Amy pressed her forehead into her knees. "One of them left dirty hand prints on a pair of panties."

"Yuck!" I wrinkled my nose. "Burn them."

"I can't. The police took them away for evidence."

Leaves rustled on a branch above me. A small grey squirrel leaped out of hiding and landed on a bare limb, exposed for the world to see. Bud cocked his head to the side, his eyes fixed on the animal.

I finally managed to speak. "Thank goodness you weren't home."

"I guess. But it feels like I *was* home. It feels like it was me they attacked, not the house." Amy's voice fell to a whisper. "It's just not fair."

I squeezed her shoulder lightly. "I'm sorry, Amy. I wish I'd been there."

"I'll be okay." Amy cleared her throat and straightened her back. "So, Dayle, what about this summer? Are we staying at the lake again?"

Her abrupt turnaround sent a blur of bittersweet images whirling through my head. I wasn't ready to think about the lake. Not yet.

"I need to know. If we're not spending summer at the lake, I have to find somewhere else to go. I have to get away from here."

I searched for something to say. "Isn't your dad off to the Yukon for the summer? You've always wanted to pan for gold."

"He won't have time for that. And I'm not interested in going on an entomology expedition. So?"

I pressed my heels into the ground. "I'm not sure, Amy."

"Because of Gram? The lake won't be the same without Gram. Part of me doesn't want to go either." A clear sadness ringed Amy's words. She watched me for a moment, waiting for me to say something.

My tongue felt swollen and dry. It wouldn't move.

Amy's face tightened. "You're staying home to be with Keith."

I quickly swallowed a mouthful of cola to wash away the dryness.

"I should have known." Her voice bristled.

My head jerked up. "But Amy, I —"

"You'd change your whole life for a guy?" Amy's eyes narrowed.

"It's not my whole life. It's just the summer. And Keith is not just any guy." I fought to keep my voice level, to stay calm. Amy made my relationship with Keith sound insignificant, but we'd been together for fifteen weeks — since the last day of January. It wasn't as if we spent every second together — Keith was too busy for that — but we shared something special.

"He's going away in the fall, anyway, isn't he? To some Ontario university. So you're just wasting your time." Hard lines settled over Amy's face.

My back stiffened. Amy had a knack for zeroing in on touchy subjects. Keith's plans for the fall were one more thing I didn't want to think about. I'd be stuck in town for another year finishing high school while Keith was miles away meeting new people, doing exciting new things, living life without me.

"Oh please," I said. "Let's not do this again. It isn't worth arguing about." I squeezed the aluminum pop can and watched brown foam bubble over the lip.

"You've got that right." Amy yanked a chocolate bar from the pocket of her faded grey cotton shirt and ripped off the paper wrapper, letting it swirl into the wind. Bud perked his ears and sprang toward her. She pushed him away with her leg. "You have to sit if you want to share. Sit." The German shepherd sprawled on his belly with a sad, pleading look in his eyes.

"That's not sitting," I said.

Amy opened the foil. She broke off a square of chocolate and waved it in front of Bud's damp, twitching nose. He whined. "Go get it, Bud." She tossed the treat past him and he whined again, but he didn't move.

"You know dogs can get sick if they eat chocolate." Amy ignored me. She threw another piece skyward. Bud leaped up and snapped it out of the air.

"He's never going to learn." I sighed. "You keep giving him treats. He probably thinks he's doing what he's supposed to. Besides —"

"You can't teach an old dog new tricks." Amy folded the foil back over the remaining bar and tucked it in her pocket. "I don't believe that. Bud's smart. He's just too independent to take orders." Bud nuzzled her pocket and gave a soft yelp. Amy opened the bar again and held it out in the palm of her hand. He swept it up in a single gulp and took off after the squirrel, who had been stupid enough to leave the safety of his tree.

Amy was such a pushover for Bud. That bugged me. She'd do anything for her dog, but she wouldn't give *me* a break. I pulled myself up from the ground. "Sure would be nice if that dog would listen."

Amy rolled the chocolate bar foil into a small ball and squeezed it in the palm of her hand. "He's a loyal friend and he's protective. I wish he'd been there last night when those jerks broke in."

Bud would have ripped them to shreds, I knew that. But that wasn't the point. I stared up at the troubled sky and I could almost see Gram gazing down at me with that little crease of worry between her brows.

I blinked to clear my vision and cleared my throat to steady my voice. "Maybe we can spend a couple of weekends at the lake." I looked from the clouds to Amy. "Mom wants to open the cabin the last weekend in May. That okay with you?"

I didn't bother telling her that it wasn't okay with me. That weekend would mark my four month anniversary with Keith, but Mom was determined to schedule our trip then anyway.

Amy's brows arched. "Your birthday's that Saturday. Isn't there a Chameleon concert? I thought you and Keith would be —" She stopped short and changed course. "The weekend after next. That'd be great."

We both turned our heads toward the river. With my eyes closed and the sound of water slapping against the riverbank, I could almost imagine Amy and me in front of a crackling bonfire with Gram. I could almost feel the pleasant, warm glow of the flames on my face and hear Gram strumming her guitar ….

Kum-ba-yah.

I shook my head and opened my eyes. An empty beer can twisted and bobbed on the river, as if to fight the current hurling it toward the Lockport Bridge. It disappeared in a froth of white at the edge of the locks. The crush of falling water would pound it into oblivion. Gone, in an instant. Like Amy's sense of security.

Like Gram.

"Are you taking the urn?" Amy hugged her knees.

"You sound like Mom. What's the rush?" I picked at a small, hard nubble of thread on my jeans.

"Sorry. Just asking." Amy's voice lowered. She stared at the ball of foil in her cupped hand. "Do you know what Olivia means?" Olivia was Gram's name. Olivia Brown.

"No. Not exactly."

"It means olive tree, keeper of the peace."

I knew what our keeper of the peace would have to say now about the tension growing between Amy and me: *Friendship outlasts romance.* Gram always spoke those words as if she had a personal relationship to them.

The sun slipped out from behind the clouds. As it warmed my face, I met Amy's gaze.

Her voice brightened. "Do you want to go to the pool tomorrow morning, swim some laps?"

"Sure." I grinned. "Just don't haul me out of bed at six a.m."

She smiled back. "I'll let you sleep till six thirty. What about tonight? What if we rent a couple of videos? We haven't done that in ages."

"Okay. We can order Pantini's Pizza, or maybe Chinese, and get that new release, the one with ..." My voice faded.

"What's wrong?"

"I forgot. It's Friday night."

"I know. So?"

I rubbed the sticky cola stain on my jeans. "I told Keith I'd go roller blading with him, but —"

"Keith would *never* understand the concept of a friend in need, would he?" Amy sprang to her feet and slammed her hands into her hips.

She didn't give me a chance to tell her I'd cancel, that Keith *would* understand. That I could go roller blading any time. I shook my head in exasperation. "Why don't you cut Keith some slack? Cut *me* some slack?"

Amy's lips stayed tight and blue for a moment. She twirled a thin strand of dark hair around her right index finger. "You've changed." She spat those words at me with a ferocity that made them sting.

I fought the urge to fling something back at her and spoke as calmly as I could. "People change. They grow up. What's wrong with that?"

"A year ago you wouldn't have liked Keith's crowd."

"A year ago we both drooled over Keith on the basketball

court."

"Yeah, and we drool over the guys in Chameleon too, but that doesn't mean we'd date any of them."

"You mean we wouldn't stand a chance of dating any of them."

"You just don't get it —"

"Get what?"

"Keith Hutton and his friends are such ... such jerks! They're nothing but a bunch of spoiled, stuck-up rich kids with nothing better to do than have a good time." Amy folded her arms across her chest and turned her back to me.

"How can you say that?" Fire laced my cheeks. "You don't know them. You've never tried to get to know them. How many times have I asked you to come along with us? But you never do. You've got homework or yardwork or that dog of yours to walk."

Amy's left hand squeezed into a fist over the ball of chocolate wrapper foil.

I swallowed hard and tried once more to reason with her. "Look, I know Jade can be a bit hard to take. Everybody feels that way. We just put up with her because she's Sam's and Marnie's cousin. And Pete is, well, kind of rough around the edges, but you need to get to know him. It's just an act. He doesn't want anyone to know he's really a pushover."

Amy glanced over her shoulder at me. "I thought he was just crude."

"That's only when he's had a few drinks."

Amy pitched the foil ball to the ground. "Guess he drinks a lot. Like Sam and Cougar and all of his other buddies."

"That's not fair. Look, if you'd just spend some time with Keith and me — or Marnie. I know you'd like Marnie. She reminds me of you, and —"

Amy spun around. "You're different since you've been with them. Like now, ignoring me when I really need —"

"I am not ignoring you."

"Sure you are. You'd rather go roller blading with Keith than watch movies with me."

"I never said that. You didn't give me a chance to —"

"Keith wouldn't hesitate to break off a date with you, would he?"

"What do you mean?" I drew myself to my feet and jammed my hands into the pockets of my jeans to keep them from curling into fists.

"I mean Keith isn't exactly dependable, is he? You never know when he's going to call."

My face flamed. Amy had struck another nerve. The truth was that I didn't always know when I'd see him, or if I'd see him. "Keith has a load of responsibilities."

"I'm sure."

I hated feeling as though I had to defend him. "He's got basketball practice and games every week, and he works hard to keep his grades up. When he's not busy with basketball or school, he's working with his father."

"So he's a busy jerk."

"That isn't fair, Amy. You're just jealous." There. It was finally out in the open.

Amy's voice rose defiantly. "How can I be jealous? I don't even *like* Keith." Her eyes narrowed. "You're out of your league, Dayle Meryk." Her shoulders straightened and she suddenly spoke in a matter-of-fact tone. "Gram would have hated him, you know."

For a second, my heart stopped beating. I stood slowly, my face cooling into a stone mask. Amy had no right to make judgements on Gram's behalf. Angry words bounced around in my head, but I couldn't hold onto any one of them long enough to formulate an equally wounding comeback.

Amy jerked her head away toward Bud, who had the terrified squirrel backed up against a rock. She whistled. Bud gave the grey lump another sniff and it leaped forward, nipping his nose. Bud stepped back, barked at the squirrel, then bounded toward us.

I pivoted on my heels and forced my stiff legs to carry me away from the river, toward the road where Amy's truck was parked. I marched across the prickly grass with Bud trotting along beside me.

"Bud, you get back here right now," Amy called after him.

The dog circled and barked and sat down beside Amy's rusty old green Chevy half-ton. I stopped there too, but only long enough to yank my backpack out through the passenger side window.

"Dayle! Wait! Dayle!"

Amy's voice burned in my ears as I stomped from the park to the highway. By the time I reached the bus stop, I heard Amy's truck rumbling up from behind. She turned north onto the highway and slowed to stare at me. The truck idled there for a moment. Bud cocked his head to the side and barked expectantly.

That made me feel worse than ever.

I could have made things better right then. I could have brushed Amy's remarks aside and hopped into the truck. I could have told her that I'd cancel my date with Keith, let her know that I missed pizza and egg rolls and Friday night movies too. That would have been the noble thing to do. Instead, the sting of her words lodged my tongue in my throat and stubborn pride welded my legs to the ground.

I stared across the highway into the trees as if the green truck wasn't there. It jerked and squealed and left a strip of rubber along the asphalt. Bud hung his head out the window, tongue lolling. He, at least, was happy — he usually had to ride in the middle.

I watched the truck speed away until it finally dissolved into a tiny green speck. Then I looked down the highway in the opposite direction, praying for Beaver Bus Lines to come to my rescue and carry me back to Selkirk.

It would be easy to avoid swimming with Amy tomorrow. What sane person got up before ten on a Saturday, anyway? But the lake. That was another matter. It wasn't the sort of invitation that could be taken back, even though now the thought of spending a whole weekend there with her twisted my stomach into a tight knot.

How can you be angry with someone and worry about them at the same time?

Two weeks. I had two weeks to find a way out.

CHAPTER TWO

THE CLOUDS THICKENED with my mood. Four o'clock. Four thirty. Dozens of cars whizzed past, but no bus. Eventually a red speck materialized over the distant grey asphalt. As thunder began to roll, the red speck grew into a rusty old Honda Civic with a colourful graffiti-like mural on the hood. An odd mixture of relief and anxiety swept over me.

Even before the car began to slow, I knew it would stop and that's exactly what it did. Stu Ingaldson leaned across the seat from the driver's side and cranked open the passenger side window. "You want a ride back to Selkirk?" He blinked and tugged at the tiny gold ring in his left nostril.

I checked the southern horizon again; still no bus in sight. Lightning flickered overhead. A gust of wind sprinkled rain on my cheeks and through Stu's open window onto the passenger seat. He brushed the water away and wiped his wet palm on the leg of his jeans, leaving a soggy hand print behind.

Mr. Chivalry, from an age long dead; charming in his own inimitable way.

Stu raised his left eyebrow and blinked at me through rain-speckled glasses. "You getting in?"

I gave him a quick smile and opened the door. As I slid onto the vinyl seat, I had to manoeuvre my feet around a plastic tray full of paints and brushes, carving tools and a lump of plastic-wrapped clay with a price tag still on it.

"Sorry 'bout all this stuff." Stu leaned over my leg to pick up the tray. He tilted and turned the tray, banging it into my legs, but he couldn't wiggle it out from between the seat and the dashboard. His long, dark ponytail slipped over his shoulder and brushed against my knee.

"It's okay, Stu." I tried to shift away from the pressure and heat of his arm, the uncomfortable tickle of his hair. "I've got enough room."

Stu put the tray back down on the floor and sat up, his face red. He shifted the car into gear and pulled back onto the highway.

"So." He cleared his throat. "What were you doing in Lockport?"

"Waiting for a ride home." I forced a smile, hoping I could sidetrack Stu with evasiveness. He had an annoying way of worming details out of me and I wasn't in the mood to share.

"Oh." The flame on his cheeks deepened and his mouth tightened.

"It's been a weird afternoon," I added quickly.

"It's probably the weather." Stu brightened. "You know, weather really does affect people. What they do. How they think about things. There's a lot of electricity in the air today."

I kept my eyes focused straight ahead. I could feel Stu's gaze shift between the highway and me, searching with an eagerness that almost made me wish I'd stayed on the side of the road. I cleared my throat. "First thunderstorm of the year."

"Supposed to get at least an inch of rain tonight," Stu said.

"As long as it doesn't rain all summer." The stiff words matched the feeling in my cheeks.

"It's going to be hot and humid until the end of the month. Then it's supposed to get real dry and stretch out into an Indian Summer. That's what the *Farmer's Almanac* said and it's usually right."

"*The Farmer's Almanac?* I didn't know you were into farming."

Stu chuckled. "Just tomatoes and the *Almanac.*"

"Tomatoes?"

"Yeah. I like cross-pollinating them. It's a hobby. I'm looking to create the sweetest, juiciest tomato ever."

His enthusiasm made me smile. "You mean there aren't enough kinds to choose from already?"

He shrugged. "Not the same as creating my own. Maybe I'll call them 'Stu's Tomatoes.'"

"Like stewed tomatoes?"

He laughed. "Exactly. And I want them to have dark red skin, almost like the colour of ripe cherries. Have you ever noticed how many different shades of red tomatoes come in?"

I shook my head and grinned. "No. But I'll think of it now every time I look at one."

Lower Fort Garry slowly materialized on the right, then disappeared. The Beaver Bus I had been waiting for flew past us on the left, dousing the windshield with water. Stu leaned forward and flicked on the radio, scanning the stations until Chameleon's latest single hummed through the speakers.

> *Perfection is haunting me,*
> *Images of your face.*
> *I'm addicted, I'm spellbound*
> *Dying for your embrace.*

"You like these guys?" he asked.

"They're pretty good."

"The lead guitarist plays some mean riffs; he's got a solo CD out now."

"Really? I bet it's great."

"Yeah. I've got it. Strictly instrumental. Lots of acoustic guitar. Maybe the rest of the band will let him play some of his own stuff at the concert on the long weekend. I know that probably won't happen, but — hey, are you going?"

"No." A cool film of sweat began to prickle my forehead. "You?"

"Yeah. Camped out overnight to get tickets. Front-row seats."

"Front-row seats? Lucky you." I licked my dry lips, searching my brain for something brilliant to say that would change the direction of our conversation.

"Front-row *centre*." A wide smile softened Stu's face.

"Wow." I felt my entire body stiffen in panic as I waited for the invitation that I was sure would follow. But Stu's smile dissolved into a deep blush and to my great relief he didn't say anything more. For several minutes, radio music and the gentle swish and whine of windshield wiper blades were all I had to listen to.

Then Selkirk came into view. Stu's back straightened and he licked his lips. He braked for a red light just before Pantini's Pizza. "Maybe," he cleared his throat and kept his eyes on the light. "Maybe you want to go to the concert with me. I've got two tickets."

My heart flip-flopped in panic. I should have changed the conversation when I'd had the chance. Why did he keep asking me out when he knew I was going with Keith? How could I say "no" without hurting his feelings? "Uh ... we're going to the lake that weekend." The words tumbled out too quickly.

"Oh. Well. That'll be nice, spending your birthday there." Disappointment flattened his voice.

Heat seared my face. How in the world did Stu know it was my birthday? Why did he have to know? I wanted to melt through the floorboards and onto the asphalt.

"You want to listen to my CD sometime?" Stu's voice cracked as he spoke.

"Sure," I said. I stared at the stoplight. Red. Like ripe beefsteak tomatoes.

Turn light, turn ....

Stu stared straight ahead through the red light. His shattered expression reminded me of the one Amy wore when I told her I had a date with Keith. I gripped the gleaming door handle, tempted to open it and run the rest of the way home. I didn't care if I got wet. The rain would cool my cheeks. It could wash over me until I was clean and free of my problems with Amy and the stickiness of Stu's crush.

Why couldn't we just be friends?

CHAPTER THREE

STU'S CAR BACKED OUT of the driveway as I closed the front door behind me. The smell of dinner filled the air, but it was overpowered by a blaring radio and a loud, off-key voice that could only belong to my sister. The real singer — whoever it was supposed to be — couldn't be heard over the screech.

From the foyer, I could see Denise in the kitchen, flipping pork chops in the non-stick frying pan, her hips swaying in time to drums. "Denise," I hollered, "I'm home."

"Oh!" Denise's shrieking instantly ceased. She reached for the small radio on the open shelf by the kitchen window and quickly turned it off. A tinge of red coloured her cheeks. Tomato red. Like overripe cherry tomatoes, I thought, if I had to choose.

"Where's Mom?" I kicked off my runners.

"Working."

"Still?"

"Don't sound so surprised. It's not even six. A last-minute interview." Denise glanced at a cookbook on the kitchen counter and sprinkled herbs over the pork chops.

"Figures." I dropped my backpack to the floor and flopped down on a kitchen chair, then ran my index finger over the hard grain in the old honey-stained oak table.

The table had been Gram's, one of the few things she had

brought with her when she moved in with us all those years ago. Every nick and scar, every little scratch in the surface of that table had a story to tell about Gram, just as the strong curved grain of the hardwood told stories about the tree it came from. Six months ago, Gram would have been sitting with a cup of tea in the chair across from mine, waiting for me to come home after school and tell her about my day.

Denise put the cover back on the frying pan and turned to look at me. "What's wrong?"

My eyes stayed on Gram's chair. "What do you mean?"

"I mean you're frowning, and you're staring at that chair ...." Denise cleared her throat. "So?" She shook her wavy, long blond hair behind her shoulders and placed one hand on her slender hip.

"There's nothing wrong," I said curtly. "When's she coming home? Mom, I mean."

"Six thirty." Denise picked up a bag of long-grain rice and studied the cooking directions.

I undid the clasps on my backpack. "She's never here."

"Well, that's not exactly true. She's just not always here when you need her."

"Who says I need her?" I pulled my biology textbook out of the backpack and plunked it on the kitchen table.

"You did. Not in so many words, but —"

"Oh, Denise. Give me a break. If you like to interrogate people so much, you should have stayed in law school."

She laughed. "You sound like Dad."

"Why didn't you at least finish the year, after doing all that work? You were so close to exams."

Denise shrugged.

I flipped open the cover of my biology text. A bright blue "sticky" note clung to the top page.

Need some help studying
this weekend?

"You had a four-point-zero average." I ran my fingers over Keith's neat, familiar handwriting — something of a cross between printing and a carefully written script — and closed the cover on my textbook again, smiling. He never signed his notes. He didn't have to.

"Doesn't mean I liked what I was doing." Denise poured a carefully measured cup of rice into a pot of boiling water. "I'm not interested in becoming a lawyer."

I'd heard all that before. "Funny that you lost interest in law and Gavin at the same time."

Denise's head jerked up from the stove. A light flush touched her cheeks. She plunked a lid over the rice and studied me for a moment. "It took me a while to realize that I didn't want to be a lawyer, that I was only there because it was what Mom and Dad expected me to do. As for Gavin, he had a lot of expectations too. I guess I grew up. He didn't." She smiled, more to herself than to me. "It feels good to be doing what I want for a change."

"Well, Gavin's no loss." I picked a freshly peeled carrot stick from the cutting board next to the stove and crunched into it.

"Hey!" Denise glowered playfully. "I just finished peeling those for supper."

I shrugged. "They're better raw anyway."

"You never liked him, did you?"

"Who?"

"Gavin. Don't play dumb."

"He was too polished. Like marble. Cold and slick." I grinned.

"Ooo, don't hold anything back. Please." Denise gave me a light shove. She smiled.

"So. Have you decided what great and wonderful thing you're going to do with your life now?" I picked up the butcher knife and began to chop the carrots into smaller pieces.

"I've thought about it, but I'm not sure." She pointed at the carrots. "Make sure you cut those up evenly, or they won't cook properly."

"Yes, oh Master Chef."

"I don't know much about cooking but I do know *that*."

I grinned. "You like telling people what to do and how to do it. Maybe you should be someone's boss. Or a teacher."

"I want to do something creative. I've always denied my creative side."

"I didn't know you had one," I teased.

Denise tore lettuce leaves into bite-sized pieces and arranged them neatly in a glass bowl, tucking bits of red leaf lettuce in between various shades of green. "Everyone has a creative side. Some people just don't explore it."

"So what changed? Why did you suddenly decide to —"

"Gram."

"Oh." I put the knife down and took a deep breath. I'd never associated Gram's death with the dramatic changes in Denise's life before, even though they were only months apart.

The delicate, curved ridges of Denise's throat moved up and down a few times. Her voice trembled. "People always say life's too short. They're right." She dropped the frying-pan lid on the counter with a rattle and poked a fork into one of the pork chops. Drops of watery juice sprang like tears from the wound.

* * *

Mom held the pork chop down on her plate with a fork and sawed through it with a steak knife. She swallowed a mouthful of meat. "Thanks for cooking dinner again," she said.

Denise grimaced at a chunk of dry meat speared onto the end of her fork. "Are you sure you want to thank me for this?"

Mom smiled. She flicked her fork through a mound of buttery carrots. "It's only overcooked because I was later than I told you I'd be. Anyway, it's better than I would have done. Never bothered learning how to cook. There was always someone else around to do it." She looked at Gram's empty chair and a long sigh escaped her lips.

I rolled a small piece of meat around my plate with my fork, but I couldn't bring myself to eat it.

Denise swished her glass of milk. "Guess there's always takeout."

Mom put her fork down and cleared her throat, then put on her fake cheerful voice. "Well, thinking of your grandmother, are we still on for the last weekend in May?"

Denise shrugged. "I guess."

All my troubles with Amy bubbled to the surface. "Can't we wait a little longer? I'm not ready to ... you know."

"I understand that, Dayle. But you might *never* really feel ready to spread Olivia's ashes. And you did promise her."

"I know, Mom." I struggled to keep my voice from rising. "But first I want to decide where I should do it. Gram never had a chance to tell me, but I know there's someplace special —"

"And how will you know where that is, unless you go to the lake and take a look around?" Mom asked softly.

I felt my cheeks burn. "I'm not sure."

"Over the water would be nice." Denise poured soy sauce on her rice.

"Maybe," I said, more calmly. "But I have to think about it."

"Just make sure you're not using that as an excuse to delay things." Mom cleared her throat. "I know it's difficult. But the longer you put it off, the longer —"

"What Mom? What? The longer it takes to get rid of every last trace of her?" I slammed my fork onto the table, angry with Mom for pressing me, angry with myself for losing my temper.

Mom's face paled. "That's not fair, Dayle. Olivia and I had our differences, but I miss her too." She clutched her glass of ice water. "I was trying to say that sometimes delaying commitments can make them more difficult to carry out."

I stared at a dark drop swelling on the side of the soy sauce bottle. "Sorry."

Denise glanced from my face to Mom's. "Why do you — did you — call her Olivia instead of Mom or —"

"Or Mother?" Mom straightened up in her chair without taking her eyes off her plate. "I've told you before. I don't really know why."

Denise gently pressed on. "But there must be a reason."

"I've just called her that as long as I can remember." Mom frowned. "No. That's not right. I did call her Mother when I was younger."

"So?" Denise put her fork down and folded her arms in front of her chest. "Why the change? When?"

"I suppose it started when I was about eleven or twelve."

"Isn't that when Grandpa died?" I wiped the swollen drop from the bottle and licked it off the end of my finger.

"Sometime around then." Mom took another forkful of meat.

"So you started calling her Olivia because Grandpa died?" Denise leaned forward. "That doesn't make sense."

"You sound like a lawyer," Mom said.

"Or a journalist." Denise grinned.

"Wonder why Gram didn't ask to be buried next to Grandpa instead of being cremated," I said.

Mom dabbed her lips with a napkin. "Ashes to ashes, I guess. Olivia was keen on that sort of thing. And her ties with the lake run deep. Anyway, I believe the cemetery Dad was buried in is full."

"So?" Denise pressed on.

Mom's eyes rested on Gram's chair again. "Everything changed when Dad died." She paused, then shook her head. "I was almost a teenager then. Must have been hormones. Did you see the mail, Dayle? There's a letter there from your father."

About face. From one prickly subject to another.

CHAPTER FOUR

A PALE VANCOUVER POSTMARK told me that Daddy had mailed the envelope over a week ago. I smoothed my hand over its linen-textured surface, hopeful and anxious at the same time.

Pushing aside the mound of stuffed bears covering my bed, I sprawled across the lacy white comforter and opened the envelope. Several photos and a cheque fell from between the creases of a single sheet of paper. My throat tightened. The cheque was larger than usual this time, dated for my upcoming birthday — one hundred and seventy dollars — ten dollars for each year of my life. Guilt money.

... Carmen ... a joy to watch ... can't wait for you and Denise to meet her ... sales soaring ... best year I've ever had ... I'll have to miss my summer visit again ... so very sorry ....

My eyes were drawn to the photographs of Carmen, Daddy's new *Sweet Pea,* a cute round baby with dark wavy hair and a toothless smile. How old was she? About six months? Her pudgy dimpled hands gripped a small pink teddy bear.

Would Daddy would buy her a room full of bears? Would he spend hours playing checkers with her as soon as she was old enough to move the pieces? Maybe he'd stick around long enough to teach *her* how to play chess.

I picked up a photo with Daddy Dearest in it, a wide smile consuming his face. One arm cradled Baby Carmen, the other clutched a young woman with long and loose dark curls. Daddy's new wife. Cassandra. She was so beautiful that, for a moment, I felt a pang of sympathy for Mom.

I rolled onto my back and stared at the white ceiling of my bedroom. Everything in my room was white, from the comforter and curtains to my dresser and bookshelf. I liked the monochromatic look, the clean and untouched image it presented.

I raised the photos over my head and studied Carmen again. The curve of her face, her cupid-bow lips; so many of her enviable features came from Daddy. Neither Denise nor I were lucky enough to inherit his dimpled cheeks or long dark eyelashes. We were blond and pale, like Mom. Like Gram. All I got from Daddy was poor eyesight.

I crumpled the photograph and let it fall to the floor. Daddy's letters were a waste of time. I glanced at the clock. Seven ten. Keith would be knocking on the front door in about twenty minutes.

After a hasty shower, I sat in front of my bedroom mirror to put on my makeup. An annoying twang and howl rose from Denise's room, digging into my flesh and raking my nerves with all of the day's anxieties. The noise grew louder. I slammed my mascara brush back into the tube and marched across the hall. I didn't bother to knock. "Would you stop it, please?"

Denise sat cross-legged on the floor, a guitar in her lap. Gram's guitar. Her eyes were closed and a dreamy expression softened her face. "Kum-ba-yah my Lord, kum-ba-yah ..."

Denise's intensity was almost comical. Laughter bubbled into my throat, but I kept it to myself and smiled instead.

"Denise," I said, more softly, "could you keep it down a little?"

Her eyes popped open. "Dayle? Oh." Her face flushed. "Why didn't you knock?"

"Uh ... you were kind of loud. You wouldn't have heard me anyway."

"Sorry. I almost had it."

"Had what?"

"The chord. I mean, I think I almost lost the buzzing sound."

"You're not pressing the strings down hard enough."

Denise looked down at the guitar and squeezed the neck with her left hand until the tips of her fingers whitened. She ran the pick across the strings with her other hand. The buzzing was as obnoxious as ever. She sighed. "Doesn't work."

"Try this." I crouched down and repositioned the fingers of her left hand. "If you press down *between* the frets instead of *on* them, it'll sound a lot better."

Denise strummed the guitar softly and the chord rang true. She gave me a smile. "Maybe *you* should be the teacher, Dayle."

I grinned. "No thanks."

"Oh, come on. It'd be fun."

"Well, maybe."

"Tell you what, if you teach me how to play the guitar, I'll teach you how to cook."

I laughed. "You call that a fair trade?"

"It'll be easier on your ears."

"Deal."

"You can borrow the guitar any time you want, you know." Denise looked thoughtful. "I always wondered why Gram gave it to me instead of you."

The lighthearted feeling that had been sweeping through me vanished. "Thanks," I said. "But I've given up on music." I left the room, closing the door firmly behind me.

The guitar was a sore spot. It had always seemed unfair to me that Gram had given Denise the guitar, when she'd never shown any interest in it. As I brushed my hair, Gram's voice came back to me in a whisper: *That sister of yours needs to learn to develop her creative energy. Have some fun. Life is too short to be so serious.*

Gram was probably right about Denise; she did seem to be a lot happier since she dropped university — and Sir Gavin Scott. I wondered how Gram would feel if she knew how much of an effect she still had on my life. All of our lives.

I laid the brush down and my eyes fell on a slender Wedgwood-blue porcelain jar on my dresser. Gram's urn. Mom had balked at the idea of me keeping it in my room — so had I, at first — but I couldn't take the thought of abandoning it to some other room. At least here I knew it was safe. Gram was safe.

Once, out of curiosity, I had peeked inside. The ashes were large and coarse, not fine and powdery as I imagined they would be. It was as if Gram had fought the heat, refusing to disintegrate, resisting the finality of the flames. I shivered. How did anyone know for sure that the dead couldn't feel themselves burn?

I picked up the photograph beside the jar. Forget the ashes. I would remember Gram by her portrait; a smiling woman with fading blond hair, thick and straight, cut in a chin-length bob that framed her face perfectly.

I studied my reflection in the mirror. I looked a lot like her, except for my hair, which had a slight wave, and my eyes. Hers were hazel while mine were pale blue, like Mom's and Denise's. I practised my smile, turning my head from side to side. Long blond hair just like my sister's fell loosely over my shoulders — framing a perfectly balanced oval face, large eyes, a slender nose and full lips. Even without Daddy's dimples and decadent eyelashes, I liked what I saw.

I glanced at the other picture on my dresser, a snapshot of Gram, Denise, Amy and me at the lake. Mom took it last summer, when I still wore glasses and my bangs were thick and blunt. I looked like a bookworm destined for spinster-hood. *You've changed.* That's what Amy had told me, disgust in her voice. Maybe I *had* changed, but as far as I was concerned, the changes were for the better. The outside "me" finally matched the inside "me."

If I were still the mousy Dayle from years gone by, I would have spent the year hiding behind schoolwork with Amy. I wouldn't have won the female lead in the school play last Christmas and Keith might never have noticed me. And being with Keith changed everything. It gave me a real social life and friends with money enough to go places and do things. Kids who had plans for the future and the means to make those plans happen. All of this would have been so much grander if Amy had tried to share the excitement with me. But Amy never gave Keith a chance.

My eyes stung. I dabbed the tears away with a tissue so mascara wouldn't smudge, then opened my drawer and pulled out a small scrapbook with folk-art angels and hearts on the cover. I put the note from my biology text inside the scrapbook with all of my other sticky notes from Keith — brightly coloured squares and rectangles with messages like *Missed you last night* or *Found your earring* or *Congrats on the math test — sure pays to study your figures!* or *Glad you told me about your Gram. I would have liked her.*

Just because Keith was planning to go the University of Waterloo with Pete in the fall didn't mean our relationship had to end.

The sound of Keith's Jeep rumbled up through my window from the driveway. I sprinted down the stairs before he had a chance to ring the bell, trying not to think about Amy and the horrible way she'd been feeling since the robbery — vulnerable and terribly alone.

It didn't have to be that way.

I took a deep breath and put a smile on my face before I opened the front door.

CHAPTER FIVE

Tuesday, May 27

THE STEADY *PA-THUNK* OF RAIN against the school cafeteria windows echoed my mood. For over a week, Amy and I had been avoiding each other. Each lonely day dragged on under a rising veil of heat, grey and damp, haunted with echoes of thunder.

As if that wasn't bad enough, I hadn't seen much of Keith since the date that had caused so much trouble between Amy and me. It had been a great evening, running on past midnight with takeout egg rolls from Lee's and enough conversation — spoken and otherwise — to keep me from brooding over Amy.

The excitement of Friday night carried me through Saturday — and a shopping trip to Winnipeg. I was so sure Keith would ask me to his grad that I had bought a dress to wear — a slim-fitting sapphire number with a low-cut back and a daring neckline.

But Keith had to cancel our Saturday night study session to help his father and Friday night's glow quickly faded. I couldn't find the courage to take the price tag off the dress.

No sticky notes in my locker. No after-school drives to Pantini's Pizza or Bertie's Ice Cream Palace. We'd only had lunch together once since that Friday. I knew that he was busy helping his father move into their new office in Winnipeg — he'd told me he would be — but doubts still prickled my thoughts.

Maybe he's losing interest, Dayle.

Maybe he's with someone else.

My apprehensions all boiled down to one simple fact: even after almost four months, having Keith for a boyfriend still seemed too good to be true.

I couldn't face Amy with all those doubts on my mind — she'd see right through me. Mom's agenda left no time for me, and Denise had found a job at a music store, working evenings, so I'd had a pretty lonely week.

That morning I had taped a note to Amy's locker. With the cold stony wall between us, using the familiar lock combination seemed like an invasion of privacy.

> Lake cancelled. Mom is flying to Toronto
> this weekend. Business. (Again!)
>
>   D.

For once, Mom's schedule had worked to my advantage. Now Keith and I would have the chance to celebrate our four-month anniversary — and my seventeenth birthday — together. And postponing the lake meant I could avoid Amy, at least until I came up with a way to bridge the gap between us.

The rain gathered momentum, pelting against the glass. I picked up my pen. One more sentence to copy from my original draft and the assignment for next class would be complete.

"Hey, Dayle."

I looked up. "Hi, Stu." I smiled cautiously.

"Whatcha working on?" he asked.

"English. Short story. Just finished." I put my pen down.

Stu hovered over the table expectantly, doodle-covered binder in one hand, cola in the other. "Can I sit?"

"Sure." I hoped he wouldn't ask too many questions.

Stu flashed me a lopsided grin and noisily scraped the chair beside mine away from the table. Every student in the crowded cafeteria must have paused to see where the racket came from. What were they thinking?

Stu Ingaldson and Dayle Meryk?

They've known each other for years, why not?

But she's supposed to be with Keith Hutton.

Told you that wouldn't last!

Jade Cannon swayed past Stu and me, her long raven hair swinging from her shoulders like a cape. She flashed me a haughty look, stopped, then turned around again.

"Hello, Dayle," she said coolly, eyeing up Stu. "And where is Keith today?"

Poor Stu turned six different shades of red.

"He's got math class," I said firmly.

"Oh. Really?" She smiled and sidled away.

My skin prickled and my ears burned. I rolled my pen between my hands and told myself that Jade was simply being Jade, trying to create conflict where there was none.

Stu rubbed his fledgling beard. He cleared his throat, and the bright spots on his cheeks faded. "So. This story you wrote. What's it called?"

"Bread."

"Bread?" Stu's eyebrows went up. "What's it about?"

"About a grandmother who's trying to teach her grand-daughter patience."

"Cool. Can I read it?"

I flushed again. I never shared my writing, but Stu was already reaching for the pages. I drew curlicues in the margins of my draft copy and tried not to watch his eyebrows bob up and down as he read.

Stu and I had been friends since daycare, when he stopped Toby Jamison from whacking me with a toy school bus for "stealing" his place at the play table. I'd showed my appreciation by sharing a box of candy-covered chocolates with Stu. He'd picked out all the red ones and laid them across my palm in the shape of a broad smile.

"This is good," Stu said finally, shuffling my pages back together.

"Thanks." A wave of relief and gratitude flooded over me.

"Is this what your grandma was like?"

I thought for a moment. "Sort of. Maybe. She liked to bake."

"Oh. I like the way you have her kneading bread dough as a way of dealing with the rough stuff life dishes out. You gonna be a writer?"

I laughed. "Me? No. I'll leave writing to Mom."

"But she's a journalist. You could write fiction."

I shook my head.

"Well, what then? Something creative. An actress, I bet. You were great in the school play last February."

"Thanks. I'd like to be an actor. Or maybe a model."

"But you could be a writer."

I shook my head. "I want to do something different. Something adventurous. And I like acting. You get to be someone else for a while, see the world like they would. Say and do things you wouldn't dare say or do otherwise."

Stu leaned back in his chair and crossed his arms as if he

were inviting me to tell him more. It felt so good to have someone to talk to that I kept right on going. "I've got everything planned out. Sort of. I'll study drama and film at university. And there's a new summer drama class in Winnipeg. It's for film acting, not stage. There's a difference, you know. Anyway they're going to bring in a real director to talk to us. Someone who's going to be here making a film this summer. We'll even get to play extras in the movie he's making. But they only take ten students. I auditioned —"

"Then you'll get it."

"Oh, I hope you're right. It would be great. Really great."

Stu grinned. "Will you still remember your lowly old friends when you're famous?"

"Famous?" My cheeks burned. "I can't imagine being famous. Listen," I added hastily, "don't tell *anyone* about the drama class. No one else knows, except Mom and Denise."

"Not even Amy?"

I shook my head vehemently.

Stu nodded solemnly. Then he pulled his cola can forward and stared into the small opening as if he had discovered something interesting inside. "I saw Amy this morning."

"Oh?"

"She told me you two aren't talking."

I picked up my pen and began scribbling again.

"She's pretty upset about it."

"Well, I'm not dancing in the clouds either. She hasn't exactly gone out of her way to apologize."

"Have you?" Stu asked.

My head jerked up.

"Sorry. Out of line. I just thought, considering what happened to her …."

I clenched my jaw. Amy, of course, would only have told Stu *her* side of the story.

But Stu looked more concerned than accusing. He took a slug of his cola. "So. You're not going to the lake this weekend?"

I shook my head slowly. Would he ask me to the Chameleon concert again? A small wave of panic swelled in my throat. I didn't have any more excuses.

"Got anything planned?" he asked.

I stumbled over a cowardly response. "Well ... maybe."

"Oh." He sighed. "I had to change my plans too. Sold my Chameleon tickets this morning."

"That's too bad." My words were sincere, but I still felt relieved.

Stu drummed his fingers over his math text. "Yeah. Well. *C'est la vie.* I've got a chance to do some work for a graphics house in the city. It'll take me all weekend to finish the job."

"You find work for the summer yet?"

Stu shook his head. "No. I'm hoping this freelance stuff will lead to something. Gotta make some money this summer. Student loans aren't cheap, so the less I have to borrow for university next year, the better. But I'll be busy anyway with a few personal projects I've got lined up. I'm going to try sculpting."

I glanced at my watch. Fifteen minutes until English. I gathered my books and papers into a neat stack and rearranged them as Stu rattled on.

"I like birds. I want to make a pelican," he said. "Lots of them to study near the Lockport Bridge. Did you know that they're particular about water temperatures? They like water that's around four degrees Celsius because the fish are more likely to swim near the surface. Pelicans don't dive so ...."

I wished he would stop talking long enough for me to make a polite escape.

As Stu described the migrating habits of pelicans, Keith walked into the cafeteria, stopping just inside the doorway to scrutinize the crowd. He didn't seem to notice — or care — that all the girls and most of the guys were watching him.

Keith Hutton was hard not to watch, with his carefully rumpled dirty-blond hair and strong, angular features. He filled out his clothes well too: designer jeans, brand name air-pump runners and one of those expensive sweatshirts with the label on the outside. A woodsy-green one, soft and warm.

I held my breath until his eyes met mine. His mouth spread into a warm grin. I smiled back. He strode across the room toward me, nodding at several other students along the way, then pulled up a chair and casually lowered himself into it.

Envious glances rippled throughout the cafeteria.

Keith took his eyes off mine for a moment and smiled at Stu. "Hey, Stu. How's it going?"

Stu shifted in his chair. "Uh, not bad, I guess."

"You ready for that physics test later this aft?" Keith asked.

Stu shrugged. "Who knows? Mr. Adams's tests are always full of surprises."

"No kidding. He got me last time with that question about green waves." Keith turned to me again. His hands were so close to mine that I could feel the warmth radiating from them. "Glad I caught you before the bell."

Stu looked from Keith to me, then pushed his chair back awkwardly. "Well, uh, guess I should go. Gotta drop off all these books. See you guys."

"Sure." Keith gave him another smile. "See you in

physics." He turned back to me. "Sorry I haven't called. Office moving is crazy. Dad's got fifteen new houses to build this spring, plus a few renovations. Can you believe it?"

"So are you going to help with construction?"

"When the ground dries up. Then I'll be able to leave the office stuff for Mrs. James." Keith paused. "You know, it's so busy that she's looking for some extra help through the summer. You interested?"

I hesitated. The offer was tempting, but there was still the possibility of drama school.

"I can talk to Dad if you want. I know he likes you."

The end-of-class buzzer rang, triggering the dull thump of moving chairs and feet somewhere in the distance.

"I'm not sure yet. I'm sort of halfway committed to something else ...."

"Oh? Tell me." He leaned in even closer.

My cheeks warmed. I didn't want to tell him about drama school until I knew I was accepted. "Well —"

Before I had time to respond, Pete Wallace sprinted up to the table. Pete was Keith's best friend, a mountain of a guy with a booming voice to match. A shock of dark hair fell across his forehead. He brushed it aside and winked at me, then gave Keith a playful jab in the shoulder. "C'mon Hutton. Geography. With Foxy Frieda. Let's check out the landscape."

Keith looked at the clock and groaned. "You mean *Frosty* Frieda, don't you? Go ahead, Pete. I'll see you there."

"Jeez, Keith. You've got no time for the guys any more." Pete rolled his eyes dramatically and jogged away.

Keith pushed his chair away from the table. "You've got English next, right?"

I nodded and picked up my books. Keith slipped his

hand over mine. An electric tingle spread heat from the point of his touch up the length of my arm and through the rest of my body.

"You doing anything this weekend?"

My heart jammed in my throat. Had he remembered our four-month anniversary? My birthday? Would he invite me out for dinner in a fancy restaurant, or maybe to the Chameleon concert? "Not exactly." I tried to steady the ripple in my voice. "We were supposed to go to the lake, but things didn't pan out."

"It's the May long weekend. The traditional date for the first party of the summer at the Meadow."

"Oh?" My tongue dried and stuck to the roof of my mouth as disappointment settled in. I'd heard rumours about the Meadow. The Party Pit, some people called it — a place far enough out in the country for kids to drink and make lots of noise without disturbing any neighbours.

"Do you want to go?" he asked. "On Saturday. We'll have a great time."

How could I refuse? I nodded and tried to think positively. It might not be the most exciting way to celebrate, but at least I would be with Keith.

He continued excitedly. "On Sunday, we're going to Grand Beach with the Sea-Doos. It's pretty early and the water'll be deadly cold, but I've got a couple of wetsuits and I want to break my record for early starts. We went out on June third last year."

"Sounds good." I managed a smile.

"You know," Keith leaned forward until I could feel his warm breath and almost taste its wintergreen cool. "I tried to get tickets to the Chameleon concert, but they were all sold out. Sorry. Saturday's kind of a special day and I know how much you like them. Guess I should have camped out overnight."

"Just to get concert tickets?" I forced cheer into my voice. "Doesn't matter. We'll have fun at the Meadow."

"Good. There's just one thing, though …" He paused for a moment and shifted in his chair, looking uncomfortable. "I found a couple of scratches on my Jeep and it goes in Friday morning for a paint touch-up. Don't want to leave it and let rust set in. Think your mom would let us take your van?"

My stomach turned inside out. I'd lost van privileges for taking it out to Assiniboine Park last week without permission. But Mom would be out of town. I nodded numbly, wondering how I would convince Denise to keep quiet.

"Great! Maybe we could use it Sunday too, to haul the Sea-Doos. I noticed you've got a hitch on the back."

We walked to my locker hand in hand. Keith dialled my combination without missing a turn. He pressed his left shoulder into the locker next to mine and grinned, then leaned forward and kissed me. I tried to imagine we were alone, somewhere other than a school hallway where a few hundred pairs of eyes were honed in on us.

When Keith stepped back, I opened my eyes to see Amy standing behind him, staring at the stack of books in her arms.

Keith followed my gaze to Amy and smiled at her warily. "Hi, Amy. How're you doing? Dayle told me what happened …."

She raised her head stiffly. "I'm fine." A pale flush rose on her cheeks. She looked back down at her books.

Keith shifted his weight from one foot to the other and looked from Amy to me. "I, uh, guess I should go, Dayle. I need to get to my own locker. See you later?"

I nodded and he left, just like that. Blown off by a cold wind.

When he was out of sight, Amy spoke again. "Dayle. I'm sorry about the lake." Her voice lowered. "And I'm sorry about what happened in the park." She shoved an envelope at me. "Peace offering and birthday gift."

I stared at the pink envelope, light as a feather in my hand.

"Go on. Open it."

I lifted the flap and pulled out two concert tickets. For Chameleon. Front-row seats. Front-row *centre*. "Amy, that's ... that's —"

"That's wonderful and generous and kind and you forgive me?"

"Well, yes ..." My voice tapered out and my chest tightened. I could see it happening all over again; Amy versus Keith, with me in the middle.

"I know how badly you want to go," she said. "And I just happened to get a great deal on these. From a mutual friend."

"This is so, so great, Amy. I mean, no one can get tickets." I tried to smile, to look appreciative.

Amy tilted her head, studying me. "So, what's wrong?"

"Well, I'm in bit of a predicament now."

"How?"

"I just told Keith I wasn't doing anything Saturday night. And it's not just my birthday, it's our four-month anniversary."

"Oh." A shadow fell over Amy's face. "Did he get tickets too?"

"He tried, but he couldn't. He wants to take me to the Meadow —"

"You mean the Party Pit." Amy's voice wavered.

"It's just that, well, he asked me and I said yes." I stared at the tickets in my hand, suddenly wishing I'd never heard of Chameleon.

Amy's voice rose. "Then why don't you take Keith to the concert?"

I shook my head and held the tickets out to her. "I can't do that."

"Yes. You can." Amy's face looked as stiff as mine felt.

"No. I can't," I said gently. "You want to see Chameleon as much as I do. Take these and find someone else to go with. But thank you, Amy. Really. You couldn't have done anything nicer." I placed the tickets on top of her binder and looked directly into her eyes, searching for a glimmer of understanding, something to help us past this horrible moment.

Amy raised her chin and the fluorescent lights of the locker bay cast an ugly greenish glint in her brown eyes. "Since when does a part-time boyfriend take priority over things that are important to you, like your best friend?" She blinked and straightened her back defiantly. "Maybe we're not friends at all, not any more."

How could I reason with the unreasonable? "Fine," I said, slamming my locker door closed.

Amy jumped backward as if the metallic clatter had startled her, bumping into Stu, who happened to be walking past. His arms flailed up and out in surprise and his books went flying.

"Here." Amy jammed the tickets into the pocket of his shirt. "You can have them back. Give them to someone who cares."

Stu shook his head, watching her march away. "What's wrong with Amy?"

"Who knows? If you figure it out, you can tell me."

Stu looked from Amy to his scattered books. "Whatever it is," he said, "I sure hope she works it out soon."

CHAPTER SIX

Saturday, May 31: Day Zero

MOM'S VAN LURCHED TO A STOP at a red light and my fingers instinctively grabbed for the door handle. An unsettled tingling wavered along my spine. Keith had never driven so recklessly before — at least not with me along. I wished I hadn't given him the keys.

He clutched the steering wheel in his left hand and flicked the rear-view mirror into place with his right forefinger, then bobbed in the seat as if to test the springs. "Ah. Nothing like driving a new vehicle. Too bad the air conditioning is toast."

Even his conversation seemed loud and coarse. He leaned out his window and sniffed the evening air.

I eyed him warily. "Well, it's still under warranty," I said. "Mom's getting it fixed next week."

Keith didn't seem to hear me. As he reached forward to crank up the radio, his arm brushed against my knee, a feathery touch that sliced through the damp heat of my skin and left a tingle behind. The familiar scent of his cologne wafted over me, but it seemed musty somehow. He smiled broadly, his green eyes brighter than usual.

And now, live from the Winnipeg Arena ... Cheering fans drowned out most of the announcer's concert update.

"Gawd, I wish I was in that crowd!" Pete's voice boomed

from behind. I felt his thick finger jabbing my shoulder. "You said your sister's going?"

I turned and nodded at Pete, who was sitting as close to Jade as he possibly could in the van's short two-passenger middle seat.

"Lucky broad. How'd she manage to get Chameleon tickets? Camp out all night?" Pete grinned, softening the stone-chiselled look of his face, then took a long slug from the cola can clutched in his left hand.

"No. She got them from a friend of ... of hers."

Stu had refused to keep the tickets, so Amy gave them to Denise. Denise had politely suggested I go with her, but I'd refused. It hadn't taken too much persuading. She and her brand-new boyfriend, Joseph-the-roofer, were both Chameleon fans. They were so grateful that Denise even agreed to keep the van business a secret from Mom. "Just be careful," she had pleaded. "And remember to replace any gas you use."

So Denise got tickets to the hottest concert of the year and I got the van.

"Denise *was* lucky to get tickets." Marnie's voice came from the seat behind Pete and Jade, where she sat between Cougar and her older brother, Sam. Her soft copper eyes darted between the back of Pete's head and me, her curly, strawberry-blond hair bobbing about her face as she spoke. "I stood in line for three hours, but they were sold out by the time I got to the window."

"The acoustics at the Arena are terrible." Jade inspected her perfectly manicured fingernails. "Otherwise I would have gone; Daddy offered me a pair of tickets."

"What?" Keith jerked his head around. "You told me you couldn't get tickets."

"I couldn't. Not to give away. Daddy's very particular about that."

"I would have paid you for them." Keith sounded indignant.

Jade flipped a long thick lock of raven hair over her shoulder. "If you'd wanted to go that badly, you should have told me. I could have taken you." Her eyes casually met mine and her lips curved into a slight smile.

I clenched my teeth. Keith rolled his eyes and shot me a grin as the light turned green again.

"Aw, Baby," Pete crooned to Jade. "You know he's a fallen man." He inched toward her. "You coulda taken me."

"Not in this lifetime." Jade slid away from Pete.

Marnie blushed and looked at her lap.

As we made our way south down Main Street, the guys let loose. We passed a girl with a Barbie-doll figure waiting on a bus-stop bench. Sam whistled. I flinched; she didn't. Pete, Sam and Cougar hooted and hollered through the open van windows, offering critical commentary about everyone we passed. People were too short, too fat or too old. They drove ugly cars or didn't know how to drive at all. Every word confirmed what Amy had said about them. I tried not to listen.

"Look! Look at that!" Keith joined in. He pointed to a thin old man who was pumping bike pedals furiously to keep up with the big, black Newfoundlander bounding in front of him. "Hey, man. Tie his leash to the handlebars and save your breath!"

My stomach twisted. Keith seemed far removed from the guy who that morning had plastered seventeen *Happy Birthday* sticky notes over my front door.

"Put a harness on that bear," Pete shouted after the old man. He turned to Cougar. "Toss me another one. Okay, buddy?"

Cougar reached behind his seat and pulled an opened cola can from Pete's cooler, handing it to Pete. Pete threw his head back and swallowed greedily. "Ah, nothing better than Dr. Cola."

"Dr. Cola?" I asked.

"Doctor as in doctored," Keith said. "You know. Premixed. With rye. It's a tradition at the Meadow."

"Oh." My throat tightened. Alcohol made me nervous and Keith knew that. Even though Pete and the others drank from time to time, Keith rarely did. But he must have been drinking tonight. That would explain his unusual behaviour and the faint musty odour that I'd first noticed before we left my house, when we'd posed in front of Joseph's camera for a birthday picture.

I didn't want anyone drinking in my mother's van, tradition or no tradition, but I wasn't sure how I could put a stop to it. I prayed no one would spill anything that could stain the interior or leave an odour stronger than the smell of new vinyl. I felt betrayed and I wished I'd stayed home.

Pete leaned forward and swirled his can beside Keith's ear. "You want another?"

"Later." Keith reached over and squeezed my knee. "I need both hands now."

Pete turned to me. "How 'bout you, Dayle? We got Dr. Cola and Brewer's Gingerale. Perfect for a Saturday night drive."

"No thanks." I studied Keith, the odd brightness of his eyes, his perpetual smile. Somehow I would find a way to take the wheel when it came time to go home. I'd have to put up with Keith's driving for now; I didn't have the courage to take over.

At the next red light, Stu's Honda Civic pulled up alongside of us.

"Hey," Pete shouted. "It's Stu." He laughed and held his nose. "Phew!"

A hard lump rolled in my stomach. I wanted to sink below the floorboards.

Cougar pressed his face to the window. "Hey, Stuey!"

"Leave him alone," I said, "Please." My voice barely rose to a whisper.

"Huh?" Cougar pulled away from the window to look at me. "I said —"

"Lay off him, guys." Keith looked over his shoulder, scowling.

But Sam had unclasped his seat belt and was leaning in front of Marnie, shouting through Cougar's window. "Hey! Hey! Hey, buddy! There's something smelly coming out of your car. I think it's fish." He glanced back at us, and lowered his voice slightly. "The Icelandic-Chinese connection. You know. Fish. For supper."

"That's racist, Sam," Marnie said, her eyes narrowing. "And it's Japanese, not Chinese."

Stu frowned and leaned out of his Honda, looking toward the back of his car. He sniffed, then sniffed again. Laughter rippled through the van. A thick lump swelled in my throat. Why couldn't Stu give some clever response to their teasing, let them see his bright and funny side? But all he did was settle back in his seat and stare straight ahead.

Stu, I tried to say, *ignore them, they're not themselves tonight,* but my tongue lay in my mouth like a hunk of dry leather.

"You're a bunch of jerks," Keith said. "Stu's a friend of Dayle's."

"Oops. Forgot." Pete looked sheepish. "Sorry."

I swallowed hard to loosen my tongue, then leaned out my window to say something — anything — to Stu. But it was too late. The light had turned green and the Honda shot straight through the intersection.

We turned sharply to the left, cutting off an oncoming station wagon. I clutched the door handle and muffled a small shriek. As soon as we had straightened out from that turn, Keith made another turn — a sharp right into the gas station.

"Cripes!" Cougar hissed. "You tryin' to kill us?"

An empty pop can whizzed past Keith's ear and clanked on Mom's dash. I sprang forward to catch the can before it hit the floor and then wiped up the spray of brown liquid with a tissue.

"Sorry guys," Keith said. "But I'm in a hurry. The Meadow waits!" He pulled up to the only free pump at the busy station. "I put the spare tank in the back beside Pete's cooler."

Cougar reached for it. "It's bone dry."

"Yeah, I know." Keith shut off the ignition. "That's why I brought it. We'll fill it for Sea-Dooing tomorrow." He stretched his arms out, lacing his hands together and cracking his knuckles, watching the two attendants scurry between customers.

"C'mon guys, let's go!" Pete thumped the side of the van impatiently.

Keith hopped out. He smiled and waved off an attendant who was fumbling with a handful of bills and a credit card, and began to gas up the van himself.

Pete grinned wickedly at Jade and made an exaggerated stumble over her as he moved across the seat toward the side door. She quickly slid out from under him and sprang from the van to stand in front of my door, blocking the sunlight. I shivered. She leaned into the van, flipping her hair, chattering to Keith as he pumped gas.

Everyone else piled out too. I squeezed the sticky cola can between my fingers and stuffed the damp tissue inside. I felt awkward sitting inside the van alone, hidden in Jade's shadow, but I wasn't sure I wanted to be outside with any of them.

Jade's perfume wafted in through my open window. It turned my stomach, but I wasn't about to crawl across the seat to exit through the driver's door for fresh air. "Jade," I said. "Let me out."

She turned and raised an eyebrow at me, then pulled away from the door, sidling even closer to Keith. I slid out of the van and sucked in a mouthful of clean air, ignoring her less-than-subtle attempt to annoy me.

Cougar leaned against the front of the van, stuffing his mouth with potato chips from a can. "Anybody else want some?"

"Sure." Sam reached out his hand.

Cougar turned the can upside down over Sam's palm and shook out a few crumbs. "Oh, gee. Too bad. All gone." The empty can flipped off the end of his fingers in the direction of the garbage bin. It fell short and rolled toward the sidewalk. Cougar shrugged and followed Sam to the store.

"Clown," Jade sniffed.

Cougar wasn't one of my favourite people, but I liked him a lot more than I liked Jade and her self-righteous attitude. "Didn't you used to go out with Cougar?" I asked as coolly as I could.

Jade's cheeks coloured slightly. "That was a long time ago."

Pete leaned against the gas pump and grinned. "Ooo, hissss!" He nudged Keith. "Hear that?"

My face flushed. Keith was hunched over the red plastic gas can, pump nozzle in hand, but I thought I detected the edge of a grin on his face.

Pete pulled a cigarette out of his shirt pocket and a lighter from his jeans. He flicked the lighter. Nothing happened. "Jeez," he said.

Marnie looked up at him.

Pete flicked the lighter again. It sparked.

"Hey!" Marnie sprang toward Pete and shook her head. "Don't light that thing. You want to start a fire?" She pointed at the no-smoking sign clearly posted on the gas pump.

Pete rolled his eyes, but he shoved the offending items back in his pockets. "Okay, *Mom.*"

Marnie quickly looked down at her runners.

Keith looked from Marnie to Pete. "Why don't you make yourself useful, Wallace, and wash the windows?"

"Naw. I leave streaks. You hate streaks." Pete hopped back into the van.

Jade straightened and reached for the bucket of squeegees, but I beat her to it and moved to the other side of the van. I was loosening a gummy insect blob from the driver's side when I looked up and saw Amy, with Bud prancing at her heels. My arm froze over the glass, squeegee in mid-air. Our eyes met.

The intensity of her stare made me feel guilty.

Defensive.

Angry.

My arm fell to my side, the smear of bug juice drying into a thin translucent ribbon of mustard-yellow.

Sam and Cougar staggered toward the van, each with an

unbalanced armload of munchies. Marnie reached out to catch a bag of taco chips before they hit the ground.

Sam snatched the package back from Marnie and stopped in his unsteady tracks to rip it open with his teeth. He spat out a strip of plastic and gave Amy a glassy-eyed stare. "Hey, who's the broad with the fuzzy hair?" His voice echoed through the gas station.

I felt my jaw drop.

Marnie jabbed an elbow into Sam's side. "Shh."

Cougar laughed. "I don't know, but she's got a nose just like her partner there."

Amy's shoulders stiffened. She looked at Bud and kept on walking.

"Aren't you two friends?" Jade spoke loudly enough for Amy to hear. She smiled smugly at me.

Touché. For the second time that night, my tongue was too thick and dry for me to speak. The *yes* hanging on the tip of it stayed there.

Amy stopped in her tracks, an angry glow on her cheeks. She looked up and her eyes locked on mine with a coldness I'd never seen in them before. "Friends?" Sarcasm iced her voice.

Not any more.

I heard the words, but I wasn't sure where they came from. Had I said them out loud, or only thought them, or had Amy been the one to spit them out?

Bud barked and pulled toward me, dragging Amy with him. She was too busy glaring at me to see where she was going and she stumbled over the potato-chip can Cougar had tossed away. Her knees hit the pavement, then her hands.

I should have run to her as soon as I saw it happening, should have stood with her in front of the others, helped her up and shown her that regardless of what she'd said — or I'd said — she was still my friend and I cared about her. But my legs wouldn't move. They were frozen to the spot with the chill of her last words and my own icy anger.

Amy pulled herself back to her feet and turned abruptly toward the road, yanking on Bud's leash. She hauled him, yelping in surprise, across the asphalt.

"Woof, woof," barked Sam.

"Sam, you're an idiot," Keith said. He jammed the gasoline nozzle back into the pump and grabbed my hand. "Are you okay?"

I dropped the squeegee back into the water bucket and shook my head numbly. Or maybe I nodded.

Something heavy settled over me as I slid back into the van. It ran cold beneath the surface of my skin, sucking air from my lungs and blotting out the evening's glow.

CHAPTER SEVEN

THE MEADOW LAY AT THE END of a long muddy trail fifteen minutes from town and several kilometres from any major road. Keith parked the Windstar just inside the clearing across from a huge pile of untrimmed logs. A mud-splattered Bronco, two GMC four-by-fours and a very mucky Jeep had arrived before us.

"Whew!" Keith shook his head. "Good thing your mother has all-wheel drive. Hope we can get outta here okay."

I didn't want to *think* about trying to get home, or how I would manage to remove the goop from the van before Mom got back from Toronto.

I stepped out of the vehicle onto a spongy mat of musty leaves and grass. The smell of decay tightened the heavy tangle in my stomach. I tried to push thoughts of Amy aside as Keith led me past the vehicles and under a green archway of willow branches that framed an entrance to the widest part of the clearing — the party area.

It was perfect. Stones and a thick pad of gravel ringed a large fire pit which lay on the north side, just far enough away from the surrounding brush to prevent sparks from igniting it. Several logs and flat-topped rocks were arranged like seats around the pit. A battered picnic table piled high with junk food lay some distance to the south. Nearly two dozen kids milled through the area. Voices buzzed through the humid air with an electric crackle and gaudy coolers littered the ground.

Pete plunked his cooler down just past the willows.

"So this is it," I said to Keith. "How'd you guys find this place, anyway?"

"My uncle's land." Keith pointed straight ahead, through the brush. "He lives about five clicks that-away."

A voice rang out from behind us. "Howdy, Hutton." I looked back through the willows. A tall boy I recognized from another school's basketball team unloaded a portable CD player from the Jeep. "How goes it?" he called.

"Babcock!" Keith squeezed my hand and flashed me a smile, then sprinted toward the boy, leaving me in front of the fire pit to fend for myself. I shivered in spite of the warm damp air and folded my arms across my chest.

Jade and Marnie had settled in with a cluster of other girls beside the picnic table. Their conversation ebbed and flowed rapidly, punctuated with barbs of laughter that pulled at the unsettled lump in my stomach and made me feel terribly alone. I thought of Amy marching away from the gas station, her shoulders squared against humiliation.

Against me.

Jade glanced over her shoulder at me and raised her chin. One eyebrow rose. Her lips curved into a slight smile. Then she turned away and leaned into the small tight circle of girls. A wave of laughter erupted. It wasn't hard to figure out that she'd been talking about me.

Marnie stepped out of the circle and gave Jade a look of disdain. When she turned and headed toward me, I felt consoled. At least a little.

"Here. Have one of these." Pete's voice rang from behind

me as something cold and wet pressed into my back.

I jumped and turned around. A pop can. He plopped it into my hand. "Gingerale?" I asked.

"*Brewer's* Gingerale." Pete grinned and wiggled his own can, sloshing "Dr. Cola" over the side. He sauntered off toward the fire pit, passing Marnie without a glance. "Hey, Ryan," he bellowed. "Don't you know how to light a fire?"

Marnie stopped beside me, swirling the gingerale can in her hand. She sighed and watched Pete for a moment, then pushed her lips into a smile. "Cheers?" She raised her drink.

I touched her can with mine then took a mouthful of bitter brew and swallowed hard. I had yet to develop a taste for beer, but I took another gulp anyway. If I finished it, I might be able to relax enough to enjoy the evening without feeling like an outsider.

The boy named Ryan hovered over a scattering of logs in the middle of the fire pit. He stood and wiped his hands on his jeans. "This stuff is too wet. It'll never light."

"Anything will light." Pete leaped over the stones into the pit. "You just gotta know what you're doing."

"So, Petey my boy." Keith dumped another log in the pit. "Show 'em how it's done! Hey, Babcock, where's the music?"

"Can't find my CDs!"

I sipped on my beer watching Pete toss firewood around and wondered if I should offer to help. He didn't look as though he knew what he was doing — or maybe he just couldn't *see* what he was doing.

Marnie nudged my arm. "Do you like this stuff?" She looked into her gingerale can.

"No," I admitted. "Not really."

Marnie giggled. "Me either." She turned the can upside

down and emptied it onto the grass, then looked up at the circle of girls just beyond us. "Sometimes I wonder why I hang around with these guys."

"You don't like them?"

"I like most of them, I guess." She narrowed her eyes at Jade, then sighed. "Besides, I have to keep an eye on my brother."

"Sam? Don't you mean *Pete?*" I teased gently.

Marnie smiled and blushed.

A warm hand fell on my shoulder. "C'mere." Keith's breath felt hot and damp on my ear. I gave Marnie an apologetic look. She smiled and raised her empty drink can in a kind of *go ahead* gesture and stayed where she was, watching the others.

Keith took my free hand and led me to a stack of large untrimmed logs that lay on the south end of the clearing. As soon as my bare legs touched the rough bark, I wished I'd worn jeans instead of new khaki shorts. Thin shapely legs wouldn't be worth showing off if they were covered in scratches. I swallowed the last of my beer and balanced on the toes of my runners to keep my legs raised above the logs.

Keith and I sat together for a while without speaking. I tried to find words to break the news about summer drama school, to tell him that I'd been accepted and how important it was to me, but I couldn't concentrate. A pleasant numbness trickled through my limbs and scattered my thoughts.

As the horizon swallowed the setting sun, the sky slipped from blue to purple and the moon began to glow. Crickets or frogs, or maybe both, sang a romantic serenade. Chatter and laughter rippled around us with the kind of anticipation that blows in with spring and the knowledge that summer is on the horizon. I managed to forget about everything that had happened earlier that evening, and the world bloomed with possibility again.

"So, what do you think?" Keith broke the silence.

"Of the Meadow? It's great. Private. It'll be perfect when they get that fire lit."

Keith put his arm around me. A stale vapour clung to him and his words slurred together in a husky drawl. "I've got something for you. Partly for your birthday and partly because it's been four months." He pulled a small white package out of the pocket of his denim shirt.

I stared at the gift, surprised and excited.

Keith grinned. "Go on, take it." He gently pushed the package toward me.

I wanted to seem nonchalant, but it wasn't easy. My trembling fingers removed ribbon, then paper, to uncover a blue velvet box. I slowly raised the lid. A thick, gold, heart-shaped drop gleamed from the end of a gold chain. I felt my jaw drop.

"Do you like it?"

"It's beautiful."

"*You're* beautiful." Keith fingered the smooth gold nugget. "Found it that weekend Pete and I went to Grand Forks."

"That was over a month ago ...."

"Yeah. But I saw it and I knew it was made for you. Wanna try it on?"

I nodded. Keith undid the clasp and slipped the chain around my neck. The heart felt cold against the little hollow at the base of my throat. I warmed it with my fingers, then let it go.

One of Keith's hands dropped to my knee. A hot flush rushed up my leg. I let my hand fall on top of his. He brushed his lips against mine, warm and soft, then put his right hand on my back and pulled me in more firmly. With the numbing sensation of alcohol floating through my body, it was almost possible to forget the crowd of other kids milling around us. I let myself sink into his kiss.

When Keith pulled away and opened his eyes, his hands slid around my rib cage, pausing close to my breasts. In spite of the beer, I felt myself tense as the heat from his hands surged through me. But he immediately let go, smiled and squeezed my hand. "You're special, Dayle." He kissed me again, quickly and lightly. "Happy Birthday. And ... uh, Happy Anniversary."

"Thanks," I said, touching the gold heart.

"Maybe you can wear that on June twenty-eighth?"

I played innocent, but the pounding in my chest picked up speed. "Oh?"

Keith grinned. "To Grad. You're coming with me, aren't you?"

"Sure." I managed to nod casually. Now I could remove the price tag from the sapphire gown hanging in my closet.

Other voices resurfaced; girls giggling, boys shouting at Pete. I looked at the fire pit, where Pete was doing a strange kind of drunken dance around a haphazardly arranged pile of unlit logs.

Cougar tossed Pete another drink. "Yeah, Pete. You're a real fire-maker. Must be the caveman in you." He whooped.

"Sure hope it doesn't get cold tonight. We'll freeze our asses. Maybe you oughta dance a little harder. Call on the Fire Spirit." Ryan threw his head back and drank from a dark bottle. "But if he answers, you better get outta there fast or you'll burn your butt."

Someone in the background started howling the chorus

of an old song from the seventies, *Light My Fire.*

"Fine," Pete snorted. "You light it." He jammed his fists into his hips and staggered sideways, glaring at Ryan.

"Since when are you a quitter, Pete?" Keith shouted. He laughed and rose from the rough logs, still holding my hand, and led me toward the willows.

"Hey, Dayle. C'mere." Marnie looked up from a handful of CDs as we approached. She stood beside Babcock, who was carefully positioning his stereo speakers in front of the willows.

Keith let go of my hand and headed toward the van.

Babcock shoved a CD into his stereo and an old Rolling Stones tune blasted through the speakers. *Satisfaction.* He hopped to his feet and threw himself into a Mick Jaggar-like dance, swallowing an imaginary microphone.

"I saw you opening a present," Marnie shouted over the music. "What's the occasion? What'd he get you?"

I held the smooth gold drop out for her to see. "Birthday gift, plus we've been together for four months now."

As Marnie leaned in for a closer look, Jade slid off her picnic table perch and sauntered over.

"Wow! That's gorgeous. You're so lucky." Marnie sighed wistfully.

"So. Let's see." Jade glanced at the necklace. "Not bad. Some girls will do *anything* for a gift like that." She looked at her fingernails.

Before I had the chance to untangle my tongue and launch a witty comeback, she flipped her raven hair over her shoulders and strolled away.

Babcock grabbed Marnie's hands, swinging her around and away, leaving me alone again. I didn't want to look like being alone bothered me, so I sat on one of the stone slabs in front of the fire pit and busied myself with a long stick, tracing patterns in the gravel at my feet. Lines intersecting ... circles ....

Suddenly, a shrill voice rose above the pulsating music. I jumped up and swirled around to see Marnie racing toward me, her sights fixed on the fire pit. "No! Pete!"

I dropped my stick and turned back to the fire pit to see what she was so upset about. And that's when it happened.

Everything unfolded in a blur.

A whiff of gasoline ....

A loud *pouf*, and a flare of yellow-white light ....

A rising ball of fire on my right, and the sensation of being hurled away from it ....

Falling ... falling ... falling in slow-motion, falling into pain, then oblivion, and another kind of light ....

I'm coming, Gram, I'm coming.

CHAPTER EIGHT

Something heavy squeezes against my temples and chest, sucking me into an inky void. As I struggle for air, a pulsating light grows from the darkness and with it comes a familiar voice, singing. I know the song. It's a lullaby, Hush Little Baby, *but I've always called it the* Mockingbird *song. It rises above the din of angry silence pounding through my head and eases some of my fear. A loud whoosh fills my ears and I'm swept into the light.*

It's Gram who's singing. She's waiting for me inside the light, a shimmering, translucent image of her former self. Her fingers stroke my hair and her light jasmin and lavender perfume wraps around me like a safe warm blanket.

Even though her lips aren't moving, I know she's speaking to me. "Remember Dayle," she seems to say, "remember that everything works together for good and that it's okay to be afraid."

What does she mean by that?

Another figure appears beside Gram. Grandpa? Grandpa is here. I've never met him, but I know it's him — I can feel it. There are others here too, floating around me with open arms — Gram's parents, her brother and his wife, and people who aren't relatives. Even though I've never met any of them before, I have this uncanny sense of who each of them is. They make me feel welcome. And safe.

It's a wonderful, peaceful place, this place of light.

But a shadow slips between the others and me and I look toward another light — a pale, cold light that lies far and away and down at the end of a dizzying tunnel of dots.

A girl lies motionless on a white sheet below me. I can't see her face because of the people who are huddled around her, but she looks terrible. Her right side balloons out with red oozing sores, except for a narrow, untouched ring of flesh around the base of her neck. Her shorts and T-shirt cling to her body in blackened tatters.

One person takes a pair of scissors and swiftly but gently tears away shreds of clothing imbedded in her skin. Another person places two small round disks over her bare, seeping chest.

Someone else shouts "Clear!" and it dawns on me that I'm looking at a hospital emergency room. As everyone steps back from the table, I catch a glimpse of the left side of the girl's face. It's bruised and bloody, with a terrible gash in her temple.

It's ME.

Images flash before me — Amy, Keith. Mom and Denise. Daddy. The urn. Feelings of regret and a sense of things unfinished thrash over me in waves until my head buzzes and aches at the same time.

"It's okay," Gram says, her voice fading. "I'll be with you. Always." I feel her fingertips brush my cheek as her image wanes. "Tell your mother I love her. And that I'm sorry."

The distant light grows brighter. Harsher. A vaguely familiar force grabs hold of my chest and sucks me downward with another whoosh, until I feel as though I'm being turned inside out. I can't breathe. I'm drowning and frightened all over again.

And then, in the dark that follows, everything changes forever.

My father fought brush fires. I've seen what happens after an intense burn. There's nothing left, nothing but black ash and skeletal remains, and the painful struggle of starting over.

— CORA MCINTYRE, RN

CHAPTER NINE

SOFT VOICES THREADED through my haze, coaxing me to consciousness.

"... earlier this evening ... difficult resuscitation."

"... chances?"

"... forty-five percent thermal burn and that nasty head wound, but considering her age ..."

"... pain?"

"... heavy doses of morphine. We'll gradually reduce ..."

A steady hiss and click surfaced along with the voices and an odd, unpleasant smell tugged at my nose. I tried to open my eyes, but only the left lid moved. It hurt. Something thick and pasty pressed against the right side of my face; in fact the whole right side of my body sagged under an uncomfortable gooey weight and a smothering kind of dullness.

I blinked and tried to focus through an eye that wouldn't quite open, as if the lid was too thick to move. A maze of wires sprouted from my chest. In spite of dim lighting and that awful dullness, I knew I was in a bed. Two blurred people — one blue, the other yellow — stood at the end of the bed, with wide bands of yellow covering their noses, their mouths. Another yellow figure, tall and slender, moved up and down the left side of the room, clipboard in hand.

Who were those people? Who were they talking about?

The image of a battered girl under a bright light flashed into my mind.

Heat and nausea washed over me. I tried to call out, but I couldn't speak. My tongue felt thick and dry and there was something in the way. A tube. There was a tube shoved down my throat.

"... scarring?"

"Yes. Plastic surgery will certainly help, but there will be scarring." A man's voice.

"My poor baby. My poor, beautiful baby." A woman's voice. A sob snagged her words.

Mom. But wasn't she supposed to be in Toronto interviewing someone? I wiggled on my pillow, trying to pull myself upright. In spite of the thick cloud padding my senses, millions of tiny, sharp, burning needles prickled over my entire body. A groan rolled deep in my chest.

Mom turned to meet my one-eyed gaze. "Dayle. Dayle. Thank God!" She charged to my side, her face dissolving from a blur into a familiar pair of eyes beneath carefully groomed brows. But the eyes weren't pale blue — they were grey and glassy, marbled in red. A yellow cap hid every strand of her hair and a yellow mask covered her mouth and nose. She grabbed my left hand with both of hers. Her touch was clammy. Rubber gloves. She wore rubber gloves.

She leaned over, gently touching her cloth-covered mouth to my left cheek. "Daddy's on his way here," she whispered. But she was wrong. Daddy couldn't visit; he had told me so in his letter.

A man with bushy eyebrows and thin-rimmed glasses leaned in front of Mom and bent over me. The mask over his face jiggled as he spoke. "Do you know where you are?"

I nodded. This could only be a hospital. Those masks they wore ... they didn't want to breathe on me. Was I going to die? I felt like I was going to die. Panic rose in my throat. So much I had to do ...

"Do you know why you're here?"

I tried to think, fighting the soupy fog in my brain and the awful pain that swallowed the rest of me. I couldn't find anything but the memory of a deep ache, something like regret. I shook my head slightly and watched the stethoscope swinging from the man's neck. His hands were cool on my left wrist.

"You were involved in an explosion," he said. "You suffered a major blow to the head and received substantial burns to the right side of your body."

I remembered the girl on the table. Was she burned? I thought burns would look black — like overdone barbecued meat — not swollen and red and runny. I didn't recall an explosion. The last thing I remembered was Keith's kiss and feeling wonderful and lonely at the same time. We were there — I wasn't sure where — with others, Keith's friends, so why was I lonely?

Because Amy wasn't there. And she wasn't my best friend any more.

I didn't want to think about it. I turned my head away from Mom and the doctor until the prickling pain in the right side of my neck told me to stop. Something pleasant had happened just before I saw the girl — *me* — on the table. What was it?

I closed my eyes and drifted through a dense fog in search of that distant peace. I thought about Gram.

CHAPTER TEN

Wednesday, June 4: Day 4

> HUSH LITTLE BABY *don't say a word,*
> *Mama's gonna buy you a Mockingbird ...*

Hold me, Gram. Make the hurt go away.

It felt like fire, the pain. I woke up with a scream tangled in my throat. Everything was worse than I remembered it — from the horrid, unrelenting sensation on my right side to the awful smell that seemed to stick to the inside of my nose. I tried to rub the odour away, but there was something jammed in my nose. Another tube. I groaned and dropped my trembling hand.

A hazy blur still clouded my vision. I brought my left hand to my eye. No glasses, no contact lenses. But even myopic eyes couldn't dim the strange familiarity haunting the room around me. Echoes of people and voices and pain lingered dully, like the edge of a half-forgotten nightmare.

A gowned figure, tall and willowy, bent over the bed. A face zoomed into focus. It was a woman — I could tell by the pale delicate skin around her eyes — but she had a man's nose. A Captain Hook nose. Her brown eyes peered over the edge of her face mask at me, soft and concerned. "Ah, you're awake. Do you know where you are?"

I'd heard her soothing voice before. I cautiously bobbed my chin.

"Do you know what day it is?"

I shook my head as gently as I could, but the room spun anyway. Through my bleary gaze, the clock on the wall past the end of the bed seemed to read seven thirty. Was that morning or night?

"It's Wednesday morning. You've been in ICU at Winnipeg Health Sciences Centre for four days now." Nurse Hook looked at her watch. "I'm going to give you something for your pain." She picked up something — a syringe — from the shelves behind her and plunged it into a bag of clear fluid swinging above me.

I moaned and blinked back my tears. It occurred to me that my right eyelid was moving again, in spite of the bandages still covering it. *Do I look as horrible as I feel?* I didn't have the strength to worry about it.

"I know everything hurts but this'll help, honey. Listen, can you tell me how many fingers I'm holding up? Nod once for each finger."

I squinted to count her fingers and nodded three times, carefully, to keep my stomach from rolling any more than it already was.

"Good." Nurse Hook scribbled on a clipboard she picked up from the end of the bed. She checked a series of machines that all seemed to be connected to me and scribbled some more, then picked up a clear plastic pail and knelt with it by the side of my bed. Liquid gushed. "This is good too." She stood up again, holding the pail which was now half-filled with yellow fluid. "Looks like your kidneys are working just fine."

What is happening to me? I opened my mouth to speak, but I couldn't make any sounds come out around the tube, or the thick L-shaped plastic contraption by my mouth. Nurse Hook studied my face. "I'll bet you have a lot of questions, don't you?"

I nodded.

"You know you've been burned?" She placed the pail on a table at the end of the bed and came to my side.

I blinked.

"These machines and tubes and wires are here to help you get better and to monitor your condition." She pointed to a thin clear tube inserted in my left hand and with her finger, followed the tube up to a bag of clear liquid hanging overhead. "That's your IV. We're pumping fluid back into your body to replace what you lost after the burn." She paused and studied my face again, as if to see whether I understood.

Nurse Hook ran her finger along the tube to my mouth. "Part of your neck was burned and you breathed in some hot air, both of which caused your throat to swell. This tube goes down your throat to keep your airway open in spite of that swelling." She lightly tapped the device by my mouth. "This little apparatus is attached to that tube. It allows us to hook up another tube to siphon excess fluid from your lungs, if we need to. It's all pretty miserable, but it'll come out soon."

I squeezed my eyes closed for a moment, trying to digest it all. I wiggled my nose. *What is that awful smell?*

"The tube in your nose? That one was put there so we could feed you. Your medication has left you pretty groggy, too groggy to eat. And you need a lot of calories for those burns to heal."

I shook my head and fought pain to scrunch up my nose.

"Oh." Nurse Hook's pale red eyebrows pulled together

and her eyes studied mine for a moment. "Ah." Her brows smoothed out again. "Are you asking me what you smell?"

I nodded.

"If you're smelling something medicinal, it would likely be the Flamozine. That's the ointment we put over all of your burns to keep bacteria from growing. To prevent infection. Because your face is burned, there's some Flamozine right next to your nose."

I shrugged my left shoulder and wobbled my chin.

"Oh. Something else?"

I blinked.

"Well ..." She spoke slowly. "Maybe what you smell is your burn." She paused for a moment and lightly touched the bandages on top of my head. "Burned hair has an odd odour. Your other burns might smell unusual too."

My stomach heaved. I remembered reading somewhere about the incinerators in Nazi concentration camps — how burning human flesh had a kind of sickly sweet smell. I squeezed my eyes shut.

"Don't worry, Dayle. As the burns heal the smell will disappear. You know, you've had one skin graft already, to your right leg. And Dr. Burke tells me it's doing quite nicely. A few more days and they'll do a graft on your arm."

I opened my eyes and tried to speak again. *How did I get burned? Why can't I remember?* The barrage of words tangled behind the tube in my throat. I made a fist with my left hand and pushed it into the bed. *Why me?*

Nurse Hook gently laid her right hand over my fist. "I know, honey. I know."

A morphine mist rose around me, sucking me into the restless world of nightmares where dreams and memories tumbled together.

Gram frowns down from the clouds. "Dayle, Dayle, don't you know friendship outlasts romance?"

I ignore her and stomp away from Amy, who stands shivering, naked, on an open field of grass littered with underwear.

Amy drives by a few minutes later and slows to stare at me through the meshed wire on the back of her truck window.

Where did the wire come from?

Bud cocks his head to the side and barks. The truck squeals its tires, painting rubber on the asphalt as it speeds away. But the wire mesh of the rear window stays behind. It surrounds me, twisting into a cage. The grey sky opens, but even rain can't stop the flames that swell from the bottom of the cage to eat me alive.

CHAPTER ELEVEN

Thursday, June 5: Day 5

DRONING VOICES FILTERED through my fog. At least a dozen gowned people swarmed the end of my bed, buzzing with medical lingo, talking about me as if I wasn't there. I closed my eyes until I heard them flow out the double doors, dragging their babble with them.

Eleven thirty, the clock read, as clear as daylight. I touched the bridge of my nose to find eyeglasses pressing awkwardly against my face. I ran my left hand over the frames and felt a wad of tape securing them to the thick layer of bandages on the right side of my head.

Nurse Hook smiled at me. "We had to remove one arm of your glasses to fit them over your dressings."

I blinked at her furiously.

"Something in your eye ... oh. You had contact lenses, didn't you?"

I nodded. *Where are they?*

"Well, they would have been removed and discarded in Emergency." She patted my arm and glanced at the window. "Ready for some company?"

My heart flip-flopped between excitement and dread. Who had come to visit? Mom and Daddy? Keith? Amy?

"Your parents are here."

A lump of relief and disappointment worked its way down around the tubes in my throat as I looked through the wire-mesh window. One yellow figure towered over another, struggling to tie a face mask in place. Daddy? Had he actually come all the way from Vancouver? It would be his first visit here in two years. The other, shorter figure reached out as if to help him with the mask, then hesitated. The gloved hand withdrew.

Those clumsy, uncertain figures couldn't be my parents. They were no more familiar than any of the other gowned strangers who wandered in and out of my room.

Panic swelled in my chest.

Nurse Hook motioned to the window. Almost instantly, the doors beside it swung open, then closed. The strangers stood frozen at the end of my bed. Shadows below their eyes revealed fear and weariness.

Nurse Hook picked up her chart and moved to the other side of the room, and the strangers came back to life. The tall one planted two chairs up along the left side of the bed, carefully leaving an arm's length between them.

"Hello, Dayle." Daddy's voice wrapped itself around me, cozy and warm, like one of Gram's crocheted afghans. But he perched himself on the edge of a chair, stiff and uncertain, and the secure feeling his voice had offered took flight. I caught a quick glimpse of his eyes before they began to dart about the room. Familiar hazel eyes, but different somehow, lined and creased in a way I hadn't noticed before. And it wasn't just that they were older. They seemed nervous. Worried. Afraid to look at me, or maybe they just *couldn't* look at me.

Mom began to speak, hesitatingly at first, as if she were

afraid that her words might interfere with the hiss and whir of the machines around me. Then her tone smoothed out and softened, and my eyes closed. She spoke about how the sun had finally decided to stay for a while, and how green the grass was after all the rain, how fresh everything smelled, as fresh as mountain air. Did I remember our trip to the mountains, when I was twelve? We did some climbing up tame slopes and stood in awe of other climbers with special boots and equipment who took on higher peaks. She spoke of the man we met who told us that the view from the top made the effort of climbing worthwhile.

For a tiny sliver of time, I almost forgot where I was.

When Mom's voice faded away, I opened my eyes to see Daddy bobbing his head and jiggling his knees, his rubber-gloved fingers laced together in his lap. "It looks like they're taking pretty good care of you in here. Doesn't it, Aileen?"

Mom nodded. Her long rubbery fingers fluttered over the bed covers, gently smoothing them over and over again.

Daddy cleared his throat and whipped a small pink teddy bear out from under his gown. "Thought this might brighten up your room." He stood and searched the tiny space, gently thumping the stuffed toy against his hip. Every inch of the room held blinking, whirring medical equipment and paraphernalia.

"On the shelf," Mom said, "behind you."

Daddy raised his eyebrows at Nurse Hook, who told him to go ahead. He tucked the bear behind a glass door, jammed between bottles and boxes. His eyes skimmed over mine, then he opened the door again and repositioned the bear. "Can you see it?"

I moved my chin up and down. I used to love Daddy's teddy bears, the ones that lined my bed and peppered my bookshelf. Big ones, small ones, white ones, blue ones, even a purple piggy-bank bear. And now a pink bear. Like the one Baby Carmen held in the photograph Daddy had sent. I closed my eyes and Mom stroked my left cheek with a touch as light as a feather. Or a fly.

Flies. Lots of them. Hovering over me under a purple sky, droning loudly, sticking to my eyes, my face ... Sirens, screaming in the distance ....

I shuddered. For a few moments, the only sound was the squeak of Nurse Hook's rubber-soled shoes as she walked around the bed to the sink.

Mom interrupted the silence. "Denise is sorry she missed you. She'll visit again soon. She's been here every day," Mom continued. "And Amy —"

She stopped abruptly. Daddy's face mask had slipped down. He gasped and quickly pulled it up again, holding it there with trembling hands while Mom retied it. When it was done, he closed his eyes and let out a long, deep sigh that made his shoulders droop. His hands fell limply into his lap.

Mom frowned at him. Their eyes met and held for a moment, just long enough for me to feel their terror. Opposing voices battered my skull. I *am* dying!

Don't be stupid! If you were going to die, you would have stayed with Gram.

Mom began to talk again, but quickly, as if her words could erase that awkward moment. Something about hospital food and the old magazines in the waiting room. Her hands flew about as she spoke.

Daddy cleared his throat again and Mom's nervous chatter faded. "Uh, your mother tells me some friends have been asking about you."

Which friends? Keith? Amy?

Mom spread her hands over her knees. "They all want to see you, but only family members are allowed in here."

Have they been here? Have they asked about me?

"The Ingaldson boy, what's his name ... Stewart?" She tapped her fingers on her skirt.

I nodded.

"He says he has something for you. He'll bring it as soon as they move you to the burn ward."

Stu, phew! Taunting words exploded from somewhere in the past and ricocheted through my brain, echoing with the sound of a familiar voice. It wasn't my voice, but for some reason, a leaden ball of guilt formed in my stomach anyway.

He can't come. I shook my head as hard as the tubes and prickly pain would let me. How could I let him visit with that unidentified guilt nagging at me?

Am I going to die? I tried to mouth the words around the tube.

"What?" Mom leaned forward, tiny folds appearing between her brows.

I shook my head and squeezed the bedcovers harder. Nurse Hook appeared with a pen and a clipboard.

"Thanks, Cora." Mom gently eased my left hand away from the sheets and placed the pen between my left fingers and thumb. "I know you're right-handed, but try, okay?" She held the clipboard firmly in front of me.

I dragged the pen across the clipboard as carefully as I could, fighting the quivering weakness in my arm and hand. I wanted to know for sure. *Die?* The letters ran together in a skew of lines and curves that even I couldn't read.

Mom squinted at the clipboard, tilting her head side to side. She frowned and handed the clipboard to Daddy. His shoulders twitched — almost a shrug — and his eyes flickered from Mom to me. "Sorry, kiddo, but I can't make this out."

I wanted to scream. I tried to scream, with every ounce of energy I could push from my lungs. A dull squeal scraped out around the tube and suddenly, a loud beeping noise erupted, keeping pace with my throbbing howl. My arms and legs flailed out, even the burned ones.

Mom leaped from her chair. "What is it, Cora? What's wrong?"

Nurse Hook swiftly moved to my side. "Easy, honey. Settle down now."

As my attempt to scream faded, so did the beeping sound.

"It's nothing to worry about," Nurse Hook said. "Just the respirator. It reflects any sudden change in Dayle's breathing pattern."

"Oh." Mom sat down again without taking her eyes off of me.

I squeezed my eyes against the tears and slammed my fist into the bed over and over again, making grunting sounds in my chest. The beeping rose again.

What happened? WHY IS THIS HAPPENING TO ME?

I heard Nurse Hook — no, Cora, isn't that what Mom called her? — telling my parents that it was almost time for my therapy and that they could visit me later. The beeping stopped. Chairs scraped against the floor. I felt the warmth of Daddy's body as he leaned over me and whispered in my ear. "I love you, Sweet Pea."

Sweet Pea. I hadn't heard that in a long time. I thought Daddy reserved it for Baby Carmen now. I jerked my head away to hide my tears. He gave my foot a gentle squeeze and held on as if he was afraid to let go.

That squeeze connected me to vague memories of other visits; my parents hovering over me in fearful silence, Denise, her pale blue eyes staring into my own for a moment, then blinking and turning away. And Keith. I could see his face and hands pressed against the glass. And I could even — almost — picture Amy peering at me through the meshed wire of the window of my room.

When I opened my eyes, Mom and Daddy were gone and Cora was injecting another syringe into the ever-present bag over my head. I watched it sway and thought of the lake and Gram, and the horrible pain of being left behind.

I swish my burned legs in the water and try to stop sobbing, but I can't. And it's not the pain of my burns that makes me cry; Mom and Daddy are getting a divorce. How can they be so cruel? Did she kick him out? Did he get tired of her being away so much? Or did he just get sick of Denise and me fighting all of the time?

Footsteps creak on the dock behind me. It's Gram, from the light, shimmering and translucent and — no. No. She's changing into someone else — Gram, like she used to look when I was younger. She hikes up her long flowered night-gown and sits down beside me. Her bare vein-puckered legs dangle in the water, then her thin, warm arm slides around my shoulders and stays there until my body stops trembling.

"Do you know," Gram begins, "that your mother was only twelve when she lost her father?" She hugs me closer and I know what she's going to say next. "He died. Your father may not be around as much as you'd like any more, but you'll still get to see him. Think of what you've got and trea-sure it. Don't worry about what you've lost." She kisses the

top of my head. "Just remember — your father loves you, even if he can't always say it."

Maybe, but I sure don't feel like his "Sweet Pea" any more.

CHAPTER TWELVE

Friday, June 6: Day 6

THE COOKIE SHEET BUSINESS was a total failure. I knew it would be even before Mom finished spreading the magnetic letters in front of me.

"They tell me your tubes will be out soon and you'll be able to talk. But I know you have questions ...."

I stared at the rainbow of letters before me.

"Go on," Mom said. "Ask me anything."

Gram would have picked up a book and read patiently while I figured out what to say, but Mom sat on the edge of her chair, tapping her rubber-gloved fingers on her knees. The steady, annoying *plaaaaat* of her fingertips kept time with the throbbing itch of my left calf graft as well as my left thigh, where Dr. Burke had peeled away skin to use for the graft. Both areas were healing well, Cora had told me; that's why they were itchy.

But it didn't matter why they were itchy. The irritation of that combined with the unrelenting pain of my burns made me mad enough to want to throw something — at just about anyone.

Mom leaned forward, staring at the letter-splattered cookie sheet. A few wisps of honey-blond hair fell forward and stuck to her mascara. She tucked the escapees back up under her cap without taking her eyes off my hands.

Don't stare at me! I tried to slide a few of the letters around with my left hand, but it wasn't easy. As an early-afternoon dose of morphine settled in, dullness took over. I had always thought drugs would kill pain, like they did for patients on TV, but they didn't. Drugs only blurred pain a little, shifting it from a direct assault into a slightly skewed echo that made me feel as though my body and brain had drifted apart.

A bright yellow letter "A" slipped across the cookie sheet just ahead of my clumsy fingers.

Grab the letter, dummy.

What starts with "A" anyway?

Agony.

Mom tapped her fingers on her knees, staring at the plastic letters in front of me as though she were willing them to move. "I know this is tough, Dayle." She sighed. "I'll be glad when we can talk again."

Why? We've never talked before. You always left that to Gram. Good thing I couldn't talk. It may have been true, but it wasn't fair. Even in my druggy state, I knew that much.

I did have plenty of questions — about Keith and Amy, and what my penalty would be for "stealing" the van. I looked back down at the cookie sheet. Those questions were too complicated for a single pack of magnetic letters. I fought the descending cloud of medication and thought of something simpler.

W-H-A-T   H-A-P-

Before I'd pushed the second pink "P" into place, Mom spoke. "There was an explosion, dear."

I know that! I scowled at her.

"Something to do with gasoline. Apparently there was some trouble starting the bonfire." Her eyes focused on something in the distance, something beyond the window to my cage-of-a-room. She spoke slowly, choosing her words carefully, as if the wrong one might cause another explosion. "Everything was wet, you know. After all the rain." She closed her eyes, shaking her head stiffly.

"No! Pete!" Marnie's voice jolted through my brain in a flash of white light and my body jerked violently, as if everything had happened all over again. This whole mess was Pete's fault. I slammed my left hand into the cookie sheet.

"I know," Mom said. "I know." She gently smoothed the wrinkles from my bedcovers and squeezed my good hand. "Your father is still in his hotel room. He'll be over this afternoon. Denise is coming later too. She's having lunch with Joseph." Her voice softened further. "I know you're worried. About a lot of things. But please, try not to. Everything will be fine. You'll be fine. Just fine."

Who are you trying to convince, Mom? Me? Or you?

Mom cleared her throat. "Denise and Joseph tidied up the van the other day. It's as clean as new. I took it in to get the air conditioning fixed and ..." Her voice tapered off. She stared at my hand, watching as I clacked a letter "K" against the metal sheet.

How did she know I was thinking about the van? And how could *she* think about it when I lay there, helpless and tortured? Breath whistled angrily around my nose tube.

"Look." Mom studied her hands as she spoke. "I know this is difficult and awkward and I imagine that you're wishing your grandmother was here." She paused for a moment and looked to the ceiling, her eyelids fluttering rapidly. "I wish she was too. She'd be able to tell me what to do." She turned her gaze to me again. "I don't know what to do for you, Dayle, but I'm trying."

I nodded, then swallowed hard and shoved a few more letters into place.

K-E-I-T-H

"Well ... he's not allowed to visit yet ...." Mom spoke hesitantly. "But he's very concerned about you. He's been here every day. Poor boy ...."

Poor boy what? I blinked at her furiously and slammed a few more letters into place.

W-H-A-T

Mom studied the cookie sheet, then met my eyes with a questioning look.

I traced the shape of a question mark on the cookie sheet. She still looked puzzled.

P-O-O-R B

"Poor boy? Oh. You want to know what I meant by that."

I nodded.

"He seems so worn out," she said slowly. She leaned back and a strange expression touched her eyes, something I couldn't quite read.

Why didn't he send me a sticky note, or have Mom or Denise deliver a few words? Something personal. Something that could connect us, even through the wire-mesh window. I brought my left hand to my throat, remembering the pendant.

Mom slipped a white envelope out of her purse. "Are you

thinking of this?" She lifted the necklace from the envelope and held it out to me.

I nodded, aching to touch it.

"They gave it to me after the accident. I polished it up a little. It was … well, they don't want you to have any jewellery in here, so I kept it in my purse." Mom gently placed the pendant in my left hand. "It's beautiful."

I squeezed my fingers closed around it, marvelling at the coolness of the smooth yellow shape and the fact that it hadn't dissolved with my skin. What temperature did gold melt at? I remembered my vision of the emergency room. There was a thin white line around the girl's neck — my neck. Keith's gift had protected me. I imagined a heart-shaped tattoo clinging to the base of my throat.

You're special, Dayle.

If I was so special, why wasn't he with me now, when I needed him most?

Mom grasped her right knee with both hands. "Ask me another question."

I jabbed my finger at the letters of Keith's name again.

Mom's eyes blinked rapidly, then creased around the edges as if she was forcing her cheeks up into a smile. "Don't worry. I'll let him know you were asking about him." She crossed and uncrossed her legs. "Let me see … ah. I've spoken to Amy several times. She's been here often." Mom pointed at the window. "She says you were sleeping every time she came. She's waiting for them to move you out of ICU so she can visit."

N-O

"No? I've asked, but they won't let her in any sooner," Mom said.

I jabbed my left forefinger at the letters over and over again. *No, no, NO!*

Mom's eyebrows dipped into a puzzled frown. "You don't want her to come?"

I stared at Mom without blinking.

"I don't understand. She's your best friend ...."

Not any more. She said so. I don't want her pity. The words screamed inside my head but I couldn't have shared them with Mom, even if there had been enough letters to choose from. I swept my left hand across the cookie sheet and knocked the rainbow alphabet to the floor. *Keep your damn cookie sheet! It doesn't help anyway!*

Mom blinked and bent down to gather up the letters, dropping them back into their box. As she folded the lid closed over the letters, a horrifying thought occurred to me. I clenched my jaw and made a soft grunting sound in my chest, limply gesturing toward the box. Mom gently rolled the letters back onto the cookie sheet and crouched beside the bed as I struggled to gather the letters I needed.

W-H-O E-L-S H-R-T

The only sound in the room was that of Cora shuffling through an open cupboard. Mom's hands trembled. She squeezed them together, massaging her thumbs. Her eyes wouldn't meet mine as she rose to her feet. "Well ...."

Panic tightened around the tubes in my throat. *What aren't you telling me, Mom? Is it Keith? Was he hurt too? You said he's been here every day, but where? Did I really see him peering through the glass, or was it just my imagination? He's worn out. What does that mean? Is he stuck in a room somewhere suffering too? Tell me about Keith! Tell me, Mom, I need to know!*

I searched through the shredded images of that horrible night, trying to remember where Keith was standing when the accident happened. As hard as I tried, I couldn't sift his image from the rubble.

Cora turned around to face us, a tray of bandages and scissors balanced in her hands. She glanced at the cookie sheet, then at Mom's troubled frown. "Maybe that's enough for now, Aileen. It's almost time for dressing changes and her basin bath."

Mom gave Cora a slight nod and scooped up the sheet, letters and all, still avoiding my eyes. She rose and kissed my forehead with her eyes closed. "I'll be back later, Dayle."

Tell me, Mom. Tell me who else was hurt!

She escaped through the door while I slammed my fist into the bed.

Traitor! Coward! Tell me the truth!

Mom stopped on the other side of the door and pulled down her mask to talk to Dr. Burke. They stood so closely together that their sleeves touched. Mom's shoulders rose and fell heavily as she spoke, gasping with every breath — someone who had just made a narrow escape, someone who had something to hide. She wiped her eyes.

Cora set the tray down on the counter next to the bed. The unexpected clatter sent my arms and legs flailing like a frightened kitten. She gently touched my left arm. "It's okay, Dayle. People who've been through traumatic experiences are often upset by unexpected noises. It's called the startle reflex."

I remembered how Amy had jumped at the sound of a chattering squirrel and how terrified she had looked when I'd slammed my locker door closed. The startle reflex? She'd been through a traumatic experience too. But I didn't want to think about that. As awful as Amy's robbery had been, it didn't compare to what I had to suffer through.

Time for her basin bath. That's what Cora had told Mom. It made it sound so simple. Close to pleasant, even. But the basin bath brought sharp, steely tools that scraped dead flesh from my body. Morphine distorted the torture but I still knew it for what it was. Debriding. Humiliating and painful, all in the name of therapy.

And while my flesh was being raked, other gowned people bent and twisted my limbs. They told me the treatment was supposed to keep me limber and prevent the scars of healing from binding me into a tight cocoon. But at that moment I wanted to curl up into a tight cocoon and die, or at least sink so low beneath the surface of the earth that no one would ever find me.

It wasn't fair. Why did I have to suffer like this? Why did Amy and I have to fight? Why did this horrible accident have to happen just when my life was coming together?

And what about Keith?

Please, God, let him be okay.

The hallway is dark and smoky, but I have to get to the room at the end. It's a room just like mine, with a wire-mesh window and wide double doors. I wipe thick, black smudge away from the glass. He's lying there, just beyond my reach, helpless, hooked up to tubes and wires, with bandages everywhere.

Suddenly, fire sweeps out from under the bed.

I throw myself at the door but it won't open, so I scream through the window. "Keith. Keith, I'm here. I'll save you." I punch my fist through the glass and rip the wire open with my bare hands, but by the time I crawl through the torn wires and shards of glass, there is nothing left but smoke.

CHAPTER THIRTEEN

Saturday, June 7: Day 7

DR. BURKE AMBLED INTO THE ROOM just before eleven, sucking his pale blue mask in and out with an obnoxiously cheerful whistle. "Ready to lose this tube?" He pointed to the one in my throat.

When I nodded, surprised, he started whistling again and proceeded to yank out the tube. After I finished gagging and coughing, he put his hand on my left shoulder. "How does that feel?"

I made an awkward one-sided shrug.

"Can you speak now?"

I cleared my throat and swallowed hard a few times, trying to wash away the rough feeling the tube had left behind. "I guess so." The voice I heard was weak. It was also low and gravelly, like someone recovering from a bad case of laryngitis. I wondered what Keith would think when he heard it. *If* he heard it ....

I squeezed my eyes closed. I had to find out if Keith was okay.

Cora patted my hand and smiled. "Don't worry, hon. A month or so and you'll sound like yourself again."

"Who else was hurt?" My weak voice gave no force to the question, even though I blurted it out.

Dr. Burke and Cora exchanged glances, as if they were conspiring about what to say, but I didn't want to hear excuses. I didn't want to be put off again.

"Mom wouldn't tell me. My boyfriend, Keith Hutton, is he ..."

Cora's eyes brightened. "Your boyfriend? He's just fine. He wasn't injured at all."

"You'll get to see him before you know it," Dr. Burke added.

"Really?" I squeaked. Relief and elation flooded through me. Keith was fine. Mom hadn't been keeping things from me after all; morphine had been playing with my mind. I blinked and cleared my throat again, then swallowed a few times.

Cora's eyes smiled. "Feels good to get rid of the breathing tube, doesn't it?"

I nodded and pointed to the tube in my nose. "What about this one?" I didn't want it around when I saw Keith.

Dr. Burke studied me for a moment. "Well, how do you feel about having something to eat?"

"Eat?" The thought of food made my stomach swill.

"If we remove the nasogastric tube, you'll have to feed yourself. Otherwise, the tube will go right back in. You need to consume about twice as many calories as usual for those burns of yours to heal."

"But why? I'll gain weight —"

Dr. Burke shook his head. "That's not likely. Tissue regeneration requires a significant amount of caloric energy."

"What do I have to eat?"

"Just about whatever you want. Any favourite foods?"

I didn't say anything. Even Lee's egg rolls wouldn't tempt

me now.

"I'll talk to your mother. See if we can't come up with something. If you eat a bit today, we'll pull the tube tomorrow morning, before we move you out of ICU. Breakfast tray is on the way." Dr. Burke nodded brusquely and left.

"I'm leaving ICU?"

Cora checked the IV swinging over my head. "You're going to the burn ward tomorrow."

Panic surged through my pain-prickled limbs.

Cora smiled. "This is a good thing, Dayle. It means you've recovered enough that you'll be okay without all these bells and whistles." She motioned to the array of equipment surrounding me. Although there was still some dull humming and a few lights glowing, the whir and click of the ventilator had ceased when they removed the tube from my throat. The room seemed strangely quiet. "We'll keep the heart monitor and these other machines hooked up until you leave. But right now, they're just a formality."

I couldn't believe what I was hearing. How could they send me away when everything still hurt so bad? They were giving up on me. I moaned and closed my eyes.

"Oh, hon. I know. It's going to hurt for a while, but you'll start feeling better soon. It's a gradual process." Cora gently touched my left shoulder.

I opened my eyes again. "How do you know? Have you ever been burned?"

Cora shook her head. "No, no I haven't. But I've seen quite a few burn patients come and go through here. And I grew up in Northwest Ontario, where my father was a fire fighter. I've heard a lot about fires and the people who suffer because of them. I know how destructive they can be. But you're strong, Dayle, and that counts for a lot. You're going to be okay. Really."

"How can you say that for sure?"

Cora lowered herself into the chair by my bed and leaned forward. "We have this way of measuring a patient's potential for survival. We call it the Rule of One Hundred."

"What does that mean?"

"We take the percentage of the patient's body with second and third degree burns and add that number to their age. If the total is less than one hundred, their potential for survival is good. If the total is one hundred or more, the patient is less likely to recover."

"So?"

"In your case, you suffered a forty-five percent burn. Add that to your age, and you have a total of sixty-two."

"Aren't numbers ever wrong?"

"We've had some patients recover who shouldn't have, others die whom we didn't expect to. But those who didn't make it usually had other outstanding medical conditions. You're young and strong, and you had a clean bill of health before your accident. And you *are* healing well."

"Oh."

Cora gently squeezed my hand. "You'll be fine on H5."

"Are you ... will you be there too?"

"I wish I could be, Dayle, but I'm an ICU nurse. I'm not trained for the burn ward. Don't worry. The nurses down there are terrific. You've met some of them already. Remember Kathy and Maureen, from your dressing changes?"

I closed my eyes again. Dressing changes weren't something I liked to remember.

Cora's attempts to reassure me weren't going to work anyway; I didn't want to cheer up. Cora was my nurse, the only one I wanted. She never left my room when she was on shift, not even for a drink of water. She was the one who explained things to me and made sure I got my morphine on time. She stood up for me when Mom and Daddy suffocated me with nervous attention. Leandra, a tiny butterfly woman who made soft sighing sounds, fluttered around my room doing Cora's job during the night. But Leandra never had much to say and I hadn't gotten to know her as well. Cora was familiar, and that made me feel safe.

She squeezed my hand again. "You'll still have Dr. Burke, Dayle. He'll be with you through all of this and he's a wonderful plastic surgeon. You're strong and determined. You're going to be just fine."

I found it hard to believe her. She was, after all, betraying me — deserting me — like Gram and Amy.

I swallowed a couple of mouthfuls of scrambled eggs from a cold breakfast tray, and threw them up all over the floor.

I'm naked and shivering, perched in a nest of twisted white sheets and yellowed tubing. A flock of older birds gather around me, clucking and cooing, pecking at my grey, peeling flesh, scraping it away and plucking out shiny silver things that hold skin patches on my right leg. They sort through my limbs like ravens clawing dead meat. When they're finished, they wrap me in a cloak of warm feathers. Their faces are nearly hidden by huge blue beaks, but human-like eyes blink behind them. "Time to fly," they seem to say, nudging me toward the edge of the nest.

I dig my clawed feet into the white sheets and think about falling. A short, dark bird with sapphire eyes seems to smile through her beak. "It's okay," she says. "You might fall,

but you'll get up again."
She hums a sweet, sad lullaby.

The sting of freshly scraped flesh surfaced through a fading morphine haze and pulled me out of an unsettled sleep. The clock told me afternoon was almost over.

"Hi, Dayle." A petite gowned person bounced in. Her voice was cheery and very familiar, although I couldn't place it. I studied her face — what I could see of it — thin, dark curls trying to spring out from underneath her cap, a sprinkling of pale freckles across the bridge of her nose. Her eyes sparkled at me, clear and mesmerizing, a kaleidoscope of blues, the eyes of a person to be trusted.

"You might not remember me. My name is Naomi. I'm your occupational therapist — or at least one of them. My job is to help you adjust to the changes in your life, find ways of doing things for yourself."

This Naomi person must have confused me with another patient. I was in too much pain and far too weak to do anything for myself. That's why I had a nurse. And what changes in my life was she talking about? Nothing had changed. The hospital stay was horrible and something I'd never forget, but when my burns healed and the pain went away, everything would be exactly like it was before. I would have no scars. I *refused* to have scars.

The door squeaked and Mom stepped into the room, leaving Daddy holding the door open behind her. She looked from Naomi to Cora. "Should we come back later? Dr. Burke told us that Dayle can speak again. But we don't want to interfere ...."

Naomi flicked her left hand and shook her head. "I just popped up from H5 to talk to Dayle for a moment. I'm usually only around during her dressing changes to do therapy, and that's not always such a good time to talk. You're welcome to come in."

"Are you sure?" Daddy stepped into the room.

Cora spoke firmly. "As long as Dayle is comfortable, it'll be fine."

All heads swung to me.

If this Naomi person had made a special trip to talk to me, she had something important to say. I wanted to digest it on my own, without feeling my parents' eyes riveted on me, waiting to pounce with nervous hugs and words of comfort. I studied the question in their pained, anxious eyes. *Shall we stay or go?* I clutched a handful of bed covers. "Stay," I said, even though my brain screamed *GO!*

Instead of sitting down and facing the side of the bed like my parents did, Naomi turned a chair to face me directly. "You're doing very well, Dayle," she said, her eyes on mine. "I don't know if you'll remember this, but the nurses removed about fifty staples from the graft on your right leg earlier this afternoon. There are a few more to go but it looks good."

I didn't say anything. I remembered birds.

"Did they tell you that you're going down to H5 tomorrow? That's the burn ward, on the fifth floor."

I nodded.

Naomi cocked her head to the side. "Can you speak?"

"Yes."

"Ah. Good. Anyway, on H5 your routine will alter a bit. Your dressing changes and range-of-motion therapy will happen in the morning instead of the afternoon as they usually do here. After that you'll have lunch if you're able — that whole routine is very tiring — and then you'll get a couple of hours rest."

"Oh."

"As soon as Dr. Burke says you're ready, you'll begin spending part of your afternoon in the physiotherapy room. We want to get you walking again."

The thought of standing on my burning, prickly right leg made my stomach roll. "I can't walk. Not yet. There's no way."

"I know it's painful. But as I mentioned before, the graft on your leg is healing nicely. Very nicely. And so is the donor site. Your pain will lessen as the grafts and healing progress. And every attempt you make to become mobile will help bring back your strength." Naomi paused as if she was waiting for me to comment. I didn't. "Anyway," she continued, "the thing about the physiotherapy room is that it's full of mirrors."

"Oh." I glanced around my room and realized for the first time that there was not a single mirror in it.

"Have you seen yourself since the accident?"

Goosebumps crawled up my left side.

"Oh, no ..." Mom's voice cut into the conversation. "She's never — "

"Yeah. I've seen myself," I whispered dully.

Mom stiffened.

"Oh?" Surprise flickered in Naomi's voice. "Where?"

"When?" Daddy's eyes widened.

I closed my eyes; it was the next best thing to walking away from everyone. I listened to the calming pace of Cora's footsteps as she moved about the room. "I'm not sure exactly. Emergency, I guess."

The room was silent. Even Cora stopped moving.
Mom leaned forward.

"Why don't you tell us what you saw?" Naomi's cheerful note returned.

I opened my eyes again and focused on her. "It was — I was looking down, through a kind of tunnel — and I saw this person just lying there. A bunch of people were poking at her and they put those things on her chest — paddles, I guess you call them — and when I saw her ... her face ... I realized it was me. I was looking at *me*. And then I came back down."

"Down from where?" Curiosity knotted Mom's brows.

"I don't know. From some kind of light."

Daddy rubbed his forehead with a rubber-gloved hand. "This is nonsense. What's she talking about? Must be the drugs. She's been on morphine since they brought her in, hasn't she? And morphine is hallucinogenic, correct?"

"It can be." Naomi spoke softly.

I felt my face flush, humiliated by my own father.

"Can you describe your injuries?" Naomi's eyes focused on mine.

"I don't want to think about it."

"Shall I describe them to you?" She was persistent, but gentle.

"No," I said sharply. I closed my eyes and tried to steady my breathing. I didn't want to think about the girl on the table — or her horrid wounds. Injuries like that would have to leave *some* kind of scarring.

"Burns can be difficult to look at, but it's something you need to do." Naomi wasn't going to give up.

I took a deep breath. "There was a big bruise on her — I mean, on my left forehead and eye. My whole right side was — when I saw it — everything was all red and swollen and dripping, like a huge blister. My hair looked like it had partly melted away on the one side ... and ... and ..."

"Couldn't she have imagined this?" Daddy whispered faintly.

"And?" Naomi coaxed me.

"And ... my face ... the side of my face ...." My voice faded.

Mom's gloved fingers gripped the armrests of her chair. "How would she know all this?"

"I told you. I saw it ..." I hesitated for a second, "... and I saw Gram too."

"You saw Gram?" There was an edge of something raw in Mom's voice. I couldn't tell if it was excitement or disbelief or a bit of both.

"Yes. In the light."

"That's not possible, Sweet Pea." Daddy shook his head.

"Yes it is. I saw her. And it was real. She was real. I know the difference between what's real and what the drugs do." I squeezed my eyes closed and clenched my jaw against the half-truth. I wasn't sure what was real any more.

"Must have been the bump on her head," Daddy said.

Loud, rasping sobs sprang from my chest.

"I'm sorry, but I'm going to have to ask you to leave ...." That was Cora, rising to my defence again.

"I know. I'm sorry too." Mom's voice wavered.

I heard Cora tell Mom something about needing to keep me calm and I felt Daddy squeeze my toes. His touch was brief this time, as if he were too busy trying to digest everything I'd said to show me any comfort. The doors squeaked open and gently thudded closed.

I'm going to live. Big deal. What kind of a freak am I going to be? Why can't they believe me? Why me? Why did this have to happen to me?

As I sobbed in anger and frustration, Naomi moved around the bed. She held my left hand and stroked my arm. "It won't always be like this," she said. "Your body will heal, and with plastic surgery you'll be surprised at how much better you'll look and feel. You'll see." And then, softly, she began to hum a familiar lullaby. I let the music take me away.

They were supposed to move me into the burn ward, but instead I'm in my room at home and it looks just as it did when I was six. Pink and pretty and perfect — like I'll never be again.

Gram sits on the side of the bed and sings the Mockingbird *song.*

"Why do you always sing the Mockingbird *song?" I ask.*

Gram tilts her head to the side and the song's lyrics fade into a gentle hum that keeps time with the evening's wind-song. She leans over and touches her strong, soap-scented fingers to my left cheek, the good cheek, and she smiles. "I suppose it just comes naturally. Mama always sang it for me."

"Did you sing it for my mom when she was young?"

"When she was young."

"Then why haven't I ever heard her sing it? She doesn't sing at all."

Even with the pale moonlight streaming through my open bedroom window, Gram's eyes grow dull, focused on some faraway place. "She left singing behind, my dear, with a great many other things from her childhood."

"What do you mean?"

Gram sighs. "I imagine it reminds her of how things were before Grandpa died."

"I don't get it. If it was me, I'd want to remember."

Gram shakes her head and slowly rises from my bed. "It

was different for Aileen. I think she felt Grandpa and I betrayed her."

"How?"

"Half-truths, my dear." I can barely hear Gram's voice over the wind whispering in the elms outside my window. "Half-truths."

CHAPTER FOURTEEN

SHE STOOD WITH HER BACK to me, a tall, slender figure whose grace could not be undone by the shapeless gown draped over her body. A knot of envy skewered itself into my chest and snaked toward my tongue.

"So you finally decided to come for a visit." Pain and weariness almost wiped the sarcasm from my words.

Denise turned away from the window and clasped her hands in front of her. "I didn't know you were awake."

"Just opened my eyes."

"Oh. Well. I have been here before, you know. You were always sleeping."

"So Mom tells me. Lucky you."

"Dayle. Honestly." Denise's hands fell to her side. As she stepped toward me and away from the window, I could see Joseph beyond the glass, talking to a nurse at the nursing station. With his faded denim jacket — the same one he always wore — and his longish crop of wild, wavy auburn hair, he hardly seemed Denise's type. But he was here, right outside my door, and my boyfriend wasn't. How fair was that?

"Why'd you bring *him* along?" I groaned, trying to shift my position on the rough hospital sheets.

A concerned frown wrinkled Denise's brow. "We're going

to a movie later."

"What does Mom think of him?"

Denise glanced over her shoulder at the window. When she looked back at me, a ridiculously happy doe-eyed expression softened what I could see of her face. She smoothed the folds of her gown. "She thinks he's charming." Denise giggled and nodded at the chair. "Can I sit?"

"Since when do you need my permission to do anything?" I said crisply.

Denise ignored my remark and calmly sat down, adding to my fury. I wanted to ruffle her feathers. "So. Does *Joseph* know about *Gavin*?"

Denise's eyebrows flattened into a thin line. She didn't speak for a moment, but when she did, her voice remained cool and even. "He knows I went with someone else for a while."

"You mean for a few years."

Denise shrugged.

"Joseph doesn't look like your type." *Lunge.*

"But he is. You'll see that when you get to know him." *Parry.*

"Think he'll be around long enough?" *Lunge.*

Denise didn't even bother to respond to that jab. It was obvious that she had no intention of sparring with me. I kept up the sarcasm anyway. "So. Did Mom and Daddy tell you how crazy I am? What I saw?"

"Are you talking about the light?" she asked slowly.

I nodded.

"Well ..." she hesitated. "Nobody said you were crazy. I spoke to Dad on the phone just before supper. He seemed a little ... uh ... unnerved by your revelation. But Mom spent the rest of the afternoon on the Internet, searching for information about out-of-the-body or near-death experiences."

"Another book," I said.

"Maybe."

"I did almost die, didn't I?"

Denise pressed her hands together. "Well, you must be feeling better now. Mom told me they're moving you out of Intensive Care."

"I feel *worse*," I snapped. "You should see what they do to me in here."

Denise shifted in her chair and clutched the arms of it with her long, rubber-gloved fingers.

"You know what the hardest part is? Always having people coming in to poke at me and look at my burns ...."

Denise looked down at her lap.

"Bunches of them come at a time. Interns. And some of them are guys, young guys. One of them is really cute — I can tell by his eyes — and he looks at me, studies me until I feel like some kind of lab rat on display. It makes me want to scream, but even if I did it wouldn't make any difference. They'd still poke and prod and look."

Denise looked up again, her eyes shiny. "I'm sorry, Dayle," she said softly. "It's not fair. What can I do? Is there anything I can do to make things easier for you? Read to you, maybe, or —"

"Can you tell me where ..." I took a deep breath. "Where is Keith?" I fumbled for the necklace Cora had pinned on the sheet just behind my left shoulder.

Denise lifted the heart at the end of the chain and dropped it into my open palm. "He just left, Dayle, a few minutes ago. And he's been here every single day. Don't forget, you've been asleep most of the time. Oh." She stood and fumbled under her gown, then drew out a long, narrow white envelope. "He asked me to give this to you."

I held the envelope down on my left leg with my right hand, and picked at the sealed flap with the fingers of my left. "You didn't say anything to Keith about ... about what I told Mom and Dad this afternoon, did you?"

"No. I thought that was up to you."

"Good. Don't say anything. To anyone." The envelope wouldn't lie still long enough for me to rip the flap open.

"Here," Denise said. "Let me." She picked it open with clumsy gloved fingers and handed me the envelope.

A sticky note lay inside, pale yellow, almost the colour of hospital visitor gowns.

Denise glanced out the window. Joseph waved at her and smiled with that same silly expression she'd been wearing a few moments ago.

"You can go, you know." I almost hoped she *would* leave so that I could read the note in private.

Her eyes smiled, teasing. "I just got here. You want to get rid of me already?"

I didn't answer. I pulled the note out of the envelope and stared at it.

> Wish they'd let me in to see you. I'm so sorry.
> It should have been me, not you.
>
> > Keith

I shook my head, in spite of the painful prickling sensation in my neck.

"What's wrong?" Denise asked, leaning forward.

"I'm not sure. He thinks it should have been him. And he signed his name."

"So?"

"He never signs his name."

"Maybe he just wants to make sure you know —"

"Why does he think it should have been him instead of me?"

"People just feel that way sometimes, when someone they care about gets hurt. But everyone knows Pete was the one ..." Denise's voice trailed off, and her shoulders rose and fell heavily. A small tremor worked its way into her voice. "You know, if there is anyone else to blame for what happened, it's me."

"You?"

"I shouldn't have taken Joseph to the concert. I should have taken you. Or you should have gone with Keith. If I hadn't been so selfish, you wouldn't have been anywhere near that meadow place and this wouldn't have happened to you."

The sob that snagged her last words yanked at something in my chest. "Denise, get a grip. There's no way I would have gone to the concert. Not with Amy's tickets."

"I just don't understand." Denise frowned and waited for me to respond. I didn't. "Amy's been here every day," she continued, "just like Keith. She's obviously concerned about you."

"I don't want her pity."

"Pity? Dayle, it's not pity that brings her here. It's friendship. Years of it. Whatever it is between you two, you should put it to rest."

"Some things are easier said than done." I closed my eyes. The effort of talking was too much.

"You want to sleep now?"

"You should go anyway," I said sharply.

"If you want me to." Denise sounded hurt. She rose

from the chair.

"You don't want to be late for your movie."

"There's a later show too ...."

I opened my eyes again, but didn't say anything. Denise looked down and played with the folds of her gown for a moment, then turned to go.

"Denise ..."

She looked back at me.

"Don't worry. It wasn't your fault."

Tears brimmed in her eyes. She quickly turned away again.

As the doors closed behind her, I thought about Keith. Why he would feel responsible for what had happened? Everyone knew it was Pete's fault. How could Keith blame himself for that? Sometimes things just happen.

Gram lies against her faded pink pillow, pale and thin, her skin as transparent as wax paper, with the same bluish undertones. I sit on the edge of her bed humming the Mockingbird *song and stroking her hand. I keep my good side facing her so she won't worry about my problems.*

"Soon," she says, "they'll be here."

"You shouldn't go." I don't want her to leave because I know that if she does, she won't come back.

A cough rattles through her frail body. "I can't stay here any longer. Your mother lies awake every night in a panic, listening for my last breath."

"How do you know that?"

"Because that's what I would do."

So the ambulance comes and takes her away. There's no sense of urgency, no flashing lights or screaming sirens, just an awkward, damning silence that wraps itself around me, squeezing until I can't breathe.

I visit her in the hospital every afternoon at two — every afternoon but one. It's the first day of school after Christmas break. It's cold and snowy and I'm tired. I know Gram has something she wants to talk to me about — something to ask of me — and I'm afraid to find out what it might be. So I go home first to gather up enough courage to face all of the tubes and wires and machines that relentlessly whisper "death."

An awful feeling clutches my chest as soon as I enter the hospital doors — an eerie sense of déjà vu. I race down the hall through clouds of smoke, ignoring the searing pain on my right side and the smell of my own burned flesh, hoping, praying, that I won't miss my second chance.

But it's too late.

By the time I get to Gram's room, all that remains is an empty bed with a small wrinkled dip in the middle where she lay, and the horrible guilt of knowing I should have done better this time. I should have been here to tell her how much I love her.

I should have been here to say goodbye.

CHAPTER FIFTEEN

Sunday, June 8: Day 8

I HEARD IT as soon as they wheeled me through the double doors to the burn ward; a low, soul-wrenching moan that ballooned into shrieks of unbearable pain. With the vivid memories I had of basin baths and dead flesh being scraped away, it wasn't hard to imagine what caused that pain.

There were others around, just like me.

* * *

After they removed the gauzy, plastic-backed sheet soaked with blood and water and bits of grey flesh from under me, they wrapped me in warm blankets. The shivering stopped, a welcome kind of numbness settled into my bones and the echo of my screams finally faded. As I clutched that tiny sliver of peace, the door to my new room squeaked open and clicked closed.

I didn't bother opening my eyes to see who it was, but as soon as his warm dry hand gripped mine, I knew. "Keith?" I forced my heavy eyelids open. He stood over me, looking down, worried shadows dulling the green of his eyes.

"It's okay. I know you're tired. So sleep. I'll stay here with you until you do." A thin line of weariness — and something else, pain? — splintered his voice. He pulled a chair up to the bed and took my hand again in both of his, and I thought that, for the moment, this was as close to bliss as I could hope for.

The Mockingbird *slips through the lake, water gently splashing as we dip and pull our paddles. Gram looks over her shoulder and smiles at me. "This is my little piece of paradise," she says.*

Even though I'm sitting right behind her, her voice has a strange hollowness to it, as if it has to travel some distance before it reaches me.

"You mean the lake?" I ask.

"The lake, the cabin, the island. Everything here."

"Did you spend all your summers here when you were growing up?"

Gram makes a few more clean strokes through the water before she answers. "Most of them. When I was young."

"Why didn't you bring Mom when she was little? She told me she never saw the lake until she was in grade one. She never knew her grandma and grandpa."

Gram lays down her paddle and hops out of the canoe, and I do the same. We pull the Mockingbird *up onto the beach along a narrow stretch of sand, the only break in the rocky island shore. There is no conversation, just the sound of water lapping and the mournful cry of a loon.*

I press harder. This is another one of those questions that has never really been answered and now that I have another chance to ask, I need to know.

"Why?"

Gram looks up at the sky. Sunlight peeks through flat grey clouds and casts an eerie glow over her face. "My father and I had our differences."

"Like what?"

"He didn't agree with all of the choices I made." Gram lifts the picnic basket out of the canoe.

"So how come he left the cabin to you instead of your big brother?"

Gram doesn't answer this question right away either. She silently pads through tangled brush and over rock to the grassy place where we'll have our lunch. I have to hurry to keep up with her, snapping twigs and stumbling on stones as I go.

We stop at the smooth flat spot in front of the wildflower garden Gram and her mother planted so many years ago. Gram sets the basket down in front of daisies and red and pink yarrow. She pulls out a heavy gingham cloth and flaps it open. It settles like a falling parachute over the grass.

"Gram?"

She sits on the blanket and stares down the rocks, over the trees and past the shore to the other side of the lake, where the cabin can be spotted through the trees. She fingers the plain gold band on her left hand before she finally answers. "I suppose it was a peace offering."

"A peace offering?"

"Yes. My father's way of forgiving me and apologizing, all rolled into one." Her long tired sigh blends with the wind. "I only wish we could have made amends before he died."

She reaches into the basket for a loaf of crusty brown bread, and tears off a chunk for me.

CHAPTER SIXTEEN

Tuesday, June 10: Day 10

THEY CALLED MY ROOM an isolation room; I called it hell.

A small cubicle — an anteroom — separated me from the rest of the living, breathing world. At least in ICU, Cora or Leandra had stayed with me. Having someone else around to share my misery had made it a little easier to take.

Here, in isolation on the burn ward, there were no distractions from my throbbing pain; I had nothing to do but brood and suffer. In spite of morphine, my whole body trembled with the fresh, raw sensation of my latest debriding — one of my last, the nurses told me. Most of my dead grey flesh had been scraped away.

Hooray.

A TV loomed before me, but I didn't have the strength to raise my arm to turn it on. I had no radio to listen to, no books to look at. There was a window in the corner of the room, but it faced the endless brownish grey brick wall of the building next door. I couldn't even close my eyes and dream about something more pleasant — images of fire and puckered flesh lurked in every corner of my mind, waiting to pounce.

If I screamed, would anyone hear me?

I tried not to think about how awful I looked. My right arm was stuck rigidly out to the side, secured in position by a formed plastic mould, a kind of brace to keep my arm stationary while a fresh skin graft healed. Bandages still wrapped nearly half of my body, including the right side of my chest — my breast. I tried not to spend too much time thinking about *that* burn or what it might mean for my future. It made me wither inside.

And then there was my face. Although I still hadn't looked into a mirror, I knew that ugliness marked every pulsating throb from my temple through my cheekbone and down the side of my neck. One-armed glasses didn't help either, but it would be some time before I could wear contact lenses again. I'd have to wait until the wounds beside my right eye were healed and free of itching — and free of medications and lotions that could irritate my eye.

I felt like a scarecrow or Frankenstein's first cousin. But as much as I longed for company, I dreaded the idea of being seen, even by Keith. All I could remember of his first visit was an overwhelming sense of relief to know, to really know, that he was there. But during his next visit — when I'd been wider awake and more conscious of how awful I looked — I couldn't meet his eyes, let alone speak.

Part of me had longed to tell Keith about Gram and the light, about seeing myself from that strange, distant place, about the sudden revelation that there was more to life than "here." But another part of me feared he would think I was crazy, like Daddy seemed to, and I had more important things to worry about.

What does he think of me now that I look so horrible?
How long will he put up with an ugly, bedridden girlfriend?

Talking — or even thinking about talking — took too much energy.

I squeezed my patient-controlled analgesic pump — or PCA. They had hooked up the special self-serve morphine pump to my IV when I moved to the burn ward. It allowed me to top up a continual drip of the drug when I felt a need for it. But there were still limits to how much morphine I could have. A computer attached to the device made sure of that — cold, cruel and calculating.

The door from the anteroom opened and two gowned figures entered, one short and swift, the other slightly taller and heavier with a slower gait. Kathy and Maureen, respectively. Kathy had brown eyes with dark lashes; Maureen's eyes were grey and more widely spaced. I could only guess what the rest of their faces looked like from the way their masks fell over them.

Would I ever see a whole human face again?

"You weren't hungry today." Maureen picked the tray off my bed.

"I had some soup and jelly."

"I'll bring you one of those supplement shakes later. Chocolate, right?" Kathy asked.

I nodded glumly.

"You need as many calories as you can get right now." Maureen placed the tray in the pass-through cupboard connecting my room to the anteroom, so that food personnel wouldn't have to gown up to collect it. "Well, now, look at this." She pulled a tube of cellophane wrapped roses out of the pass-through cupboard and handed me the small card accompanying them.

For my Rose,
Keith

As I greedily drank in Keith's note, Maureen arranged the soft-pink roses in a blue plastic water jug and placed them on the counter at the end of my bed where I could easily see them.

Kathy wrapped a beige-coloured elastic type bandage around my right leg. "We're going to help you sit on the edge of the bed for a while before your nap."

"I don't feel like it." I stared at the loops and tails of Keith's words.

"I know." Kathy clipped the bandage in place. "This tensor band will keep blood from pooling in your injured leg."

"I don't want to sit up."

"You can't face the world propped up against pillows in a hospital bed. The sooner you sit, the sooner you'll adjust to being upright." Kathy gently moved my trembling legs toward the edge of the bed as Maureen eased me into a sitting position. I squeezed my eyes closed to steady myself against a dizzying wave of nausea.

Maureen supported me with her arm behind my back. "How does that feel?"

"Like —"

"You're sitting up!" I heard Mom sweep into the room behind me.

"Barely." I swayed forward, like a tower of blocks ready to tumble.

"This is wonderful!" Mom slipped around the bed to watch.

"Can you hold out a few minutes longer?" Kathy crouched before me, levelling her eyes with mine.

"No. I want to lie down again." I licked my dry lips and squeezed my eyes closed as they helped me back down.

"Morley — Dr. Burke — told me you were doing well, but I had no idea you'd be moving around." Mom eased herself into a chair by the window.

"That wasn't moving, Mom."

Maureen gently removed the tensor bandage.

Mom leaned forward. I followed her gaze to my injured leg. It was the first time since the night of the accident that I'd been able to bring myself to look at any part of my injuries. Pockmarks appeared around the border of the graft where staples had held it in place as it healed. Red skin speckled with tiny white lines spread from just above the ankle bone to the upper mid-thigh, front and side. I gasped. "Why is my leg covered with those white marks?"

"You mean where the graft is? You have a meshed skin graft. A meshed graft comes from stretching the harvested skin — the healthy skin they took from your left thigh, the donor site — before grafting it onto your burn."

"They stretched my skin?" I asked in disbelief.

Maureen explained that meshed skin allowed wounds to drain. It was also more efficient because it covered more burned area than non-meshed skin, and that way, less skin was needed from the patient's donor sites. If less healthy skin were removed, there was less raw area exposed and that meant faster healing. For a meshed graft, a small strip of skin went through a machine that poked holes in it. The holes made it easier to stretch the skin to cover a larger area, up to four times the size of the original harvested skin. As the holes were stretched, they pulled into thin lines.

Gross. "Will the red fade? Will the lines disappear?" My gravely voice croaked more than usual.

"The red will eventually fade. After a while, the lines will be much less noticeable."

I felt my chin wobble. "You mean ... they won't go away?"

Mom straightened in her chair.

"Not completely. But their appearance will improve dramatically," Maureen said matter-of-factly. She looked from Mom to me. "Don't worry. We won't use a meshed skin graft on your face or your hand."

I closed my eyes to hide from everyone.

Kathy gently pulled the covers back over me. "You're doing well, Dayle. A few more days and we'll fit your leg with a temporary pressure garment. By that time, you should be up and walking."

My eyes popped open. "You can't be serious."

"Oh, Dayle, you want to be mobile again, don't you?" Mom asked.

I didn't answer. If I were mobile, more people would see me. What would they say?

Poor, poor thing ....

If I looked like that, I'd hide ....

Shh. Don't stare. It's rude ....

Partly digested vegetable soup soured my throat.

I wiggled my right leg against the sheets, trying to scratch an itch that seemed to have grown roots. I had to admit the throbbing had faded, if only slightly. My left calf hurt more than my injured right leg did because a chunk of skin had been removed from it to graft over my right arm.

Mom went to the counter where Maureen had placed my roses.

"Your call bell is there if you need anything," Maureen said to me. "Otherwise, we'll put a Do Not Disturb sign on the door so you can get a couple of hours of rest." She turned to Mom. "Mrs. Meryk, you can have a few minutes with your daughter first."

"Thanks, Maureen." Mom touched one of the blooms with a rubber-gloved finger as Maureen and Kathy left. "Keith is so thoughtful." She shifted a few flowers around and stood back to admire her work. "I brought you something too." She pulled a thick pen and a smooth chocolate-brown leather journal from her purse.

"What am I supposed to do with those?"

"I thought you might find it helpful to write about what's happening to you."

I thought of Gram's journals, the ones she wrote in faithfully every day and kept hidden. I had always longed to read them to find out about her secrets. About why she and Mom had so much trouble getting along, why Gram rarely spoke of her own parents. Maybe her journals could give me an idea of where she wanted her ashes spread. But if I could read Gram's journals, couldn't someone just as easily read mine one day? I shuddered at the idea. What would people think if they knew how awful I could be? "I can't write." I pointed to my suspended right arm. "Remember?"

"Well, you could try using your left hand. And Morley — Dr. Burke — told me that Naomi can fit your right hand with a device that will make it easier for you to hold a pen. When your arm graft is healed."

"What is it with all this Morley stuff?"

A red band washed across Mom's face and she looked at her lap.

"You're kidding, right?" I shook my head.

"We've had lunch in the cafeteria a couple of times."

"You're not supposed to date your doctor. It isn't ethical."

"He's not my doctor, he's yours. And I wouldn't exactly define lunch in a hospital cafeteria as a date."

"What does Daddy think?"

Mom tucked the pen in the spine of the journal, and placed them on the counter next to the roses. "I don't discuss my personal affairs with your father," she said crisply. "Did you see him last night?"

I nodded. "He said goodbye. He took the earliest flight to Vancouver that he could find. He couldn't wait to get away."

"Oh, Dayle, that's not true. He was very torn about leaving. He'll be back as soon as he can."

"Sure he will. If he can pencil me into his schedule."

"You know that's not fair." Mom sighed. She leaned back in her chair and stared at the pale yellow cover on the bed, tracing the line of my legs with her eyes. "It's going to be all right," she said. I didn't know if she was talking to me or to herself. She closed her eyes, sighing wearily through her mask.

I squeezed my eyes shut too, silently choking back rage and despair.

I'm standing in a room built of mirrors. Everywhere I look I see me. Me without bandages, me without clothes; puckered and red, ugly and raw. The wounds spread as I watch, consuming me one cell at a time. I close my eyes and feel my way around the room, searching for a door, for a way out, but there isn't one.

When I open my eyes again, the mirrors are moving in on me, closer and closer, until my breath steams the glass. All I see is my face and dark angry eyes, windows to my soul. It's terrifying, what I see. So I scream. I scream as loudly as I can — a piercing, high-pitched wail.

Glass shatters. Walls and ceiling collapse into silvery shards that run through me, cold as ice.

CHAPTER SEVENTEEN

Wednesday, June 11: Day 11

THE SOUND OF KEITH'S VOICE flowing through the telephone line brought more relief than a flush of narcotic. "Hi, Dayle. You get my flowers yesterday? I did get down to see you, but I was late and you were asleep ...."

Kathy brought the jug of flowers out of the tiny bathroom in the corner, water replenished.

"I know. They told me. The roses are beautiful," I said. "I'm looking at them right now."

"Sometimes it's hard to time things right, to juggle everything." Keith sounded halting and weary.

Juggle what? "That's okay," I said.

"No it isn't. It just seems ... everything seems so ... it's so wrong." His voice was jagged and raw.

I struggled to find something cheery to say, even though lunch roiled in my stomach and my body trembled from exhaustion. "Well, at least you can come right into my room now."

"Yeah. I can see *you* without a wall of glass in front of me."

You? What did he mean by that? Before I could ask, he spoke again. "I have to see you, Dayle. I mean, there's something I need to talk to you about. Something I need to tell you ...." His voice broke.

Kathy jotted notes on my chart, close enough to hear everything. My voice fell to a gravelly whisper. "I wish I didn't look so awful ...."

Silence on the line, just for a split second. Then something that sounded like a deep, unsteady breath. "What you look like ... that's not what's important. Not to me. I just want you to get better."

I'd been longing to hear those words from someone, anyone — especially Keith — but somehow, hearing them only made me feel worse about the time that had been slashed from my life. Time that I should have been spending with Keith. With summer and drama school. With my life.

Keith told me that he had two last-minute exams, one tomorrow, another on Friday. He'd come Friday evening, just after supper.

"Okay." My throat tightened around a sob.

"Oh shit. Forget the exams. I'll come right after school today and —"

I squeezed my eyes closed and concentrated on steadying my voice. "No. No. Don't do that. You need to study. You've got straight As. You can't blow them."

"I won't blow them. I'll just study a little later and —"

"You can't do that. You're tired enough already. It's just a couple of days."

"Are you sure?"

"I'm sure. Absolutely." Even as I managed to make the words ring true, part of me hoped he would ignore everything I had said and come to visit me anyway. My hand fell to my side still clutching the receiver as dial tone buzzed through the line. A strange combination of relief and dread, hope and despair, tumbled over me. Kathy hung up the phone and left me to my scheduled afternoon rest.

As a cloudy morphine haze drew me into sleep, I stared at the counter. Keith's cluster of roses, dewy and half-opened, lay just beyond my reach.

* * *

I wasn't sure how long I slept, but when my eyes fluttered open, the first thing I saw was Keith's bouquet. The second thing I saw was my sister. "Hi. I was hoping you'd wake up before I had to leave," she said softly.

"*Joseph* waiting?"

"Not today," she said smoothly. "But I don't want to take up too much of your time; you've got other visitors coming before supper."

"Who?"

"Wait and see."

"Keith? He said he wouldn't be able to come before Friday but —" Before I had a chance to finish, the door from the anteroom opened and Amy appeared at the end of my bed, a thin, wispy figure dwarfed by an oversized gown. Another figure stood behind her, tall and slim, shifting from one foot to the other. Stu.

I searched what I could see of Amy's face for any hint of smugness, a trace of you-got-what-you-deserved, but there was none. A dull bluish wash shadowed her eyes.

Even though I'd been telling myself I didn't want to see her, I was glad that she'd come. That they had come. "Hi," I said. My gravelly voice didn't make it sound like much of a greeting.

Amy's eyebrows wrinkled. "Your voice is different."

"From the tubes they shoved down my throat when they brought me here. It'll go away. Eventually."

"You can have my chair," Denise said, rising. "I should leave anyway. They only allow two visitors at a time."

"Don't go! Wait until they kick you out. Please." Tension still radiated between Amy and me; I felt it in the air. I didn't have strength or courage to face her — or Stu — on my own.

Stu shifted his weight from one foot to the other again and stared at the floor.

I pointed to a chair in the corner by the door. Amy hesitated, then pulled it up beside Denise. "Small room," she said.

"Well, at least it has a window to the outside world." I tried to sound cheerful.

Stu glanced over his shoulder at the bricks beyond the oblong glass. His eyes smiled and one eyebrow lifted up. "Nice view too."

I forced a laugh. He let out a long whistle of air, as if he'd been holding his breath. Then he hopped up on the counter with one hand on either side of his legs.

"How are you feeling?" Amy spoke stiffly.

"Lousy. But they tell me I'll live."

"Good." Amy picked at the folds in her gown. "I came to see you in ICU."

"I know. Denise and Mom told me. And I think I remember. Sort of. The drugs ... you know."

Stu began to swing his feet against the cupboards, the clunk of his shoes muffled by paper slippers. His eyes darted between Amy and me. "So, uh ... I've got something for you, Dayle."

Stu, phew! My face warmed and the pain in my limbs surged. All the events before the explosion suddenly flooded back. I had let Pete and the others tease Stu, without defending him. Why would he bring me anything, or even come to visit at all? I jabbed the button on my PCA and tried to meet his eyes. I couldn't.

Stu pulled a small battery-operated cassette deck out from behind his back. It tumbled onto the counter beside him. His face flushed as he clumsily retrieved it. He fiddled with the controls until guitar music filled the small room, then set the deck down. "Recognize this guy?"

"Jeremy Firenza, from Chameleon," Amy said.

Stu nodded. "It's his solo album. I made a copy of it for you, Dayle. Made some other tapes too." Another four cassettes tumbled out from under his gown. He looked like a disorganized juggler as he fumbled, gathering them up. "Missing one," he said. "Must have left it in the car."

"It doesn't matter. Thanks." His kindness made me feel more guilty than ever.

"Thought it might take your mind off things." Stu pushed his dark heavy glasses up on his nose. The bottom of his frames covered the top of his face mask, just enough to pin it into place.

My left hand automatically flew to my own glasses, but I couldn't adjust them, not with all the tape welding them in place. My arm dropped back on the bed.

"Stu, what's that on your forehead?" Amy asked.

"Huh?"

"Just above your left eyebrow."

Stu scratched at his skin and his face flushed again. He looked at the dry grey dust on his rubber-clad fingers.

"Clay," he said. "It's clay. I ... uh ... I was trying to sculpt something."

Denise leaned forward, her head cocked to the side. "What were you making?"

"A bird. But I gave up. Clay didn't seem right for the project." Stu drummed his fingers on the edge of the countertop. "I'm going to carve it from wood instead."

"What kind of bird?" Amy asked.

"A pelican," I said.

Stu looked at his shoes. "I'll show you when I'm finished."

"I didn't know you carved wood," I said.

"I haven't done much. Not for a while. But I found a neat log at the lake. Driftwood, actually. I thought I'd —"

"The lake?" I interrupted. "What lake?"

A moment of awkward silence followed. Denise spoke first, gently. "We went up on Sunday. Stu drove us."

"You went to the lake?" Every trace of disappointment I felt spilled out with those words. "What did Mom say?"

"We didn't tell her," Denise said softly. "You know how she feels about us all going together ...."

"Don't worry," Amy said. "We didn't touch any of Gram's —"

"You went too?" I stared at Amy in disbelief.

"Why not? I usually go, don't I?"

"But not without me." I sounded whiny.

"We just went for a day," Denise said. "To get away."

"We needed to be a little closer to Gram," Amy added.

"She's my grandmother, not yours." The words flew out before I could stop them.

Amy's eyebrows settled into a flat line. "I loved her too," she said softly.

I nodded, but my tightly clamped jaw refused to release any words of apology.

"It's okay," Amy said, but I knew it wasn't. She had been almost as close to Gram as I had. She'd never had a grandmother of her own, so she'd adopted mine. And Gram had adopted her right back.

Silence stifled the room.

***

The three of them had been gone for almost fifteen minutes when I heard the door open again. Stu stepped into the room. He waved a cassette at me. "Hi again. I ... uh ... I found this. Chameleon, their newest recording, *Shades of Change.*"

"You didn't have to make a special trip," I said.

He shrugged. "I was here anyway and Amy went home with Denise." He picked up the leather journal Mom had left on the counter. "You keeping a diary?"

"Mom wants me to. But I can't."

"Why not?"

I pointed to the contraption holding my right arm out to the side.

"So try using your left hand for now. You could vent all your frustration."

"I don't have the energy."

Stu shifted his weight from one leg to the other, eyeing the chairs beside my bed.

"Why don't you sit?"

Stu nodded and sat with the journal on his lap. He opened it to the first page. "It must be hard to be stuck in bed. Kind of like being stuck in a prison."

I nodded. "You've got that right."

He pulled the pen out from the spine of the journal. "I'll bet the worst part of keeping a diary is getting started."

"I guess."

"The pages are so fresh and clean, you want to keep them that way. Whatever you write has to look good on the page, like it belongs there." He pointed the pen at my right arm. "I'll bet you'll be anxious to start writing when your arm's feeling better."

"Maybe."

"So what are you thinking, right now?"

"Like I've been convicted for a crime I didn't commit." Or maybe one of the many I did.

Stu clicked the pen open, ready to write. "Can I?"

I shrugged. "If you really want to."

He carefully drew the pen over the pages of the journal. Even from where I lay I could see his neat lettering, crisp and black against the clean white pages.

He closed the cover. "There. It's started." He smiled. I could tell by the way his eyes crinkled up behind his glasses. He looked different behind the mask, with only his eyes showing. In spite of his glasses I could tell he had nice eyes. Light brown with little gold flecks, framed by thick dark lashes. Soft and warm, with the almond shape his mother's eyes had.

Funny, I'd never really looked at his eyes before. Eyes became awfully important when they were all you could see of a person. "I'm sorry, Stu." I swallowed hard. "About —"

"You've got nothing to be sorry for."

Why were people so good to me?

I closed my eyes and sank into the comfort of his kindness and his company. It delayed the misery of being left alone with my nightmares, the ones real and not.

I pitch my glasses to the floor and unravel the bandages on my head, layer by layer.

"Goodness, Dayle! Whatever is the matter?" Gram picks up the glasses and sits down on my bed.

I stare at the two-sided face in the mirror. "I'll never get asked out on a date. Ever!"

"What makes you say that?"

"Those." I point to the glasses. "They make me look ugly."

Gram holds the one-armed glasses up and looks through them. "Well, the frames could use a little fixing, I'd say, but they don't look that bad on you. And besides, any boy worth dating is going to look past your appearance."

"Yeah, right."

"It's true. Dating isn't all it's cracked up to be. Much better to be friends with someone first, really get to know them. Friendship outlasts romance."

"How would you know?" I can't imagine Gram dating anyone. The only man I've ever seen her with is Grandpa, and even then, only in old photographs.

"Well, I dated a little in high school. Looked for all that romantic fluff, the stuff that makes your spine tingle and your legs go weak —"

"Gram!"

"Fact of life, dear. Anyway, the tingle doesn't last forever. And any boy who's only after the tingle isn't worth your time. On the other hand, look at your Grandpa. He wasn't exactly handsome, and he wasn't the smartest or the most popular boy in school, but he was a good friend. We built our relationship on that, and the tingle came later."

"It did?"

Gram nods. "And it was a pretty good tingle too."

CHAPTER EIGHTEEN

Thursday, June 12: Day 12

NAOMI SAT BESIDE THE BED with a small hand mirror in her lap. "I know this isn't easy for you, Dayle. That old saying, *the eyes are the windows to the soul,* have you heard it?"

I nodded and let her remove my glasses.

"Look at your eyes first. They haven't changed."

"How would you know?"

She smiled. "I've seen pictures of you. You've got beautiful eyes, just like your mother." She handed me the mirror and I clenched it tightly in my left hand.

"Go on," she said. "This is something you need to do."

I closed my eyes and raised the mirror, then took a deep breath and did what Naomi suggested. I focused my eyes on the mirror, blue into blue. But I couldn't escape the horror of the rest of my face. Part of the hairline on the right side of my face had melted into a strip of shiny red goosebump flesh that looked as though it had been brought to a boil, then frozen with the bubbles still in place. That same ugly pattern rippled into the front of my ear, down through my right cheekbone and neck, covering nearly half of that side of my face. The hair on my right side lay in a singed fuzzy tangle, while the hair on the other side lay long and full — a striking, taunting contrast.

I dropped the mirror. "Shave it off."

"Pardon me?" Naomi asked.

"Shave my hair off. I'd rather have none at all than ... than this freaky mess!"

"Are you sure?"

I nodded fiercely.

"Your hairline won't be like that forever," Naomi said. "It's amazing what plastic surgery can do. It'll just take time."

My life was over. Everything good about me was gone, every hope I had for the future shattered. How could I ever become an actress or a model with a face like this? Who would want to *look* at me, never mind be *seen* with me?

Naomi picked up the mirror and showed me my face again. "Remember, focus on your eyes, Dayle."

I turned my head to the right, just enough to conceal the burned side of my face. But even the other side of my face was marked. A thin red line ran through my temple, just under the only decent hairline I had, a souvenir of my collision with a jagged rock.

"The scar on your left temple will fade and in time you probably won't even notice it. Camouflage makeup will highlight your eyes and minimize any scarring. You'll be surprised how much better you'll look — even before plastic surgery. We're only just beginning."

Nothing Naomi said mattered. People would see the ugly part of my face first, before they checked out my eyes. Why would they bother to look any further? Burns were hideous but fascinating — as long as they belonged to someone else. Maybe people didn't care about eyes anyway. I hadn't thought to look into Stu's eyes until yesterday, even though I'd known him for years.

I hurled the mirror to the floor and cried like a baby, squeezing my PCA pump over and over again.

I'm falling through a tunnel of smoke, down and down, as images whirl by. Photographs. Pictures of me from the time I was young, my eyes hidden behind glasses.

And then I see other eyes. Eyes peering at me through the smoke, watching me with an accusing intensity that makes me squirm. One pair of eyes grow larger — a pair of robin's-egg blue eyes fringed with dark lashes. They belong to a young man — a boy — in a photo that lies in Gram's bottom drawer beneath a neatly folded stack of scarves. It's an old picture with cool undertones and lots of contrast, taken when colour photography was new. I pull the photo out of the drawer and study it more closely.

"What are you doing in my drawer, Dayle?"

I spring up from the floor at the sound of Gram's voice. "Oh. I was looking for an old family picture. For school. A social studies project."

I can tell by the look on Gram's face that she's not pleased. "You should have asked me first."

The level of disappointment in her voice makes me feel ashamed, but I protest anyway. "But Gram —"

"Everyone needs a certain amount of privacy." Gram gives me that look, the one that asks if I got the point, before she continues. "Did you find what you need?"

I shake my head and hold out the photo of the boy with the blue eyes. "Who is this guy anyway?"

Gram glances at the picture. "He's nobody."

"Then why do you have a picture of him?"

"Forgot I had it." Gram holds out her hand.

I glance at the picture once more before I give it back to her. The boy, who looks to be just a few years older than me, seems familiar somehow, yet I'm sure I've never met him. "Well, he's awfully handsome for a nobody."

Gram studies the picture and sighs. "He may be handsome, but there's more to him than that. Look at his eyes. He's arrogant." She tosses the photo back into the drawer and closes it. "Don't forget, Dayle, you have to look beyond outward appearances."

Gram turns and leaves the room, dissolving into a glowing transparent form as she goes.

CHAPTER NINETEEN

Friday, June 13: Day 13

ALTHOUGH THE BATHROOM was only a few feet from the end of my bed, it might as well have been a million miles away. Naomi and Maureen held me up, but I had to propel my sore aching legs on my own and cope with the awful nausea that accompanied movement. As if that wasn't enough, they lowered me to the toilet when I finally arrived.

"Try and pee or have a bowel movement," Naomi said. "Wouldn't it be great to get rid of the bedpan?"

Death by embarrassment.

By the time I fell back on my sheets, I longed for the blissful escape of a dreamless sleep, if such a thing was possible. With a squeeze of the PCA button, I closed my eyes — both eyes, now that the bandages had been removed from my right one.

Maureen turned on one of Stu's tapes before she left. I fell asleep before the first song finished.

> *Perfection is haunting me,*
> *Images of your face.*
> *I'm addicted, I'm spellbound*
> *Dying for your embrace ….*

The door creaked. My arms and legs flailed and my eyes

flew open from a dream of despair.

"Dayle ... oh. Sorry. I didn't mean to scare you." Keith's masked head peeked in around the door. He froze. "What happened to your hair?"

My heart leaped into the wild rhythm of panic. I blinked and struggled to push myself higher on the bed, smoothing the remaining bandages over my face, straightening my ever-present glasses. "They shaved it off this morning. I told them to." I sounded more confident about the whole deal than I felt.

Keith shook his head slightly. The surprised look in his eyes dissolved into a twinkle. "Dayle, you've got some kind of spunk, you know that?"

"Well, c'mon in." I tried to steady the flutter in my chest.

His voice lowered. "You've got a couple of other visitors too."

"Oh." What could I say?

Keith disappeared behind the door into a low buzz of voices. A few seconds later he reappeared with a slightly shorter female figure at his side. Her eyes were unmistakable. Jade. Why on earth would he bring her along?

"Oh, Dayle. And you had such beautiful hair." Without any invitation, she pulled a chair right up to the side of the bed and scanned me with her emerald eyes, carefully avoiding my own. "Keith told me you were in rough shape, but I had no idea .... Are you in a lot of pain?" She pointed to her right knee. "I got burned too and it hurt like hell."

Something vile rose in my throat. Did she think she was being sympathetic?

Act like you don't care. Don't let her faze you.

"It wasn't a bad burn, Jade. They treated you and let you go." Keith picked up my hand and gave it a gentle squeeze.

"She got hit by flying debris."

Jade looked at Keith. "I know it wasn't bad. That's exactly my point. If mine hurt so much and it wasn't serious, well, poor Dayle must really be suffering with half her skin gone."

Keith's shoulders stiffened. Anger flashed in his eyes. But Jade didn't seem to notice; she stared at my bandaged arm. "What do they give you for the pain?"

"Morphine."

"Oh, really?" She leaned forward as if to study the bandages on my face, but she wouldn't look into my eyes. The strong scent of her perfume drifted over me, clogging my throat. "I wanted morphine, but all they would give me was something with codeine. Doctors. What do they know?"

Keith cleared his throat and shifted in his chair. "So. You moving around now?"

"Some," I said. "Mostly just sitting up, standing a little." I had no intention of telling anyone that I'd had the privilege of walking to the john that day. "I'm supposed to start physiotherapy tomorrow."

"Will you be out of here in time for grad?" Jade blinked innocently and adjusted the cap covering her hair.

Keith raised his head to look at her, his brows dipping into a frown.

"Grad?" Her question caught me off guard. "I doubt it." I remembered the dress hanging in my closet, with its low-cut neck and back. I'd never wear it now. Even if by some miracle I did get out on time.

"Such a shame." Sympathy oozed from Jade's voice.

Keith spoke quickly. "Don't worry about it, Dayle. I didn't really want to go anyway."

"You can't miss your own graduation," I said.

"He'll go." Jade smoothed the rubber gloves on her

hands. "I'll see to it. Even if I have to —"

"Jade?" A shorter, rounder figure opened the door a crack and peered around the corner. Marnie.

"Oh. Already?" Jade sighed and rose from her chair. "Guess I better go and let Marnie have her turn. They only let two visitors in at a time you know."

I felt like a side-show exhibit with admission limitations.

As Jade made her exit, Keith leaned forward and whispered. "I'm really sorry, Dayle. She wouldn't take 'no' for an answer. You know what she's like."

Marnie stepped slowly into the room. "Is this a good time to visit?"

"Sure," I lied, not wanting to hurt her feelings. At least Jade was gone.

"I won't stay long. I just wanted to say hello and see how you're doing." Marnie tucked her hands behind her back, but not before I noticed the redness of her forearms rising above her rubber gloves.

"What happened to your arms?" I asked.

"Nothing to worry about." Marnie's weary eyes smiled at me.

"She was the first one there when you ..." Keith's voice wavered. "She tried to help —"

"You got hurt trying to rescue me?" I asked, amazed and dumbfounded at the same time.

"It's nothing, Dayle. Really." Marnie rubbed her foot over the linoleum. Her voice lowered. "Not like you and Pete."

"Pete?" A gush of horror flooded my limbs and jerked me upright. Bits of conversation flashed through my mind.

... Sometimes it's hard to time things right, to juggle everything ....

... I can see YOU without a wall of glass in front of me ....
Small remarks and unanswered questions, the expression on
Mom's face when I asked who else had been hurt — all clues,
if only I'd paid close enough attention; if only I hadn't been
so consumed with my own problems. "Why didn't you tell
me any of this?"

Keith's eyes darted from Marnie's to mine. "We didn't —
your Mom and I — we thought that hearing all that stuff at
once might upset you too much."

"Oh, Dayle. I'm sorry. I just assumed you knew ...."
Marnie sank into a chair.

"And you — are you okay?"

Marnie nodded. "Like I said, it was nothing. Really.
First-degree burns. They kept me here for a couple of days
for observation because they weren't sure. But everything is
pretty much healed now. More red than anything."

"Pete?"

Keith cleared his throat. "He's not great."

"How bad is it?"

Marnie's voice fell to a whisper. "He's still in ICU ...."

Keith pressed his fingertips together and stared at his lap.

Marnie steadied her voice. "The logs were wet and
wouldn't light ...."

"I remember," I said.

"He was standing right in the middle of the fire pit when
... when —" Marnie's voice broke. Keith's head jerked up, his
eyes on Marnie. She squeezed his arm, then wiped her eyes
with the sleeve of her gown. Her voice wavered again. "Look.
I should go. Let you and Keith visit."

Keith watched her leave. "She's been here every day since
the accident. First as a patient, then upstairs with Pete. The
nurses up there have this idea that she's his sister. Mrs.

Wallace didn't tell them any different." His expression seemed dazed, his eyes glassy and distant.

"Have you seen Pete?"

Keith nodded, looking at his lap. "Only through the window. His room, then your room."

"I can't believe no one told me."

Keith finally looked back into my eyes. "I was going to tell you today — about everything — but ...." His voice cracked. "I'm sorry. I'm just so sorry."

"You don't have anything to be sorry about. It was Pete's fault."

"Don't be too hard on him. Please." Keith stumbled over his words.

"Right. He had too much to drink and wasn't thinking clearly." I couldn't keep the venom out of my voice.

Keith sucked in a mouthful of air. "He didn't ... it wasn't ... it shouldn't have happened." His voice broke and I lost his eyes again, but he took my hand and squeezed it.

"I'm sorry," I said softly. "I know he's your best friend."

Keith held my hand for a very long time, with a grip that surprised me, like a drowning man clinging to a raft.

As I lay there thinking about Pete, an odd sense of bitter triumph washed over me. Pete was suffering because of his stupidity. An eye for an eye, a burn for a burn. *Suffer, Pete, suffer.* Somehow, spewing out vengeful thoughts made my own suffering a little easier, even though I knew it was wrong.

Gram and I sit on the stone steps of the cabin looking at an old photo album: pictures of Gram and Grandpa with Mom when she was young. In spite of the warm sun there's a chill in the air. It has something to do with Mom and

Gram and another subtle war of words.

"What is it between you and Mom?" I ask.

Gram sighs, a sound like the distant water breathing. "She can't find it in her heart to forgive me, and I don't seem to be able to apologize."

"For what?"

Gram smiles sadly. "It doesn't matter. Things are always more complicated than they seem."

"So why not just forget about it? Both of you?"

"Guilt settles in like a cold front over the lake. If you're not careful, it can become a habit. Just like anger. Don't harbour either one of them, Dayle. They'll eat you alive …."

Eat you alive … eat you alive … alive ….

Gram's voice reverberates into a long, eerie wail, and a cloak of darkness falls over me. The weight and dankness of it terrifies me. I reach out for Gram, but she's not there.

Another sound rises softly, then grows louder, a kind of liquidy crunching sound. I feel something crawling against my skin and look down to see maggots working their way up my legs, my arms, toward my chest. They settle in around my heart, dissolving it into a pulsating mass of unrelenting hate and anger and pitiful remorse.

CHAPTER TWENTY

Saturday, June 14: Day 14

AMY FOLDED OPEN the greasy paper bag and a cloud of heavenly smelling steam escaped; the sesame-vegetable scent of deep-fried Chinese. For the first time in two weeks, my stomach growled. "Egg rolls," Amy said. "Want one?"

"Sure. Thanks. What made you decide to bring food?"

"Heard you need to eat more — and you've never turned down an egg roll in your life." Amy's voice sounded cheerful enough, but a strained note underlined her words.

"You having some?" I asked.

"Already did, on the way here. Easier to eat without this thing." She pointed to her face mask, then pulled a can of cola from another bag on the counter "So. When did you cut your hair?"

"Cut? Don't you mean shaved?"

"You always had such nice hair."

"It'll grow back." I felt defensive.

"Oh, I know," Amy said quickly. She swirled around to face me again. "I just meant ... well ... I think it's really cool, what you did. You've got a very nice head."

"Gee, thanks."

In the past an exchange like that wouldn't have fazed

either one of us, but this time, I saw my own discomfort reflected in Amy's face. A deep flush rose up above her mask and she turned away again. I heard the cola can fizzle as she tore back the tab. "You think bubbles will hurt your throat?" she asked softly.

"No. My throat's fine. Just sounds bad."

Amy put a bamboo placemat on my bedside dining table. She arranged a paper plate with four egg rolls and a foam container of plum sauce in front of me, then plopped an elbowed straw into the drink can. "Enjoy." She stood beside my bed, her hands clasped in front of her.

I felt as uncomfortable about everything as she looked. I pointed to a chair near the window. "Why don't you bring that over here?"

Amy repositioned the chair by my bed and sat down. "Are they okay? The egg rolls? I mean, they're not too hot — or too cold? They taste really greasy if they're too cold —"

"Amy, they're just right." I spoke through a mouthful of crunchy wrapper and vegetables. "Trust me. This is the best thing I've eaten in two weeks."

She lost her stiff posture as she settled into the chair to watch me eat. Her eyes crinkled around the corners as if she was smiling.

"What?" I spoke through another mouthful of food. Glorious food. Food with flavour and texture, calories and grease. "Why are you smiling?"

"What makes you think I'm smiling?"

"Your eyes. They're doing that crinkle thing. So?"

"Well," she said slowly. "I can tell you're really enjoying yourself."

I slurped a mouthful of cola and reached for another egg roll. "What makes you say that?"

"You're eating like a pig."

I jerked forward from my pillows with a laugh and cola snorted through my nose. The sudden movement and stinging spray of bubbles triggered a wave of pain, but the laughter felt so good that I barely noticed.

Amy reacted with her own fit of nervous giggling. She caught her breath for a moment. "You remember at the lake, when we were about twelve —" She choked with laughter.

I gasped for air, wondering why I was laughing so hard. "Yeah. Yeah. We sneaked down to the kitchen after everyone else was asleep —"

"For drinks and chips —"

"And woke Gram up when you snorted cola through your nose and started coughing," I finished for her.

Amy giggled. "Maybe it wasn't the coughing that woke her up, but the noise you made tripping over your drink can. What a mess! You know, Gram had that stern look on her face and made us clean up everything, but I don't think she was mad. Not really."

"She couldn't have been mad. Don't you remember? The next night we found junk food under our pillows. I know Mom didn't put it there."

"I sure miss Gram." Amy's shoulders rose and fell in a heavy sigh. "Well." She sprang to her feet. "Your mom said there was a cookie sheet in here somewhere."

"What do you want that for?" I asked. I poked at another egg roll, thinking how much Gram used to like Chinese food. Especially egg rolls and wonton soup.

"A puzzle. Thought we could put a puzzle together. I found a really neat one of two little kids walking on the beach. Three hundred pieces. We could put it together inside the box, but the sides are so flimsy that I thought they'd tear."

"It's in the closet." I pointed. "There. Top shelf, I think."

Amy pulled out the cookie sheet with the box of magnetic letters on top. "Hey, look at these letters. I had some when I was a kid. Remember? Dad and I used to leave messages on the fridge for each other. We had to abbreviate a lot though; not enough letters."

"Yeah," I said. "I know what you mean." I dipped my last egg roll into plum sauce and bit into it. Amy was right; they did seem greasier as they cooled.

As Amy cleaned up after my snack, I studied the cover of the puzzle box. It reminded me of greeting cards that had been popular a few years back, the black and white ones with lots of contrast and texture, the only spot of colour belonging to a small flower or a bit of clothing. The puzzle had two children walking hand-in-hand with their backs to an unseen camera, oblivious to anything but each other. A light-haired girl with her head thrown back in laughter, a dark-haired girl whispering into her ear. White ruffled waves, hair tossed in the wind, and footprints in the sand — all leading into a deep blue horizon.

A clear sky. Friends. *True Blue.* That's what the puzzle title read. It should have made me happy that Amy had chosen that particular puzzle, but it didn't. It made me feel sad for the tension that still lingered between us, for the closeness we'd lost.

Amy propped the puzzle box cover against a spare pillow at the foot of my bed for reference. "So, what's Keith up to tonight?"

My fingers tightened over a puzzle piece.

"I didn't mean anything by that, Dayle," she said quickly. "I was just asking."

"He was here a while ago." I fingered through the other

puzzle pieces without looking at them. "Said he was going to go up to ICU and see Pete, then go home and watch a movie or something."

Amy sat down again. She spoke stiffly. "I guess he's really tired. Between school and the time he spends here —"

"So what's happening in school?" I asked quickly. Thinking about Keith's absences made me gloomy and resentful.

"Nothing exciting. Lots of last-minute tests. And the grad committee is busy making decorations ...." Her voice petered out and her gaze fell to her lap.

"It's okay." I tried to sound as though I didn't care. "Grad goes on without me. You going?"

Amy looked back at me. "Stu asked me the same thing."

"An invitation?"

Amy shrugged. "Kind of. But not like a date. Like buddies. You know."

I nodded. "So you'll go, right?"

"I guess."

A tiny bubble of envy rose in my chest. "What are you going to wear?"

"Guess I'll have to go shopping. I don't own anything that formal. What do you suppose it costs for a dress like that?"

I thought of the sapphire dress hanging in my closet, the one with the price tag still attached. One I'd never wear; one Amy could never afford to buy. "I bought a dress a few weeks ago. Why don't you check it out, see if you like it?" The question left my lips before I gave myself time to consider it.

"That doesn't seem right."

"Why not?"

"You should keep it for later. For —"

"I won't wear it, Amy. Not ever. It drapes low in the back and front." I took a deep breath. "It'll fit you, and it's a beautiful dress."

"What colour is it?"

"Sapphire blue."

"I don't know …."

"It's a nice dress. Wear it."

"Well, maybe I'll try it on."

"Good." I made a mental note to ask Denise to remove the price tag before Amy could find it.

Although giving Amy the dress seemed like the right thing to do, an awkward silence wrapped itself around the room as we carefully — almost too carefully — pieced the puzzle together. Eventually, a fresh flush of morphine from my PCA pump made me relax a little, but it also made my fingers too clumsy to manage puzzle pieces.

Amy glanced at the clock. "How late are visiting hours?"

"Nine o'clock. An hour to go. And if you don't leave by then, the nurses turn you into a pumpkin."

Amy looked at me sharply. "I'm not just waiting to leave, you know." She spoke defiantly.

"I know," I said. "I'm kidding."

"Oh." A light flush rose above her mask. "It's hard to tell, with your voice so rough."

"I don't think they're too strict about visiting hours on this ward anyway."

"Really? You know, there's supposed to be a Whoopi Goldberg movie on tonight. I don't remember what it's called. Something about nuns. A comedy. Wanna watch? It'll just be starting."

"Okay." I reached for the remote control and aimed it at

the TV. "What channel?"

"I dunno. Just scan." Amy slid the partially finished puzzle back off the cookie sheet and into the box and scattered the remaining pieces on top. "There. I'll put it in the closet for safe-keeping."

* * *

The movie was, as Amy put it, "full of whoops." We laughed ourselves silly. When Cecilia, the night nurse, came in to check my temperature and take my blood pressure, it was after nine o'clock, but she didn't ask Amy to leave. In fact, when Amy hopped up from her chair mumbling something about forgetting the time, Cecilia told her to stay.

"I heard laughter coming from this room," she said, in her flowery French accent. "Laughter is good medicine."

Maybe Cecilia was right. For the first time in a long time, I slept without dream or nightmare. In fact, I must have fallen asleep before Amy left, because I didn't remember her leaving. And when I awoke the next morning, the cookie sheet was propped up on the counter with a magnetic letter message attached.

A-T L-S-T
E-G R-L-L-S
A-N-D M-O-V-I-E

I couldn't help but smile.

Come dance the dance with me,
Dance in the flames and you'll see,
What you desire
Can be found in the fire ....
And the price?
Misery.

— *Devil's Advocate*
CHAMELEON

CHAPTER TWENTY-ONE

Wednesday, June 18: Day 18

THE ORANGE-AND-YELLOW STRIPED CURTAIN around my bed turned my share of the new room into a cramped, airless tent. Old Mrs. Sheffield, my roommate, was there before me so she had first dibs on the window.

I smoothed my left hand over my cleanly shaven scalp. It still seemed strange, even after five days, but I felt less grotesque than I had with Dr. Jekyll and Mr. Hyde hair.

Naomi chirped cheerfully as she checked the mobility of my various joints. "What do you think of your new surroundings? Nice to finally be on the ward and out of isolation?"

"It's okay, I guess. I'm glad the gowns and face masks are gone." I couldn't take my eyes off of Naomi's face. A cheerful smile dimpled each of her full round cheeks.

She picked up my right hand in both of hers and gently but firmly pulled my index finger toward the back of my hand. She had slender fingers with perfectly manicured nails. The modest diamond solitaire on her left hand glittered. I wondered who she was engaged to, if he was as outgoing as she was, or if their relationship was based on the attraction of opposites.

"I hate this." I groaned as she tugged on my middle finger.

"Needs to be done," she said.

I decided her fiancé would need to have a strong, outgoing personality too, or she would railroad him into submission.

"Does the pressure garment help your leg at all?"

"It's tight."

"That's the idea. It helps keep your burn scars from becoming thick and lumpy. Does it help keep the itching down a bit?"

"Some."

"Well, aloe cream will help too. Just ask, any time you feel you need it. How does the new graft feel?" Naomi laid my hand back on the bed.

"Rotten. Hot and sticky." I inhaled as gently as I could, to avoid stretching the freshly patched wound on my right torso.

Naomi gently touched my forehead. Her hand felt cool against my skin.

"I hate lying flat on my back," I said.

"If you don't keep still, the graft won't take properly. It'll only be for a few days." Naomi smiled. "Your right hand is healing very well. You won't need much grafting on it when the time comes. Tomorrow I'll bring a tube that will help you hold small objects in that hand — like a pen or a fork." She reached for the curtain. "There, now. We're done for today."

I sucked in a slow, deep breath. It was time to ask *the* question, if I could unscramble my tongue. "Is it ... after my graft ... is my ... umm ... you know, front ...."

"You want to know what your breast will look like when the graft heals?" Naomi's hand fell from the curtain and she studied me for a moment. "Your breast was protected by two layers of clothing, your bra and your T-shirt, so the burns weren't as severe as they were on other parts of your torso. Much of the area has healed well without grafting. You'll have some light scarring on the side of your right breast, but nothing too terrible."

Any scarring was terrible. This was my *breast* she was talking about. I refused her offer to show me the graft; I didn't want to add to the horrid images that haunted my dreams and I didn't need to fuel my rage with the sight of more ugliness.

I wished with all my heart that Pete had burned something important too.

* * *

"So your father sent you a magnetic checkerboard." Mrs. Sheffield leaned her short, doughy frame against her walker and shuffled over to my bed.

"Yeah. We used to play a lot when I was little. It's got chess pieces too. He was supposed to teach me how to play, but he never got around to it."

Mrs. Sheffield's grey eyebrows dipped in weighty concentration over each step. Her voice belied her pain. "Why don't we have a game of checkers then?" She lowered herself into a chair before I had a chance to say no.

"You want black or red?" she asked.

"Black. Like char."

Mrs. Sheffield winced, her pale cheeks puffing out with concern. "That new graft giving you trouble, dear?"

"It doesn't feel right. It's different than my other grafts somehow. And it smells like ... I don't know. It's too faint to tell. Something yucky. But nothing feels or smells right anyway."

"I know what you mean." With gnarled fingers, she plucked the checkers out of the box and lined them up on the board. "You make the first move."

I flicked a black checker forward with my left index finger. She carefully turned the board around and made a move of her own.

"So, Dayle, how were you burned?"

"Some idiot tried to light a bonfire with gasoline."

Mrs. Sheffield made a clucking noise with her tongue. "I'll bet he — or she — feels perfectly dreadful about what happened."

"He should. He got burned too."

"Oh my goodness. Such a lot to bear."

I felt obligated to ask how she was burned. Her pale face sagged like soft putty. "An accident, dear."

"What kind?"

"A fryer of hot grease spilled over me."

"How did that happen?"

"My great-granddaughter, Jessica — she's only six — accidentally knocked the deep-fryer over when we were making doughnuts. Poor darling. She feels terrible about it."

"I guess." I was sympathetic, but I thought at eighty-something, Mrs. Sheffield should have known better than to deep-fry doughnuts with a six-year-old.

"They won't let her visit because she's so young and her parents can't coax her to the phone so I can talk to her. She needs to know I'm not angry with her. I don't know what to do."

"Well, she'll be more careful the next time."

"That's not the point, dear. She's suffering every bit as much as I am, if not more. Guilt can be a terrible thing."

* * *

I dragged the pen across a sheet of white paper with my left hand. The checkerboard, lying flat against my left side, served as a makeshift writing table.

Dear Pete ...

I couldn't think of what to write next. *Serves you right ... I know how you feel ... May you burn in the fires of hell ....*

I clicked the pen closed and open and closed again. Mrs. Sheffield snored softly from the next bed; I felt like throwing my pen at her. Pete had made a great target for my rage. Why did she have to try and take that away from me? And why did she have to sleep now? Company — even hers — would have helped me take my mind off my hot, aching miseries.

A tap on the door gave me an excuse to lay the pen down. Amy and Marnie stood there, dressed in shorts and T-shirts. I couldn't help but stare at them — normal human beings with mouths and noses below their eyes.

"It's only us." Amy clutched a large manila envelope to her chest.

"I know, but I almost forgot what people looked like without gowns and masks." I shoved the note under my covers. "I didn't know you two were friends."

Marnie smiled at Amy. "We kept bumping into each other in the hallway." She showed me a bouquet of freshly picked deep purple lilacs. "From home. Hope they don't smell too strong." She tucked them neatly in a glass.

"Thanks, Marnie. Have you been up to see Pete today?"

She studied the flowers and rearranged them in the glass. "For a while. He's in pretty rough shape. I don't think he even knew I was there."

"The drugs'll do that to you. How bad is his burn anyway?"

"Eighty percent."

Eighty plus eighteen — Pete's age — equalled ninety-eight. That was too close for comfort to the tragic line in Cora's Rule of One Hundred. I tried to steady my voice against the shock. "But that means —"

"It means he's got a rough go of it." Marnie turned to face me. Her lips trembled as she spoke. "With the grafting they've done, he's down to about seventy percent, but he's not healing as fast as they'd hoped. As fast as he should."

After a moment of uncomfortable silence, Amy pulled a sheet of white poster board from the envelope she carried. Smeared, overlapping purple paw prints topped the page. A short message was neatly printed below.

> Goodness nose I miss you,
> Pawtner.
>> from your buddy,
>>> Bud

I grinned. "Nice to see Bud hasn't lost his sense of humour. How'd you get him to do that?"

"I put a pie plate full of paint on the grass and stuck his front paws in it."

"No, no. That's not what I meant. How'd you get him to print?"

Amy laughed. A real laugh, the infectious kind that had Marnie and me laughing too. When the laughter petered out, Amy propped up the card on the counter beside Marnie's flowers. "I found a job."

"Where?" Marnie asked.

"At the Highway Garden Stop. Selling plants and gardening supplies. Long hours and not-so-great pay, but kind of fun for the summer. And it'll keep me busy while Dad's in the Yukon."

"He's the bug doctor?" Marnie asked.

Amy nodded and grinned.

I felt a pang in my chest then, realizing that I would miss my seventeenth summer completely. No days at the beach, no drama school, no midnight outings under the stars with Keith. No life, no future.

I HATE you Pete! How could you be so stupid?
But he's suffering too, and so much more ....
He got what he deserved.

I couldn't let anyone suspect that I had such a hateful side. I took a deep breath. "Marnie, would you deliver a note to Pete for me?"

Dear Pete,
I just found out that you're a captive in this prison too. I'll visit as soon as I can, even if it's just through that awful cage window.

Your friend,
Dayle

That small gesture clung to my conscience with the guilty sting of a lie and wrestled with my dreams that night.

Pete and I stand inside the fire pit. A circle of smouldering embers surrounds us.

"I can beat you out of here," I say. "Wanna race?"

Pete snickers. "No way a woman is going to beat Pete Wallace. On your mark ...."

I crouch into a starting position and wait for the signal. A loud "pouf" sends me shooting across the embers as they burst into flame. Pete stumbles and falls. I hear his cry for help, but I keep running.

CHAPTER TWENTY-TWO

Thursday, June 19: Day 19

SWEAT PRICKLED over my body and a hot flush swept through my limbs. I swallowed both of the pills the nurse gave me and gulped down a glass of water before she swept out of the room with her tray of medications.

Naomi wrapped the fingers of my right hand around a thick tube of foam and taped them in place. My pen fit neatly inside the core. "If you're going to write, you should try and use your right hand."

"I don't feel like writing. I don't feel like doing anything." I wiped my sweaty brow with my left hand.

"Fever making you feel lousy?" Naomi asked.

I nodded, then groaned. "Why me?"

"It's not uncommon, Dayle. Many burn patients contract some degree of infection because of so much exposed body tissue. But the antibiotic Elaine gave you should take care of it and the acetaminophen will ease your fever."

After Naomi left, I opened my journal to read Stu's entry. His writing was perfectly centred in the page, crafted like a work of art.

Wednesday, June 11

Lying in a hospital bed is like being stuck in a prison, convicted for a crime I didn't commit.

Dayle's thoughts, recorded by her friend,
Stu Ingaldson

I turned to the next page and tried to write the date. A feverish sweat dripped down my brow and my hand quivered so badly that my letters were barely legible. I grabbed the outside corner of the page with my left hand and ripped it out, then scrunched the stiff paper into a ball.

It crackled.

An image of roaring flames exploded in my mind and my whole body lurched forward. When I swallowed my embarrassment long enough to stop trembling, I tried again. I thought of Stu when I wrote, drawing my pen over the page slowly, moving my hand and arm together in the same sweeping motion an artist might use to brush paint on canvas. The work was painstaking and my writing wasn't terribly neat, but at least I could read it. I kept going. Even the thought of someone else reading my words couldn't stop the tide of emotions spilling over the page.

Day 19

I can just picture Pete lying in ICU, wrapped in layers of bandages, smelling of burned flesh and Flamozine. It makes me glad. Glad! His stupidity ruined my life. I know my anger fuels the infection in my torso graft and stirs my fever, but even the fever of streptococcus bacteria can't purge the horrible way I feel inside. Anger can eat you alive. Gram told me that, and she was right.

Just look at me! I'm a freak! Visitors flow in and out of my room; my family, my friends, and others I hardly know. They say they come to wish me well, but that's not it at all ....

Step right up to the side-show!
See the woman with the melted face!

That's what they must be thinking every time they look at me.

The only bright side to any of this is that Keith has decided to go to the University of Manitoba in the fall instead of moving to Waterloo. He wants to be here with me, with Pete. But I don't want to share him with Pete. I want him to be as angry at Pete as I am.

Why does it feel so good to have someone to blame?

CHAPTER TWENTY-THREE

Saturday, June 28: Day 28

STU JUMPED ME one last time. The game was over. He rubbed his hands together gleefully. "Ah, I love checkers."

"Obviously." I raised the checkerboard lid and slammed the game pieces inside. Even though my infection was gone, something hot still bubbled in my chest and lashing out with my tongue seemed to be the only way to cool it. "You've got dirt on your glasses."

"Oh." Stu pulled his glasses off and wiped them on his T-shirt.

He looked much better without glasses. His rather large nose seemed a natural extension of his face then, softened by his eyes. That unmistakable nose, his pale skin, wavy hair and height came from his Icelandic father, but the dark colour of his hair and the almond shape of his eyes were more like those of his Japanese mother. His artistic talent must have come from her as well; Michi Ingaldson had won several awards for her watercolour paintings.

"What are you looking at?" Stu asked.

"Nothing."

"Why are you so out of sorts today?"

"I can't go to grad. And Keith can't visit. He has too

much to do to get ready for tonight. His Jeep. His tux." I couldn't keep the whiny sound out of my voice. "It's your grad too. How come you can visit and he can't?"

Stu shrugged. "You could be a little more sympathetic, Dayle. He comes almost every day. At least you're not missing your own grad."

"So?"

"So, what about Pete? He's lying in ICU instead of graduating from high school."

"He put himself there."

"Dayle." Stu shook his head, his brown eyes clouding over. "It was an accident. A stupid one maybe, but an accident." He paused and wrinkled his brow. "You haven't been up to see him yet, have you?"

"Only family can visit in ICU, remember? Shouldn't you be going? You don't want to be late for your graduation ceremony."

Stu pushed his chair away from the table. His voice matched the acidity of mine. "I guess I should. You want help back to your room?"

"No thanks. I can do it myself," I lied. I used the table to pull myself to my feet, ignoring the pain in my right arm and shoulder. I glowered at him. "Have fun."

As I hovered over the table, afraid to reach for my walker, Stu escaped down the hallway with long even strides. Watching him go, I felt lonelier and more helpless than ever.

Who would Keith dance with? Would he flirt with anyone? How many other girls were trying to get his attention now that I wasn't around to stake my claim?

Even Amy, who did not date or socialize — or even try to — would be going tonight. With Stu, wearing my dress.

It would look good on her, although she wouldn't fill it out as well as I did — as I would have. Before.

How did she have her hair done? Would she wear more makeup than just mascara for a change? Whatever possessed me to offer her my dress in the first place?

Life went on without me and it made me furious. It would have been nice to have someone to commiserate with, but who would understand? I could think of only one person.

Naomi poked her head inside the lounge. "Mrs. Sheffield told me you were here. Visitors?"

"He's gone. Can I go see someone in ICU? Pete Wallace." I blurted out the question without giving myself time to consider it. "I know I'm not family but we were in the same accident and my infection is gone ...."

"I'll see what I can do. But you'll have to go to physiotherapy first."

"Great. When that's over, I should be as good as dead."

The physiotherapy room was in a newer part of the Health Sciences Centre, miles from the burn ward, so Naomi took me there in a wheelchair. I was grateful for that. Bending scarred joints took a great deal of energy. By the time the physiotherapists were done tormenting me each day, I barely had the strength to crawl back into the chair, let alone manage the long trek back with a walker.

Karen smiled from the reception desk. "How are you doing today, Dayle?"

"Great, just great," I snarled.

Karen's eyebrows went up slightly, but her smile didn't fade.

Go ahead. Tolerate me.

Naomi wheeled me around the corner and to the right.

I lowered my eyes to avoid catching a glimpse of my reflection in the huge mirrored wall at the end of the room. The wheelchair came to a halt. "I'll leave you with Mike," she said cheerfully. "He'll see you get back to your room, safe and sound."

My response came out as a grunt.

Mike winked at Naomi, then smiled at me. "Good afternoon, Ms. Meryk. Ready to work?" Mike never seemed to lack energy.

"No."

He ignored me. "Let's start out with the parallel bars again. See if you can pull yourself out of the wheelchair today." He wheeled me up to the bars, which were just wide enough apart to accommodate the chair and just lower than waist height — making the job of pulling myself up much tougher than it had been from a regular chair using the table in the visitors' lounge. "Okay, hands on the bars."

I had no interest in obeying his command, but I knew Mike wouldn't let up until I did what he told me. Like Naomi. I leaned forward and kept my eyes down to avoid the mirrored wall, then gripped the bars. I wiggled forward until I could place my feet on the ground. With every ounce of strength I could muster, I pressed my hands into the bar and hauled myself to my feet. Fire ripped through my torso and across my burned shoulder. I tried to stifle a groan. Pressure garments squeezed my right arm and leg, aggravating the itchy pins-and-needles pain prickling through them as I stood.

"How are you feeling?"

"Lousy. It might help if I didn't have to wear these damn pressure garments." Swearing made me feel better. I kept my eyes on the fuzzy pink slippers Mom had brought from home.

"You need pressure garments," Mike said calmly, "to keep your burn scars from becoming thick and lumpy."

I snorted. "You sound like Naomi."

He smiled. I looked at his left hand. He wasn't wearing a wedding ring. "Okay," he said, "eyes straight ahead, and take a step ... That's right, but don't be afraid to bend your right knee ...."

"How well do you know Naomi?" I watched my left foot move forward again.

"Oh, fairly well." I glanced at his face. A smile twitched the side of his mouth, and I knew, even before he said it. "She's my fiancée."

Another happy couple. Everyone but me had a life.

As Mike coaxed me forward, he pulled my IV pole along. "C'mon Dayle. Your posture will be much better if you look up instead of at the floor."

"I don't want to look up."

"So I see ... okay, another step ... watch the knees ...."

When I'd made it to the end of the parallel bars, Mike had me do weight exercises for my arms and legs. "Pull the weight in a little closer to your shoulder. You have to work each joint through its full range of motion. Remember, if it's burned —"

"I know. I know! If it's burned, stretch it." Burned skin shrank and tightened as it healed, binding knees and elbows and any other affected joints. I had to keep stretching my injuries so that I could bend. At that moment, I didn't particularly care.

* * *

I almost slept through supper that evening — not that I would have minded skipping rubbery meat loaf and sticky mashed potatoes anyway. As I jabbed my fork at a runaway pea, I listened to Mrs. Sheffield jabber like a caged monkey.

"... and the best thing of all is that Jessica is happy again. I took your advice, you know, Dayle. That note you suggested did the trick."

Serena, the night nurse, swayed into the room and smiled broadly. "Naomi told me you wanted to visit the young man with the burn in ICU. It's not usually allowed, but his nurse thinks you might be good for him, so you've been given the green light. You still up to it?"

I bit my lip. My entire body trembled with exhaustion and I wished I'd kept my mouth shut about Pete.

"Oh, go on dear," Mrs. Sheffield said. "It'll cheer him up. Maybe you too. We can chat some more when you get back."

If I stayed away long enough, Mrs. Sheffield might fall asleep, and I could spend the rest of the evening in peace. "Sure," I said. "Why not?"

Serena wheeled me through the double doors to Pete's room in ICU disguised in a yellow gown, hidden behind a mask. It wasn't the same room I'd been in, but it looked almost identical. An eerie kind of *déjà vu* slammed against my chest. Another body, not mine, lay flat against the sheets, beeping and bleeping, whirring and whistling. My stomach swirled.

There was nothing familiar about the thin wasted form before me. Burn dressings covered over half of Pete's body. Tubes sprouted from his mouth, his wrist and from under the bed. I couldn't see anything of his face but two small holes where unfocused eyes peeked through. Netting —

something like an onion bag, but white instead of orange — held all the dressings in place.

I thought the eyes blinked at me. Pete raised his left hand a couple of inches from the mattress, in what might have been a greeting. His hand was wrapped to look like a fist.

But it wasn't a fist. His fingers were gone.

I sucked in the breath of a horrified gasp, then hid my shock by rolling it back out in the form of a cough. "It's me, Pete. Dayle. About time, eh?"

Serena wheeled me up to the bed. Remembering how awful it felt when people avoided my eyes, I gazed right into Pete's. "It does get easier," I said. "Even the dressing changes hurt a little less when you get used to them."

Pete mumbled an incoherent morphine-induced reply.

CHAPTER TWENTY-FOUR

Sunday, June 29: Day 29

THE WOODSY-GREEN LEATHERY SCENT of his cologne reached my nose just before my eyes fluttered open. Keith sprawled over the chair by my bed with his head back and his eyes closed, his mouth slightly open. Air softly tangled and unfolded from the back of his throat in a gentle snore.

I watched him for a moment, then reached out and touched his knee.

His head bobbed up. He blinked and rubbed the dark circles under his eyes with balled up fists like a little boy, then stretched his arms and yawned.

"Good morning," I said.

"It is now." He grinned and reached behind his chair. "Brought you something." He handed me a long-stemmed ivory rose. "From the dinner table last night."

"They actually had roses? Wow. So, how was everything?" I pushed myself up against my pillow and held the creamy flower to my nose.

"Okay. But it would have been a lot better if you could have been there." He leaned forward to brush the rose away from my face, then kissed me on the mouth, gently but firmly — the first real kiss since the accident.

In that one brief moment, all the memories I'd been avoiding flooded back — images of life before the explosion. A longing ache swept over me.

Keith leaned back in his chair again, holding my hand. He kept his eyes on mine with a look that made me want to leap out of bed and wrap my arms around him. But I wasn't quite ready for leaping.

He told me about the ceremony, how everyone had been soaked with sweat because the school's cooling system had broken down. How Marnie had nearly fainted from the heat, but Cougar caught her. How Sam had tripped on the steps as he walked up to the podium to receive his diploma, then bowed to the audience in a wave of uproarious applause.

The ache burrowed into my bones. *It's not fair! It's not fair! It's not fair.* Somehow I managed to find a cheery voice. "How was the dance after?"

"Okay, I guess. I danced with Amy."

"Really?" I carefully turned to face him and dropped my legs over the side of the bed.

"Yeah. Looked like she was having fun too. You know, Amy's okay. Guess I misjudged her. I used to think that she was a bit stuck-up, but maybe she was just watching out for you. You know, sizing me up or something."

"Oh. I never thought of it like that."

"Hi, Dayle!" Amy bounced into my room holding another cream-coloured rose. She stopped short and nodded at Keith. "Hi." She looked at the rose in her hands, then at the one in mine. "I see Keith beat me to it." She sounded cheerful enough, but I thought her lips moved a little too stiffly as she spoke.

"Hey, Amy." Keith hopped up from his chair and gestured to it with a smile, then glanced at his watch. "Guess

I should go wave to Pete now. I'll come back later." His lips brushed against mine again. I wanted to hang onto that moment and never let it go, but he gave me a smile and sprinted out of the room before I could think of a way to do it.

Amy sat in Keith's chair and brushed a wispy tendril of hair from her face. Her hair was twisted into a casual knot that showed off the delicate lines of her face, her bangs swept back to reveal a slight widow's peak. In all the years I'd known Amy, I had never seen her hairline. I wondered what else I'd missed. "So, how was it?"

Amy sighed. "Not as much fun as it would have been if you were there."

I laughed softly. "That's what Keith said. Did you and Stu dance?"

"A few times. He doesn't dance as well as Keith does, but he sure tries hard." Amy laid her rose on the table across from the end of my bed and picked up a blue plastic water jug.

"Keith told me he danced with you."

Amy went to the sink. "A couple of times. Fast numbers. Guess he was saving the slow ones for you." She turned on the tap and held the jug under it.

I chewed on my bottom lip for a moment, then blurted out the question I'd been dying to ask. "Who else did he dance with? Did you see?"

"Didn't pay much attention. He didn't come with another girl, if that's what you're asking." Amy set the jug on the table, carefully broke the tip of the stem off her rose, then plunked it into the water. "Would look better in a bowl, don't you think?"

"You must have noticed something." I stared at my bare feet: clean, smooth white flesh that had been protected from the flames by ankle socks and runners. Feet that could still dance, even if one of the attached legs was temporarily clumsy.

Amy sighed. "Like I said, I didn't pay too much attention."

"Don't try and hide things from me."

"I'm not. Look, if it makes you feel any better, he seemed pretty miserable for most of the night. I guess he missed you. The only other people I remember seeing him dance with were Marnie and Jade."

"Jade?"

Amy nodded.

"Figures." I dropped back on my pillow.

"You asked."

"How did she look?" I closed my eyes.

"Gorgeous as ever. An emerald gown to match her eyes, and that bright red lipstick. You know, nothing too subtle." Amy dropped back into the chair.

"Who'd he leave with?"

"Cougar and Sam, I think." She paused for a moment. "You know, Dayle ... after all this time and ... and everything, you really should trust him. Keith's a stand-up guy. I take back every rotten thing I ever said about him." She took a big breath when she finished speaking, as if she was relieved to finally have that off her chest.

I looked at her face as my fingertip traced the soft velvety edges of the rose. "I do trust him, Amy. I just think he might have been lonely and well ... never mind." My hand tightened over the stem. A sharp sting drew my eyes downward. The sheet was speckled in blood.

CHAPTER TWENTY-FIVE

Tuesday, July 15: Day 45

"CHECKMATE." Pete spoke in a gravelly whisper, pointing at the magnetic chess board with his fingerless, bandaged hand.

I shook my head. "You're cheating again, Pete. You can't move your pawn backward. Remember?"

"Hey. Who's the Chess Master here? Besides, I never cheat." He paused to catch his breath. "You've lost, woman ... admit defeat."

I snorted and began to pack up the chess pieces. I'd started bringing the game with me when Pete had moved from ICU to the isolation room. Room 529. The same room I'd been in. Pete was a pretty good chess teacher, but I couldn't bring myself to tell him that. "I don't know why I keep playing with you," I said. "You cheat too much for your own good!"

"You don't know enough about chess ... to know if I'm cheating." Pete made an odd noise I thought might be intended as laughter. It turned into a stifled groan. He coughed and pressed his only thumb into his PCA button for another shot of morphine. His eyes closed.

Neither of us spoke for a moment.

"Who'da ever thought we'd get drugs for free?" Pete wiggled against his sheets and sighed. "You know what's funny? I'm dying for a cigarette."

"Wanna rest?" I squirmed in my chair. "I can come back later."

He shook his head slightly and opened his eyes again. "Naw ... if you go, I'll lie here and feel sorry for myself. If you stay, you can feel sorry for me too."

"Sure, Pete." I laughed because I knew he expected me to, but I did feel sorry for him. He could barely move because of the recent graft to his stomach. He didn't have much energy, although I could still sense the sarcasm in his words.

Don't feel sorry for him, Dayle. It's all his fault.
But just look at him, look at all he's lost ....

"You see Marnie yet today?" I had to say something to silence the abrasive chatter in my head.

"Nope. But she phoned this morning. She's coming tonight. There's a good movie on. A Tom Cruise action flick." Pete waved his bandaged hand at the TV hanging over his bed. He lay silent for a moment, then spoke with a touch of wonder in his rough voice. "Can't figure out why she keeps hanging around. I mean, jeez, I hardly even gave her the time of day before ... So why would she? A woman like that, she's gotta have better things to do."

"I think Marnie's doing exactly what she wants to do."

"Yeah. Well. I tell her not to bother coming and she shows up anyway."

"She knows you don't mean it."

"Right." He coughed. "So why do *you* keep coming?"

"Why?" I asked numbly.

"Yeah. Why?"

Why DO you keep coming Dayle? Honour? Pity? Self-satisfaction?

"What else am I going to do here all day long?" I shrugged. "Everyone else on this floor is too old to be good company."

"I dunno. Mrs. Sheffield sounds like a cool old lady. At least you've got a roommate."

"A nosy roommate."

"But you're not alone." He stared at the ceiling for a moment. "I hate being in isolation. You ever wake up screaming, and there's no one there to hear you?"

Pete's frankness caught me off guard and it hit home. I had asked myself that very question when I'd been in isolation. Did he feel as tortured as I'd felt — as I still felt — and as vulnerable? How could I be angry with him? I swallowed hard a few times to soften the lump in my throat and nodded, then dropped the lid on the chess box. It clattered.

Pete's whole body jerked at the sound. "Gawd! Talk about skittish. It's like I keep expecting something to happen again."

"I know what you mean." Tears stung my eyes.

"You ever wonder ..." His voice sank to a lower whisper than usual. "You ever wonder if it's worth it?"

"What?"

"This." He made a subtle waving motion about the room with his bandaged arm. "I mean, this is hell, isn't it?"

I nodded and looked down at my lap, determined not to cry.

"Dayle?" Pete's hushed whisper seemed softer than usual. I looked up.

"Keith's a good guy, you know. Even if he does dumb things sometimes."

"I know that." I frowned, wondering where Pete's comment had come from.

His tone suddenly changed. "Hey. Maybe we oughta go out to dinner, someplace real nice, you and me, when we're both outta here. You know, to make up for both of us missing grad." He paused, sucking air like an out-of-shape runner. "A place with real low lighting."

"We could." I smiled.

"If you don't mind waiting for me, that is. Looks like you'll kick this joint long before I do."

I thought I detected a note of envy in his voice when he said that. For a moment, it felt good. Then I looked back into his eyes, shiny behind the bandages.

"Who's to say," I said. "Maybe I'll get another skin graft infection. Or maybe I'll catch that new pneumonia, the kind that antibiotics can't touch."

It was easy to be crass about everything now that I felt a little strength returning, now that Pete was in isolation. Making it to the ward from ICU seemed like an assurance that everything would be okay. That we'd both make it out of here — in some shape or form.

"Don't ever say that, Dayle." The fierceness in Pete's whisper surprised me.

"I was only joking."

"Don't. You never know what might happen."

My cheeks flushed. An awkward silence hung for a few moments. I looked at the clock. Almost four.

"You gonna stick around long enough to meet Ma this time?" Pete asked.

I shook my head. I'd always tried to avoid Mrs. Wallace, sure that she'd somehow sense my vengeful thoughts and banish me from Pete's room. I didn't think I could handle that. "Denise will be here any minute with pizza."

"Pizza?"

"From Pantini's — extra large — with ham, pineapple and double cheese."

"Jeez. All I ever get is cabbage rolls. Save me a piece, will ya?"

"I'll try. Gotta go," I mumbled. I placed the chess set on the end of Pete's bed and reached for my walker.

He shifted on his bed again, and coughed softly. "You oughta get rid of that thing. It makes you look like an old lady."

"Good. Maybe people will think I'm old instead of just plain ugly."

"You're not ugly, Dayle. You'll never be ugly. You're just a little, well, funky, with that new hairdo and all."

"Gee, thanks, Pete." I edged toward the anteroom door.

"No problem. And Dayle ...."

I glanced back over my shoulder at him. "... if you ever decide to dump Keith, give me a call, okay? We'll date by proxy until I get outta here. I'll send what's-his-name ... Winston ... in my place. You know, that janitor with the green stripe in his hair. See you tomorrow?"

"Only if you promise not to cheat."

He raised his fingerless hand in a farewell salute.

* * *

The pizza sat heavy in my stomach that night. I couldn't shake Pete's question from my thoughts.

You ever wonder if it's all worth it?

CHAPTER TWENTY-SIX

Monday, July 21: Day 51

IT MIGHT HAVE BEEN an actor's dressing-room mirror with the line of soft glowing bulbs around it. But I saw nothing glamorous in the mottled, swollen red side of the face glaring back at me.

Building Self-Esteem. I studied the poster by Naomi's mirror, a list of steps for improving self-confidence. Sure. Tell myself I'm worthwhile and wonderful, smile at everyone even if it hurts. Pretend nothing has changed and life will go on as if it hasn't. Might work for someone whose face didn't look like the parboiled underbelly of an old chicken.

Isn't this *the role of a lifetime?*

Naomi applied a layer of concealing foundation over my red skin. She pulled two shades of cream blusher from the large drawer in front of me. "Either of these would work well for you. Do you have a preference?"

I pointed to the lighter shade, wondering why I'd need blush on a red-tinged face.

"Good." Naomi worked her brush into the cream. "That poster interest you? I can give you a copy of it. Those steps are part of a program designed to help burn survivors adjust to their appearance."

"I'm not that gullible." I didn't feel like a survivor; I felt like a victim.

Naomi applied two different shades of shadow to my eyes, a light touch of liner and light brown mascara. She outlined my lips with a pencil and filled them in with a tube of lipstick. Sun-kissed Rose.

"What do you think?" She stood behind me, dimples showing.

I slid on the new glasses I'd picked out from a case of samples brought by a local optician. Denise and Amy wanted me to choose something thin and light, but I settled for a heavier frame, something that let me feel like someone else. Something I could hide behind.

The face in the mirror came into focus. It wasn't as red as it had been before the makeup, and the line of uneven skin around the edges of my graft had softened a little. Naomi had done what she said she would. My eyes looked pretty, even through my glasses. But nothing else came close to looking like the me I used to be.

My right hand flew up to rub the tender, itchy skin of my scalp burn. Naomi had applied foundation there, but it still looked like a large, ugly bug burrowing into the feathery scalp around it. My hand fell to my lap.

Naomi placed a gentle hand on my shoulder. "Plastic surgery will help that too."

"How?"

"Well, first of all they'll insert a valve underneath the healthy scalp behind your burn. Over a period of time they'll infuse air under the skin, forcing it to stretch. After a few months there will be enough 'new' skin — or scalp — to pull forward and create a new hairline."

"Great. I only have to wait a year and a half for them to

get around to it. Why can't they do it now? Just go in and get it over with and give me a face. Some hair. A life."

"The scars developing on the side of your face need time to mature and settle before cosmetic surgery will be effective. You could wear a hairpiece — "

"Then I'd be a total fake."

"Well, think about it. In the meantime ...."

Naomi whisked a brightly coloured scarf off the shelf. "May I?"

"I guess."

She carefully wrapped the scarf around my head, over the burn and the stubble around it, and tied it at the back of my head. "Add a pair of clip-on earrings, and you're set. Feel better?"

"Nobody wears clip-on earrings any more. And who wears a scarf over their head unless there's something wrong with them?"

"We'll do the makeup together a couple more times," Naomi said pleasantly. "Then when you're released from the hospital you'll know exactly how to apply it for the best effect."

Released. From one hell into another. "Great," I said.

"Only two weeks until you go home. You'll spend some time away from the hospital before then to adjust to your new routine. Your mother will need time to get used to helping you with your care."

Mommy, Mommy, I need you. Help me.

Get real.

"A home-care nurse will visit you each day for a couple of weeks to do the dressing changes until your mother is comfortable with it." Naomi turned off the lights around the mirror. "You go home for your first day visit on Friday, right?"

Yahoo.

I nodded. Dr. Burke had had a twinkle in his eye when he gave me the news, as if it was some great gift he was bestowing, something I'd been waiting for. But leaving the hospital meant venturing onto the street — and that meant being seen in public. People would stare, and I didn't want to be stared at. I didn't even want to be glanced at.

"Any plans?" Naomi asked.

Mom wanted me to spend the day at home with rented movies and Chinese take-out, like Denise and I used to do with Gram. But I didn't want to spend a day at home. Not with dear, sweet Morley — Dr. Burke — and Joseph-the-roofer hanging around. Keith and I would have no privacy. How different would that be from here?

I had told Mom that Keith was going to take me out to the lake instead, to visit Gram's cabin. She thought that I wasn't ready for such a long drive and that there wouldn't be enough time to spend there after the trip to make it worthwhile. Keith had told me the same thing. I guess it made sense — I really wasn't ready to face the lake anyway — but I was tired of other people telling me what to do.

I shrugged my shoulders. "I probably won't do anything. Hide. What do other people do?"

"Most people just like to get home for a while. But once in a while someone will choose to do something different."

"Like what?"

"Go to a movie, or for a trip to the park. I had a patient last year who went to a wedding."

"A *wedding*? Your patient must have been a masochist."

"It'll be nice to get away from here. You'll see."

* * *

I walked back to my room on my own two feet. Being on my right leg that long made it tingle with a pins-and-needles irritation I couldn't rub away, but it did feel good to be mobile without having to depend upon a wheelchair or a walker. I wished I had hard-soled shoes so I could stomp on the cold hallway floor and drive the horrible image of my face into oblivion.

My journal lay in the top drawer of my bedside table. I smoothed it open, and began to write.

Day 51

I can't let myself think about what I look like. I can't. I just can't. But what I can do is complain, and that makes me feel better, even though I complain to everyone but Pete. He's the one I should gripe at. But I refuse to do that. It's much more satisfying to pretend everything's great for me and silently rub his nose in his own misery.

That's pretty easy to do right now. He's got an infection in his stomach graft, and he's hot and sweaty and uncomfortable, just like I was when I'd had my torso infection. I can tell by looking at him, by watching his lousy chess moves. He jokes about it, but I know he's just trying to hide the way he really feels.

He's a lot braver about all of this than I've been. As mad as I am at him for what he did, I have to admire his attitude. That makes me even more angry.

If we really were having a race, he'd be losing. One part of me is glad about that. The other part of me wishes there was some kind of consolation prize.

CHAPTER TWENTY-SEVEN

Tuesday, July 22: Day 52

A DISTANT ROLL OF THUNDER added to the gloomy sound of rain pattering against the visitors' lounge window. I jammed buttons on the remote control and watched bright, noisy images flash across the television screen. A talk show. Dancers. Cartoons. Football. An old movie.

Frivolous. Annoying. Boring. Nothing seemed worth bothering with.

Why did Denise leave to meet Joseph for lunch? She should have stayed here with me. But then, maybe thirty minute intervals were all she could stand. Ugliness was tough to look at.

I could go and visit Pete, but I didn't have the energy to face his determined cheer or listen to the nagging cough that he'd developed. And the way I felt right now, I'd probably try to strangle him for what he did to me.

I dropped onto the sofa, banging my head on the wall behind it. "Stupid wall," I said sharply.

"What did the wall do?"

Stu's voice. I looked toward the door to find him there with Amy at his side. Water dripped from their clothes and hair, but they were both smiling. Smiling so hard I thought their smooth, perfect pink cheeks would crack.

"What are you guys so happy about?" I jammed the remote control a few more times and avoided their eyes.

Amy wiggled out of her jacket. "We bumped into Denise as she was leaving. She told us you're getting a break from this place."

"Yeah. On Friday. Whoopee." There it was again; my impending venture into the exhibition grounds of the real world.

"Maybe we can do something." Amy draped her jacket over a chair.

"Sure. We'll go dancing. So. What's new with you?" I tried to fold my arms across my chest in a show of defiance, but my right elbow wouldn't bend. I slammed my hands into my lap instead.

Amy's smile broadened and her eyes met Stu's. He grinned at her.

I looked from one to the other. "You can't be *that* excited just because they're springing me for an afternoon."

"Well, sure we are," Amy said quickly.

"Right. What else is going on?" I turned off the television and tossed the remote onto the coffee table in front of me.

"Tell her." Stu sat in a chair so low that his knees seemed to rise higher than his waist, making his long legs look even more gangly than usual.

"You'll never guess what happened." Amy squeezed her hands together.

"Give me a clue," I said dryly.

"They found the stuff. The stolen stuff. Not all of it, and I can't have it back right away because they have to keep it for evidence until the court business is finished, but —"

"Slow down," I said. "You're talking way too fast. You mean —"

"From the robbery. It's like a miracle or something." She sat beside me.

I felt my jaw drop. The look of pure joy on Amy's face pushed my sullen mood into the background. "But they said you'd never see it again."

"I know." She nodded happily. "That's what I mean. A miracle."

"What about ... did you get —"

"They've got her mom's jewellery," Stu said. "All of it."

"That's fantastic. How'd they find it?" I asked.

"Following up on some other break-in," Amy said. "Stu has good news too."

Stu's cheeks flushed crimson. "I got a scholarship."

"So no student loans," Amy said.

"Wow! That's great. Really great." I gave Stu a thumbs up sign and as big a smile as I could muster.

Everyone but me has good luck.

So? Be happy for them.

"And now everything is perfect. You're getting out of here for a while on Friday, so we can celebrate. For all of us."

"I'm not exactly up to celebrating," I said shortly.

Look at me! Look at me! Your local freak show star is free!

Amy's cheeks flushed. "Nothing fancy. I mean, we can just rent a movie and eat egg rolls or something.

"That's what Mom and Denise wanted to do."

"So they can celebrate with us. Marnie and Keith too. Maybe we could have a party. I know. We'll have a tea party."

"A tea party?" I laughed in spite of myself.

"At your house, of course," Amy said.

"That's a great idea," Stu said. "I'll bring the china. Mom

just finished painting a really cool china tea set, tray and everything. And she *did* say I could use it anytime —"

"You're going to *bring* china?" I shook my head.

"We can order a special cake ...." Amy's eyes narrowed into thinking mode.

"We'll need balloons," Stu said.

"Definitely," I said sarcastically. "What would a tea party be without balloons? Helium ones, with congratulations written on them."

Stu's head bobbed up and down enthusiastically. "And some plain ones too. Lots of balloons."

"Oh, goody," I said. "And let's not forget the fancy table linen."

Amy pulled a pad of paper out of her purse and began to take notes.

* * *

By the time Stu and Amy left, the rain had stopped and I was almost looking forward to a temporary escape from my prison.

Day 52

... I haven't seen Amy look so light and cheerful since last Christmas. I'm glad for her, really glad. We phoned Mom and Keith, and they both think this crazy tea party idea would be a lot of fun. So it's a go. Everyone who'll be there has seen me before, so I won't have to worry about how awful I look. Stu is even going to make some invitations for us — any excuse to be creative — and ...

"Dayle?"

My arms and legs fluttered helplessly and the pen flew across the room, landing on Mrs. Sheffield's empty bed. She had been discharged that morning. I flipped the journal upside down on my lap.

"Sorry. I didn't mean to scare you." Keith's voice trembled. Red ringed his eyes. He moved zombie-like across the room and retrieved my pen, then held it in the palm of his hand and stared at it.

A cold rush of fear flooded my chest. "What's wrong?" I pushed my journal aside and worked my legs over the edge of the bed to face him.

"It's Pete."

"He's feeling pretty lousy, isn't he? I'm going to see him after supper."

Keith dropped onto Mrs. Sheffield's bed and stared at his shoes. "He's gone."

"What?" My heart leaped in panic. "They sent him back to ICU?"

"No. No. I mean ... he's ... he's really gone. He ... he died." Keith's voice fell to a whisper.

"No. No. I was just there. We played chess last night. He told me I was a lousy player and I told him I let him win. We had a rematch for tonight. He can't be dead. He can't be ...."

"That infection he had ... it turned into pneumonia and his lungs weren't strong enough ...."

I walked across the room on quivering legs and sat down next to Keith. I put my arms around him and held him while he trembled.

My own sobs came silently.

Pete and I stand inside the fire pit, surrounded by flames. "I can beat you out of here," I say. "Wanna race?"

Pete snickers. "No way a woman is going to beat Pete Wallace. On your mark …."

I crouch into a starting position and wait for the signal. It rises above garbled hospital talk crackling through an intercom speaker.

Room 529. Stat. Streptococcus bacteria ….

White blood cells on the increase ….

Code Blue.

"… get set … GO!"

I fly through the wall of fire, barely singed, but Pete stumbles and falls. I hear his cry for help and I'd like to leave him there, but something makes me turn around and reach for him instead.

" Pete! I'm here. Pete!" I grope through the smoke and flames until I feel his sticky, burned flesh. I pull as hard as I can and his dead fingers crumble off in my hand. As he falls backward into the flames, I hear him screaming my name over and over and over ….

CHAPTER TWENTY-EIGHT

Friday, July 25: Day 55

WHAT A SHAME ....

But look at her good side ....

The other victim ....

Whispers swirled around me, sucking my breath away. Were they really talking about me or was it just my imagination? It didn't matter. I could still feel their eyes boring into my back; burning, prying, curious.

Mrs. Wallace kept glancing at me, too. Was she shooting bullets my way from the other side of the funeral parlour? I couldn't blame her; I survived and her son didn't.

I wished I'd never left the hospital, or that I had at least gone home with Mom and Denise instead of coming to Pete's funeral. But I'd made my choice.

An oppressive kind of ache had wrapped itself around me from the moment I'd found out that Pete was dead. It might have been guilt or anger at myself for my vindictive thoughts, or it could have been grief. Maybe it came from all of those things combined, but whatever the reason, I could not stay away from his funeral.

Pete, my friend — in spite of everything. What we shared no one else could know, and that made a powerful bond. I'd never told Pete how I felt — maybe I didn't even realize how I felt myself until it was too late. Worst of all, I'd never forgiven him and I'd missed my chance. Just like I'd missed the chance to say goodbye to Gram, to tell her how much I loved her.

Anguish slid over me like a tight rubber glove, squeezing my breath away. The world swam before my eyes.

I felt a light hand on my left elbow. "Dayle, what's wrong?" Amy's worried whisper rose above the drone of mourners waiting to give their condolences to the Wallaces.

Stu frowned. "You're hyperventilating."

"I can't breathe." As I sucked in mouthfuls of air, I kept my eyes focused on my shoes — real shoes, not slippers. Navy, to match my dress, the one I'd borrowed from Denise, the first real clothing I'd worn in nearly two months.

The dress rubbed uncomfortably over my back and chest, even though it draped like a sheet over my thin frame. How much weight had I lost? Five kilos? Ten? My feet hurt, my head throbbed and my stomach ached. I would have given anything at that moment for a healthy dose of morphine, but they'd taken my morphine away and replaced it with codeine a few days earlier. Jade had been right about codeine. It didn't seem to help much.

"We should go." Amy spoke firmly. "Keith?"

Keith blinked and turned to look at me, his dull eyes ringed with shadows. "I know ... we should ...." His arm slipped gently around my waist.

"I'll be okay." I tried to steady myself without leaning on Keith. "You need to be here. I'll be fine."

"The Wallaces will understand, Dayle. This is too much ...." Marnie spoke softly, but her voice was rough and raw, her eyes red and weary.

"I just need a little fresh air. I'll go outside and —"
My knees buckled, but Amy and Keith caught me before I fell.

Curious glances became outright stares and the drone around me intensified until my lungs felt as though they would burst.

Keith stared at me through pained, glassy eyes. "There's a bench outside —"

"You stay. I can go myself."

I wiggled free of Amy and Keith and pushed my way through the crowd, trying not to look at anyone else for fear of seeing pity.

Jade touched my elbow as I passed. One look at her wan face almost convinced me that she was worried.

"Dayle? You okay?" I recognized Cougar's voice, but it carried a level of concern that I'd never heard before.

I nodded and kept going. Another hand touched my elbow. I turned, hoping — no, expecting — to see Keith, or maybe Amy. It was Mrs. Wallace.

"Dayle." Her eyes met mine — controlled, focused — but wet around the edges and red from nearly two months of tormented, futile hope.

I nodded, trying to squeeze a tangled ball of emotions back down to my stomach.

"I know this must be very difficult for you. I wanted to thank you before you left. The time you spent with Peter before ... well, it meant a lot to him. He felt terrible about his part in what happened ...."

His *part?* The whole thing was his fault. Didn't she know how furious I was with him? I'd been expecting her rage and she was thanking me. It was just too much. All of it.

My cheeks burned and the makeup on the right side of

my face began to itch. Naomi had warned me it was too soon to wear it for any length of time. A thin layer of fog rose over my glasses from the damp body heat filling the room and I felt myself sway again.

Mrs. Wallace leaned forward and gently hugged me before I had a chance to collapse. "Good luck, Dayle. And thank you again." Her voice broke then, but she turned away before I could see any tears fall.

* * *

Amy and Stu found me sitting on a bench under an elm outside of the funeral home.

"Keith?" I asked numbly.

"He's gone with Marnie to the cemetery." Stu said gently.

I nodded. "Good. That's good."

"He'll call you later." Stu held up his car keys. "You want us to take you home?"

"I don't want to go home." I didn't have the strength to explain my sorry state to Mom and listen to her say she'd told me so, that I wasn't ready for a funeral. "I want to go to the cemetery."

"But you really shouldn't be on your feet." Amy smoothed her skirt and sat on the bench beside me.

"I want to see where they're putting him."

I wouldn't let them talk me out of it.

* * *

Pete was laid to rest in the shade of an elm. I stayed in the car as the minister spoke over the grave. I couldn't hear most of what he said, but I did catch a few simple words written by Tennyson.

God's finger touched him, and he slept.

I knew he was wrong. Pete wasn't sleeping. He'd be somewhere else — with Gram, I hoped. He didn't deserve that other place, not even after all he'd done, all the misery I'd wished on him. But wherever he was, he'd be watching. What if he knew what I was thinking, that I'd silently challenged him in that awful race?

Other words about death by Tennyson sprang to mind — words that chilled me.

Come not, when I am dead,
To drop thy foolish tears upon my grave,
To trample round my fallen head,
And vex the unhappy dust thou wouldst not save.

In my heart, I had asked for revenge. Now I had it. What right did I have to be here grieving?

* * *

I stumbled into the house to find Mom and Denise waiting anxiously at the kitchen table in front of several unopened boxes of Chinese take-out food and a two-litre bottle of cola. Mom leaped from her chair. "You're okay?"

"Of course I'm okay," I snapped. "Why wouldn't I be?" And then I broke down and sobbed. "I didn't know this would happen, Mom. I really didn't know. And it's just not fair. Poor Pete. It could have been me. Poor Pete."

"Oh, Dayle." Mom opened her arms, tears in her eyes. I leaned against her shoulder and she held me close, just like

Gram would have. "It's okay. It'll be okay." She rocked me and stroked my hair and let me cry until I couldn't cry any more.

* * *

It was almost a relief to return to the hospital that evening, where burn scars were normal, and people didn't stare or whisper about what a shame it all was.

CHAPTER TWENTY-NINE

Sunday, July 27: Day 57

A THIN TRICKLE of hot night air stirred over the sheets on Mrs. Sheffield's bed — my bed now. I thought I'd be glad to be free of her continual chatter, but since she left five days ago — the day Pete died — solitude had closed in around me like a shroud. Every anxiety I had lurked behind my eyelids, ready to pounce. Solitary confinement. What worse curse could there be?

I glanced at the clock. Ten thirty. Stillness cloaked the room; even fresh air from the window couldn't lighten the gloom. My eyelids flickered and I let them close, just for a moment. Long sinewy fingers of a familiar Chameleon tune crept toward me.

> *If lust is the need consuming your soul,*
> *I can cut you a deal.*
> *No forms to fill out, no money down,*
> *Just sign your name on the seal.*
>
> *Come dance the dance with me.*
> *Dance in the flames and you'll see,*
> *What you desire*

Can be found in the fire ....
And the price?
Misery.

Vengeance, they say, belongs to the Lord,
But if you're too impatient to wait,
I'll help your cause for a signed credit note,
And catch up with you down by the gate.

I tossed and turned in my bed, trying to escape the accusing throb. Was the tape player on? I didn't remember turning it on. My eyelids flickered, but I couldn't force them open. I tried to shut out the savage beat, but it sucked me deeper and deeper into a dark abyss.

"Dayle! Wait! Dayle!" Pete calls out to me, his voice an eerie wail. I run faster, blindly, through a dense fog of smoke and heat. I hear his footsteps thudding behind me, closer and closer ....

His charred fingers grab hold of my wrist and creep up my arm. The pungent stench of burned flesh sears my nostrils and fills my throat until there isn't any room for air, and the world around me explodes in a ball of fire.

A silent scream rippled through my chest and I jerked up from my pillow. Beads of sweat trickled down my back. I looked at the clock. Only ten forty. I didn't dare close my eyes again, not even for a second. How would I manage to make it through another night alone?

I needed to see Keith.

I pushed myself off the damp sheets and picked up the receiver; it felt cool in the palm of my hand, cold against the hot flush of my cheek. But I hung up before the first ring.

How could I ask him to come? Or wake him if by some miracle he was sleeping? For the past two days, his visits had been short, spent in near silence and when he *did* speak, the despair in his voice raked my soul.

Marnie told me that she'd gone over to the Wallaces with Keith on Saturday. "I've never seen him look so awful," she told me. "He's just so ... so full of regrets."

I asked Marnie what she meant by that. She had opened her mouth as if she was going to respond, but took a deep breath instead and stared at the floor for a moment. "Just give him time." Her whisper had barely reached my ears.

I looked at the clock again. What about Amy? I'd been very careful not to ask her for anything since I'd been here. In spite of how well things were going between us, pride held me back. Or it might have been fear; what if I asked too much? But maybe pride and fear were all used up. I dialled her number and let the phone ring a dozen times. I knew she couldn't be at work; the Highway Garden Centre would have closed over two hours ago. Was she sleeping? Out with Marnie or Stu?

A click and a cheerfully recorded message, Amy's voice. *Please leave your name and number ....*

I thought of the last message Amy had left me — the one about the break-in — the message I'd never bothered to check on. I slammed the receiver down so hard it toppled over the side of the phone, bobbing toward the floor. I picked it up and slammed it again a few times. "Damn, damn, damn!" Cursing gave me a split second of satisfaction, but as the words exploded from my mouth they left behind a vacuum that sucked in more rage. I savagely punched another number into the phone, the only other number I could think of.

Denise picked up on the eighth ring. Her voice was groggy.

"It's me. Where's Mom?" I demanded.

"Out with Dr. Burke. What's wrong?"

"I can't sleep. And there's no one around to talk to." I tried to soften my voice, to hide my fury and frustration. "What are you doing?"

"I *was* sleeping." Denise yawned noisily.

"Oh. Sorry." Did I sound sympathetic? "I'm tired, but I can't sleep. Everything still itches and hurts, and they won't let me have morphine any more." I gave her a moment to offer to come. She didn't.

"Why don't you come over?" I swallowed my frustration long enough to try and sound pitiful.

"Now?"

"Well ... yes."

"It's a long drive from Selkirk this time of night, Dayle, and I'm tired." Denise sounded very far away.

"No limit on visiting hours in this ward." I tried coaxing her.

"I was planning on visiting you in the morning."

"You didn't come yesterday." I laid in a little guilt.

"I was busy, and —"

"If you cared about me, you'd come *now* — when I need you!" I didn't have to try too hard to add a few loud sobs for emphasis.

* * *

About forty minutes later, Denise stood in my doorway with her hands clasped in front of her long pale cotton dress. The warm yellow light of the burn ward hall illuminated her from behind, surrounding her with a soft glow. If she had let her hair fall down around her shoulders instead of hiding it under a baseball cap, she would have shone like an angel.

The sight of her sagging shoulders nagged at the ball of guilt that had grown in my stomach since I'd hung up the phone. "Thanks for coming," I said meekly. "I just couldn't stand being alone here for another minute."

Denise tugged the peak of the cap down over her eyes and stepped into my dimly lit room.

"When did you start wearing caps?" I sat on the edge of the bed and pulled the sticky nightgown away from my chest.

Denise shrugged. "Joseph gave it to me." She pointed the crest above the peak. "See? Raleigh Roofing." She folded her arms across her chest. "Well, I'm here. What was so awful that it couldn't wait until morning?" Her voice was tired, her words clipped.

My guilt evaporated. How could she ask a question like that after all I'd been through? I glared into the shadows at her oval face where I knew perfect cheekbones and a clear complexion lay. People always told us how much we looked alike. At least they used to. "How can you *be* so mean?" I stood up. "I just need some company. You don't know how lucky you are to be able to go and do whatever you want whenever you want. To be normal. To be beautiful. Your life is perfect."

"Dayle, my life isn't perfect. Nobody's is."

"How can you say that? You have everything."

Denise adjusted her cap again.

"Why don't you take off that stupid cap so I can see you? Are you afraid to look me in the eye?"

Denise slowly raised the cap from her head. I expected to see her hair cascade around her shoulders. It didn't.

I squinted into the shadowy place where she stood. My

mouth fell open. "Denise Meryk, what did you do to your hair?"

"Don't look at me like that." Denise smoothed her hands over her cleanly shaved scalp and tossed the cap on my bed. "Do *you* like it when people stare?"

"Why would you cut your hair off?" I circled her, amazed and horrified at the same time.

She smiled. "I liked your new style. It has a certain aura of sophisticated spunk."

"What does Mom think?"

Denise laughed. "She never said, and I didn't ask. She smiled, though, when she saw me. Joseph likes it. He says I have a lovely head."

"You're crazy." I sat on the edge of my bed again, still staring. "And so's Joseph."

"The good thing about hair is that it grows back." Denise moved to the empty bed across from mine and sat down. "We'll let ours grow back together."

I couldn't speak, overwhelmed.

"Is it Pete," she asked softly. "Is that why you can't sleep?"

"I guess. Pete and a lot of stuff."

"So, tell me."

The stories poured out, haltingly at first. All of them, from my concern about Keith's despair, to the tension still lurking between Amy and me. My own despair, my fears. I even confessed the horrible truth about my unspoken race with Pete.

"Oh, Dayle." Denise moved next to me. "Anyone would feel angry over what happened, and I think most people would contemplate some kind of revenge. Nice or not, it's human nature. But the point is, you didn't *behave* vengefully. Look at all the time you spent with him before he died.

He taught you to play chess and you gave him hope. I'll bet he took that as a sign of forgiveness. I don't think anyone could have done anything more."

As Denise spoke, I studied her, maybe for the first time ever. She was beautiful and she had that poise, but she had something else too, a kind of strength rippling below the surface.

"You and Amy will work things out," she continued, "and as far as Keith goes, he just lost his best friend. He'll be grieving for a while."

"You know what I wish?" I asked.

Denise shook her head.

"I wish that I could have told Pete and Gram how I felt about them before they died. I wish I could have had the chance to say goodbye."

Denise took my hand. "People don't always get that chance." She frowned thoughtfully. "You know, maybe that's why Gram wanted you to be the one to spread her ashes. The rest of us *did* see her that day, in the morning. She was so weak ... maybe she knew ...." Denise shook her head and closed her eyes. When she opened them again, tears ran down her cheeks. "Oh, Dayle. So many awful things have happened this year. But we'll be okay. Really, we will."

Tears sprang from my eyes too. I put my arm around my sister. "Of course we'll be okay," I said softly.

Denise nodded and ran her hands over her bare head in what looked to be an absent-minded gesture. Then a smile slowly crept over her face. "This is good. Especially now, in summer. A lot cooler than a full head of hair."

"And no tangles to worry about," I added.

"No shampoo. No cream rinse. No blow dryers. That should add an extra twenty minutes to each day."

"If we don't have to shampoo, Mom'll expect us to cut down on shower time."

Denise groaned. "I hope not. Love that hot water."

"The only bad thing is ... have you noticed how shiny bald heads are? Gotta get some powder to dull the shine."

Denise giggled, then laughed, and then we both laughed, and the sound was enough to drown my anxieties, at least for the moment.

* * *

Denise fell asleep before I did, on the bed across from mine. I pulled the covers over her and closed the window. Enough fresh air had blown through the room for one night.

There's this mythical bird called a Phoenix — a beautiful bird with sweeping, red-hued tail feathers and a pure sweet singing voice. Every five hundred years or so, the Phoenix consumes itself with fire. But the fire doesn't kill it. The old bird becomes ash, and out of those ashes another bird rises, a kind of purified resurrection of the old one.

— STU INGALDSON

CHAPTER THIRTY

Tuesday, August 5: Day 66

HOME SWEET HOME. A light wind clipped through the trees around the white brick house before me and stirred the scent of freshly mown grass and potted petunias. Birds — robins, mostly — sang a cheerful greeting in spite of the day's dry heat and I felt good. Tired, itchy and sore, but good, wanting nothing more than to climb the stairs to my bedroom and sleep. I closed the van door softly and breathed it all in.

"C'mon, Dayle." Denise sounded impatient. "Mom's waiting."

As Joseph pulled my suitcase out of the Windstar, I wondered again why Mom hadn't been there to pick me up at the hospital. Or why Keith couldn't have taken a little time off work. Wasn't this cause for celebration? But Keith didn't feel like celebrating anything. I knew that.

The house seemed empty when I stepped inside, with no one in the kitchen before me, or on the stairs to my left. I turned to my right and saw a wall-length poster coloured with bright felt markers hanging above the living-room sofa: *Welcome Home Dayle!* The artistic hand-lettering reminded me of the entry Stu had made in my diary all those weeks ago.

Just as I began to suspect that the poster and the unnatural silence meant something was up, Mom stepped out from the dining room holding two wine glasses filled with lemonade. She handed me one and smiled. "For the bravest girl I've ever known."

They came out of hiding then — Keith, Amy, Stu, Marnie, Dr. Burke, even Daddy, Cassandra and Carmen — bursting with laughter, chatter and gurgles.

Wild thumping exploded in my chest. Excitement. Gratitude. An overwhelming feeling of claustrophobia. So many people all at once, when I had become accustomed to two or three at a time. Why hadn't anyone warned me? My limbs trembled. I grabbed hold of the wall between the foyer and the living room to steady myself, then took a deep breath and smiled for the well-wishers crowding around me.

We missed you, Dayle!

Glad you're back ....

You look well ....

Denise touched my elbow and leaned toward my ear. "Gram would be proud of you." It was then I realized that even though the house was nearly full with people I loved, emptiness lingered. I made an excuse to escape and hid in the bathroom to compose myself.

* * *

Gram's lupines were still blooming, even though by the middle of July the tall flowery spikes were usually finished, leaving only their palm-like foliage. I twisted one stock and plucked it free from the cluster. Deep blue. Like the colour of the sky in Amy's puzzle, *True Blue*. I sat on the broad, limestone slab in the rock garden, a spot that overlooked the entire backyard but still kept me out of direct sunlight.

Keith stood beside Marnie across from Amy by the corner fence at the end of the yard, on the other side of a cedar arbour thick with engelmann ivy and bright splashes of purple clematis. Marnie sipped a glass of lemonade, apparently intent on whatever Amy was saying. Keith seemed to be listening too, but his arms hung limply at his sides and his face had no expression. Amy, on the other hand, was fully animated. She leaned toward Keith and Marnie as she spoke, her hands flying about for emphasis. I watched, amazed at the transformations: Keith and his silence, Amy and her newfound confidence.

Denise rushed past me with a tray of lemonade. "Salad bar open soon. Need a refill?"

I shook my head and repositioned my broad-brimmed straw hat. I wondered if I'd ever get used to wearing it, or if my injuries would *ever* heal enough for me to face the harsh rays of the sun again.

Amy's shoulders rose and fell as if she'd just expelled the last of whatever it was she had to say. Keith looked my way, then headed toward me. "Hey. Room for two?" He nodded at the rock. I shifted toward the edge of the rock and Keith sat down. "Nice to be home?" He smiled but his eyes were glazed over, as if he was caught in a space somewhere between past and present.

"Yeah. I was getting a little bored with the hospital routine." I smiled too, hoping to cheer him up.

Keith gently swirled his glass. Ice cubes clicked against the surface, cold and wet. His poker-straight back slowly curved into a more comfortable posture and his legs loosened a little. His left knee brushed against my right leg. "Oops. Sorry." He tensed again and sidled away from me.

"It's okay. It doesn't hurt that much unless I stand on it a lot. It's just itchy."

His eyes narrowed slightly, as though he didn't believe me.

"Honest."

"Good." He twirled his glass between his palms and breathed more easily again. "I'm uh … I'm sorry about the past couple of days, about not visiting." He clutched the glass in one hand and grabbed my hand with his other. "It's not that I didn't want to see you … it's just …" His voice tapered off and he shook his head.

I squeezed his hand. "I know."

As we sat there hand in hand scrutinizing the lawn, a pair of sandals slipped through the grass. The long, hairy toes protruding from them wiggled like nervous worms. I followed the toes up past khaki shorts and a beige T-shirt to Stu's flushed face. He had one hand behind his back; the other fiddled with his wavy pony tail. "I've uh … I made you something, Dayle. A kind of welcome home gift." He thrust an oddly shaped, tissue-wrapped bundle toward me.

Stu's gesture caught me off guard. I handed my flower to Keith and took the package with trembling hands, staring at it.

"It's not going to open itself." Keith grinned at me.

Stu scratched the thickening stubble on his chin and cleared his throat.

I untied a trail of curly red ribbon, then ran my finger behind small, neat strips of tape. Inside the tissue lay a wooden bird about twice the size of a man's fist. Its tail feathers fanned out like those of a peacock, but they were fiery red instead of blue and green. The rest of the bird's feathers ranged from deep orangey yellows through emerald greens and sapphire blues. I turned the carving around, examining the careful details from the finely textured plumage to the sleek narrow beak and polished eyes that seemed to glitter knowingly. "What kind of bird is this?" I ran my fingers over the rough grey base from which the bird rose.

Stu jammed his hands into the pockets of his safari shorts. "Uh ... it's a phoenix."

"Any relation to the Phoenix Suns?" Keith asked.

Stu raised an eyebrow and his mouth tweaked into a grin. "Basketball birds?"

I gave Keith a playful jab with my elbow. "Isn't the phoenix extinct?"

"Not exactly. It's a mythical bird that's supposed to die and then rise from its own ashes. It's a symbol of rebirth. Of starting over."

"Is this the bird you were carving earlier this summer from the driftwood you found at the lake?" I asked.

Stu nodded and looked at his toes.

I swallowed hard and tried to think of something to say that would express my gratitude for his gift, his effort, and everything it meant.

Keith touched the bird's tail feathers lightly and shook his head in wonder. "I knew you were talented, Stu, but this is really amazing."

I finally managed to find my voice. "It's beautiful. I've never had a gift like this. Thanks." I clumsily hauled myself to my feet and kissed Stu's cheek. A wave of red washed over his face.

"Hey, Keith!" Denise rushed past. "Come and help me set up a few extra chairs."

Keith stood and gently thumped the lupine against the side of his leg. He shoved his free hand into the front pocket of his jeans and followed Denise.

Stu watched Keith go. "How's he doing?" he murmured.

"He's not himself, that's for sure. Especially since Pete ... you know."

"Maybe he feels a little responsible," Stu said. "I mean, it happened at his uncle's place and Keith's the one who organized everything, right?"

I nodded, watching Keith dutifully arrange chairs with Denise.

"Maybe he figures if he hadn't had the party, Pete would still be around and you'd be okay."

"Maybe that's it." I remembered how Denise had felt responsible for what had happened to me, even though she wasn't. I watched her arrange food on the picnic table, then pop a bright red cherry tomato into her mouth. Denise had moved past her feelings of guilt; surely Keith would too.

Stu pointed to the table of food. "Let's go eat. You can try some of my new tomatoes. I used a mini-green house this year to plant them earlier so they'd be ready sooner. I kind of like them. They're not as sweet as I want, but next year ...."

* * *

"I'm so glad you're out of the hospital." Cassandra bounced Carmen on her hip, oblivious to the thin string of drool running from the baby's mouth to the sleeve of her white silk blouse. "Stephen is thrilled too. In fact ...." She glanced over her shoulder to the picnic table where Daddy stood sipping beer from a frosty mug, talking with Dr. Burke. "We've got a little something for you."

Daddy nodded at Cassandra, then strolled toward me with his hands behind his back. A broad smile played across his face, as if he was about to present me with something wonderful, something that would brighten my life and take my mind off the horrible things that had happened to me.

Isn't that what Daddies did — rescue their princesses?

"I ... uh ... we weren't sure what you might want or need so ..." Daddy whipped a thin white envelope out from behind his back.

My heart sank. I opened it. Another cheque — for five hundred dollars.

Daddy cleared his throat. "Not as original as Stu's gift, I guess. But maybe you can use it to buy some new contact lenses and a wig —"

"Or a portable CD player ..." Cassandra gave Daddy a small, quick frown. "Or clothes or whatever you want. Treat yourself." She hugged me with her free arm and smiled warmly. "You deserve it."

I stared at the cheque and swallowed hard to squelch the lump in my throat. "Thanks." I gave Daddy a quick peck on the cheek and realized that for the first time in my life, I didn't have to stand on my toes to do it. How long had it been since I'd stood next to Daddy? Two years? I had grown up and not just in height.

Bright sunlight paled my father's tan and highlighted his thinning hairline, and it suddenly occurred to me that he wasn't as tall or as handsome as I remembered him to be. He wasn't as sure or as right. The image I'd been clinging to was the flawless vision conjured by an adoring ten-year-old. It was really all I knew of him; a snapshot from the past. And all my father knew of me was what he remembered from that same moment in time. So he relied on teddy bears for comfort and money when all else failed. Daddy — Dad — did the best he could with what he had. I suddenly understood that his gestures were as much a show of love as anyone could expect.

I leaned forward and gave him a left-armed hug with all the strength I could muster. "Thanks, Dad, Cassandra. This is great. Really. I'll let you know what I decide to do with it. I'm glad you could fly out early in the week like this."

"It's good to see you home, Sweet Pea." Dad kissed my forehead.

* * *

"She's adorable, isn't she?" Marnie sat next to me on the sofa, bouncing baby Carmen on her lap.

"She sure is," Amy said. "Can I hold her?" She took Carmen from Marnie and began to twirl around the living room with her. Carmen's infectious giggle soon had Amy, Marnie and me laughing too.

I fingered the gold heart drop around my neck and leaned forward for a better view through the patio doors between the dining room and the backyard. Keith stood between shadow and sunlight, holding an empty glass. He shifted his weight from one leg to the other, watching Joseph and Stu talk as Joseph tuned his guitar. From time to time Keith would nod, but his lips never seemed to move. His despondency knotted my stomach.

"... and we'll bring stuff home and go over it with you, okay?" Amy's voice filtered in through my thoughts.

"What?"

"Schoolwork," Marnie said. "For grade twelve. It starts in a few weeks."

Amy stopped prancing around with Carmen and looked at me. "Aren't you glad?"

"Glad for what?" I asked.

"That you still passed, even though you missed the last month of grade eleven?" Amy kissed the soft curly hair on Carmen's head.

"I guess."

Keith set his glass on a small side table. He picked up Gram's lupine and opened the patio door. "Uh ... you guys want to come back out?" he asked. "Joseph's going to play us a few tunes on his guitar."

Amy looked at me, her eyebrows raised.

"I'd like to," I said, "but the bugs and stuff out there ... it just makes me feel itchy."

Keith stepped into the dining room and closed the door, nodding at Carmen, "Cute baby."

"You want to hold her?" Amy didn't wait for an answer; she plunked Carmen against Keith's chest. He thrust out his arms to catch her, one hand still clutching the lupine.

"Let's go find out how well Joseph can play, Marnie. And maybe get some more cheesecake." Amy plucked her dessert plate off of the coffee table and Marnie followed her outside.

Light, easy notes of a classical guitar rose in the background. Carmen wiggled and cooed at Keith and the tightness bled from his shoulders. He ruffled Carmen's curls, then smoothed a finger over her plump, rose-kissed cheek. "Sure is soft," he said, as he sat down beside me.

"Babies are." My hand flew to my own cheek — the rough, imperfect one. I felt jealous of Carmen all over again.

"A new life with a clean slate." Keith kept his eyes on the baby as he spoke.

The background music darkened and a ribbon of anxiety wound itself around me. Stu was wrong about what troubled Keith. He had to be. Keith seemed too morose for Stu's theory to make sense. Sure, it was his uncle's place, but how could he have known what would happen? How could he have stopped it? Even in his grief he had to realize that. I reached out and squeezed his knee, hoping that I could change the subject and take his mind off whatever plagued him. "You're finishing up a few houses now, right?"

Keith nodded.

"I'd like to see what you're working on."

He shrugged. "No big deal."

"What about the big one on Highland? I bet it's gorgeous. Why don't you show me?"

"Sure. If you want." He kept staring at Carmen. "We'll do whatever you want."

It was a solemn pledge, a vow to fulfill a debt.

I rubbed the side of my neck, soothing the itch of rubbery, scarred skin, and tried to tell myself that Keith just needed a little more time and he'd be fine. That we were fine. And that it really was great to be home again.

CHAPTER THIRTY-ONE

Monday, August 18: Day 72

THE DOOR TO GRAM'S ROOM was closed. I took a deep breath. As I pushed it open, a trace of her favourite perfume enveloped me. For a split second, I expected to see her sitting in her rocker reading a book. But the chair was empty and the parquet flooring rang hollow beneath my feet.

Boxes of things Mom had planned to discard or give to the Salvation Army still lay on the floor, flaps open. The few cartons we'd managed to finish packing after the funeral and before my accident were piled by the closet, neatly labelled. Proof of Gram's existence had been sorted and filed into categories, reduced to cheap packing crates and felt-pen categories — *Scarves, Knick-Knacks, Clothing*.

A box with a whiskey logo stamped on the side sat on Gram's bare mattress with the flaps folded closed. Her favourite painting, *The Tangled Garden*, by J. E. H. MacDonald — a painter from the Group of Seven — leaned against it.

The print seemed so dark, with drooping sunflowers and overgrown weeds framing a patch of flowers, that I wondered why Gram had liked it as much as she did. When I picked it up to study it more closely, I realized that there was much more to it than an unkempt garden. MacDonald played with light and colour, drawing my eye through the centre of the painting, leaving me curious about what lay beyond. He seemed to have captured the garden at a precise moment, when a sliver of sunlight had swept out from behind clouds, lighting a bounty of flowers hidden by the disarray.

Perspective is everything.

I propped the painting against Gram's dresser and stood back to study it from a distance. There was something hopeful in the tangles of green, something inviting. The Tangled Garden would warm the chill of my white bedroom.

A cushion of quilted squares, fashioned from my great-grandmother's collection of fabric scraps, lay on the seat of Gram's rocking chair. I slipped into the chair and held the cushion to my chest. With my eyes closed, I swayed back and forth. The familiar creaking rhythm hypnotized me into sensing Gram's presence almost as clearly as I had on the nights I'd fallen asleep listening to her rock.

So, Gram, what about Keith?

I almost expected to hear her answer, to give me an idea or two about what I could do to bring him back from that dark abyss he floundered in. I wondered if her old journals might hold some answers — but where did she keep them?

I dropped the cushion on Gram's bed and searched through the boxes on the floor. Nothing. I opened the louvered doors to Gram's closet. Every inch of the space was crammed. Hangers held clothing that must have dated back to the 1950s. The top shelf was packed with books, shoe boxes and collections of odds and ends. An old steamer trunk, a few pieces of other luggage and dozens of pairs of shoes lined the floor of the closet. Sorting through it all would be a daunting task.

"What are you looking for?"

I jumped and swirled around, gasping.

"Sorry. I didn't mean to startle you." Mom put the quilted cushion back in the rocker and sat on the bed, her hand on the box. "If you tell me what you want, I might be able to help you find it."

I managed to catch my breath. "You know where everything is?"

Mom laughed. "That would take a while. She saved everything from old shoes to hair ribbons, and even though it's all as neat as a pin, I can't say I've ever figured out her method of organization. I haven't even touched the closet yet." Her smile faded. "After the accident ... well, it was just too much. And I think you and your sister should have a say in what stays or goes."

"I'd like to keep the painting." I pointed to *The Tangled Garden.*

Mom nodded.

"Tough job, deciding." I sat on the other side of the box.

"It brings back a lot of memories." Mom closed her eyes for a moment. "I spent many nights lying awake rehashing things while you were in the hospital. What went wrong between Olivia and me. Why you and I are often at odds." She opened the box. "When I finally found the courage to go through a few more of her things, I began to see her differently, as someone more than simply my mother. She was a real person with strengths and weaknesses. Someone who made a few mistakes along the way — but she always tried to do what she thought was right."

Mom pulled a card out of the box. A twelfth anniversary card. "This was the last anniversary my parents shared."

To Livy, my love,
for now and always,
Fred

She closed the card and ran her fingers over the heart-embossed surface. "You know we didn't get along all that well. I think my attitude toward her was just habit." She looked up. "Sounds awful, doesn't it?"

Her raw, moist eyes gave me another glimpse of the emotional side that I'd never seen before the accident. I was still trying to get used to it. "Maybe that's what's wrong with you and me sometimes," I said slowly. "Bad habits."

A smile softened Mom's face. "Habits find a way of working their way into any relationship. But that's only part of it. The truth of it is that up until now you and I just haven't gotten to know each other as well as we should have. And that's my fault. I spent too much time on the road when you were growing up. I missed so much along the way."

I looked at my feet. "Maybe we both did."

"That can change."

I looked back up again and smiled. "It is changing, isn't it?"

"You're right." Mom leaned across the carton to give me a quick hug. "Now, what were you looking for?"

"Gram's journals. Do you know where they are?"

"The only one I've found so far is the most recent one … the last one. It's in there with a few other things." Mom motioned to the open box and I peered inside.

There were a couple of scrapbooks and photo albums, a well-used leather-bound Bible, along with several loose photos and cards, a faded and frayed book about Australia and the small cloth-covered book I recognized as Gram's journal.

I pulled it out of the box, but I couldn't bring myself to open the cover. I was afraid it might break the flow of discovery unfolding between Mom and me.

Mom folded her hands in her lap. "I wish I could have seen Olivia for the person she was while she was alive. Especially after your father left. She did so much for us, but I was too absorbed in my own problems to notice."

I ran my fingers over the linen-like texture of the journal cover, smooth in places, rough in others. "You sound like Gram, wishing she'd made peace with her dad before he died." I raised my legs to the bed to relieve the pins-and-needles feeling in my right calf and leaned into the headboard.

"Maybe that's why I found your experience after the accident so interesting." Mom rubbed her brow thoughtfully. "If Olivia — Mother — is still out there somewhere, maybe she knows what's happening here, with us. Maybe she knows how I feel."

"Maybe she does. She told me something that night, after the accident ... something I was supposed to tell you ...." I closed my eyes, searching through a distant mist. "She told me to tell you ... that she loved you, and that she was sorry."

Mom sucked in a quick, sharp breath.

My eyes popped open again. "What? What would she be sorry for?"

"Probably for the same things I am."

"And what exactly does that mean?"

"For not trying harder to see things from each other's perspective."

I groaned. "You and Gram are a lot alike. You both love to talk in riddles."

A faint smile tugged at the corners of Mom's mouth. "It

runs in the family."

"Oh really?" I smiled and pointed at the formidable closet. "Maybe if we tackle the closet we can solve a few riddles. And then ..." my voice lowered, "... there's the lake. Have you gone through any of Gram's things there?"

"No. No. I haven't gone to the lake yet this year ... it was always much more of a home to her than this place was. I still think we should all go together." She placed Gram's card back in the box. "Are you ready yet, to spread her ashes?"

I closed my eyes.

"It's okay. I don't want to push you. Would you like to go up there for a weekend? Summer isn't over yet."

"Maybe." I leaned forward and ran my hands over the pressure garment squeezing my right leg. "It's a long drive when you can't stay in one position very long." I couldn't think of any other excuse to avoid the trip.

"I know. Well, you can think about it. I'll see if I can find Gram's other journals for you. I suspect they're in her steamer trunk in the closet."

"Okay." I leaned forward and rubbed my right leg again.

"Looks like you're getting pretty itchy," Mom said. "Let's go find the aloe cream." She held her hand out to me and I took it, surprised at the warmth and strength of her grasp. She helped me to my feet and we left Gram's room together.

CHAPTER THIRTY-TWO

GRAM'S PAINTING lay propped against the wall by my closet, the only spot of colour in a wash of white. For some reason, the clean untouched look that I used to love about my room seemed too perfect now. I felt out-of-place in such a pristine environment. I buried myself in Gram's journal to take my mind off my discomfort.

The journal had a pattern of line-drawn gardening tools on the cover. It crackled when I opened it, still stiff with newness, rich with the scent of fresh paper. She'd only written on a few pages and what she had jotted down was loosely formed and difficult to read, as if it had been recorded by a weak hand. Her last entry was dated only days before she went to the hospital.

December 20

... I tell myself that it's time and that there is nothing I can do to stop it, but I'm not ready to go. There are so many things I still want to do, for Aileen, for the girls, even for myself. Australia. That photography course at the high school ... it just isn't fair. Still, I know I'll soon see Fred again and that is a comfort ....

A box of Gram's other journals lay beside my bed. Mom had found them in the old steamer trunk and brought them to my room, as promised. I dug through the collection looking for an old one to begin with. I opened a faded pink plastic-covered diary with a broken lock. It had been written in Gram's sixteenth year.

September 12

Dear Diary,

Robert really is a dreamboat! Not only is he tall and handsome, but he's a true gentleman. He took me for a walk by the lake after the football game today and held my hand, and when I began to shiver in the nippy wind, he draped his football jacket over my shoulders. It nearly reached my knees.

"Olivia," he said, "you're very special to me." And he kissed me, right on the lips. I thought my knees would give way.

I think I'm in love.

Now all I have to do is find a way to break my date with Fred Brown for the Fall Dance, so that I may go with Robert. I never really wanted to go with Fred anyway. He's very sweet, but rather dull.

I couldn't imagine Gram breaking a date with Fred Brown, my grandfather, to spend time with Robert Whoever-he-was, no matter how handsome or wonderful he might be. From the stories Gram had told me, Grandpa had been anything *but* boring. He was the kind of man who orchestrated surprise candlelight picnics at midnight and would go to see the same movie three times in one week, just because Gram had been crazy about it.

I wondered if Robert might have been the young man in the picture I'd found in Gram's dresser years ago. Why had she pretended she didn't really know who he was, or that she didn't care about him? Maybe she was just embarrassed about me finding out that she'd ever dated anyone besides Grandpa. Obviously, Robert had been a mistake. I found it hard to associate the enthusiastic, infatuated young girl who wrote that entry with the wise, patient woman who was my grandmother.

There was a lot more about Robert, and her father's aversion to him.

October 15

Dear Diary,

Papa has forbidden me to see Robert again. He's too worldly, Papa says, but he won't explain what he means by that. How can I stop seeing Robert? He is so wonderful and kind, and he makes me feel like I've never felt before. My heart actually flutters whenever he looks at me. A wild kind of static, a kind of magnetic force surges through me whenever he's around and I want to crumble into his arms.

Papa has a terrible temper. I know there will be consequences for continuing to see Robert, but I really don't care. This is my life and I will not live it by someone else's rules.

Was this Gram? I knew her to be strong and determined, but here she seemed defiant. I flipped the page to find a thick ridge of torn edges where the rest of the pages should have been. An angled tear had removed the top half of one remaining page. The date and the first part of the entry were missing and what was there had been hastily scrawled:

> ... my apartment here in Winnipeg is cold and lonely, and I'm afraid I won't make my rent this month. I had to miss three shifts at the dry cleaner's this week and Mr. Dobson is not pleased. If only I could go back to school and get my teaching certificate, or even find the time to improve my secretarial skills, then I might not have to depend on such a crotchety employer. But there just isn't time to improve myself, not with all of the responsibilities I have now.
>
> Fred drove all the way in from Kenora last night. He asked me to marry him. I think I will say yes. He is a kind and thoughtful young man, and right now, I don't have the strength or courage to manage on my own.

I reread that passage several times. I couldn't imagine Gram without strength or courage. The whole thing sounded like an episode from a soap opera. Her father must have kicked her out for continuing to see Robert, but what had happened to Robert? And how did she end up alone in Winnipeg?

Friendship outlasts romance. Gram really was speaking from her own experience when she told me that. Her friendship with Grandpa obviously outlived whatever she'd had with Robert.

I tried to read the rest of the journals in order. They covered the early years of Mom's life, with very little reference to Gram's parents or her older brother, John. It seemed that Gram and Mom and Grandpa — Fred — were very happy together until Grandpa died in that awful car accident.

July 15

Aileen found out everything about her father last night. She's been so despondent since Fred's death. Why couldn't she have asked me about him instead of snooping through all my old letters and journals? I shall burn them all! Or at the very least, find a better hiding place.

She is terribly angry with both Fred and me, accusing us of deceiving her when all we tried to do was protect her. How can I make her understand when she won't speak to me?

I think we'll go to the lake today. Perhaps if we spend some time in a family place, she'll be able to see what she has and put her disappointments aside.

God how I miss Fred, and the feel of his strong arms around me, and the way he always knew how to make things right. I think I'll wear this old grey cardigan of his forever, just so I can keep the smell of him, the feel of him, close to my skin.

I closed the journal with trembling hands. Poor Gram. And poor Mom. What had she found out about Grandpa that was so terrible? Why didn't she ever mention any of this? Could it be that she'd pushed it too far back in her mind to remember? Or was it just too painful to think about?

My heart ached for Gram and the loneliness — the helplessness — she felt when Grandpa died. I knew all about feeling helpless myself, with Keith and with the horrible twists and turns my life had taken.

I missed Gram terribly. I rolled onto my side and clutched my pillow to my chest. The urn stared at me from my dresser. I thought of the note beneath it, the one Mom had brought home from the hospital after Gram died. It wasn't in Gram's handwriting, but the words were clearly hers.

My dearest Dayle,

We may not have time to say goodbye, and I have something important to ask of you. As you know, I would like to be cremated, and I would like you to be the one to take care of my ashes. At the lake, in the spring ....

The note ended there. Gram's voice had faded before the nurse could find out what else she had wanted to say.

I studied the urn for a moment, then carefully raised the lid. The coarse grey flakes held no hint of the colour and life Gram had once had. When I thought of Gram, I remembered her words and deeds and warmth, not her ashes. So what was the point of clinging to them? Why couldn't I just go to the lake and spread her ashes?

I still need her. I don't want to let her go.

I fell back on my bed and closed my eyes against the glaring white walls of my room.

CHAPTER THIRTY-THREE

Thursday, August 21: Day 75

"YOU WANTED TO SEE what I've been up to." Keith opened the front door of Number Five Highland Bay. "This is it."

The wonderful fresh smell of newly cut timber filled the air. Much of the interior existed only as framework, but I could tell from the wide open rooms and vast expanses of sunlit glass that it would be a showpiece when it was completed.

"I promised Dad I'd finish drywalling before university starts. Just the main floor left to do." He shoved his hands into his jeans pockets and gave me an easy smile that made my heart feel light. "This is absolutely my favourite house so far." His eyes glowed with some of his old energy.

"It's going to be beautiful. Do I get the grand tour?"

Keith led me up the stairs without letting go of my hand. "Gotta watch out here. Railings don't go in until the rest of the drywall is up. Wouldn't want you to fall." The look of accomplishment never left his face as we travelled from room to room. "Three thousand square feet in all," he said. "I helped design it."

"Sure sign of a guy who wants to be an architect. Did you get into the classes you wanted?"

"Yeah. Registered on Monday. I'm glad I decided not to go to Waterloo." He kissed my cheek and smiled, and I felt good.

We finished the tour in the family room which was just off a large area where kitchen cabinets would go. Keith opened the French doors to let in a light breeze, then stood in front of them, looking off into the distance with his hands on his hips; a broad, shadowy silhouette against a deep blue sky.

I framed that image of him in my mind and savoured it.

So many things about our time together had lost their glow lately. Lee's egg rolls didn't taste the same when they were consumed with everyone else in tow. I didn't enjoy big-screen movies any more either. My prickling, aching, right side made it difficult to sit still for two hours, especially when I felt everyone staring at me, even in the dark.

Pool nights at Sam and Marnie's house were horrible too. I knew I couldn't pull my right arm back far enough to strike the ball, so I sat on the sidelines watching. Everyone else tried to mask the ringing silence of Pete's absence with busy hands and loud voices and too much laughter. Forced laughter. Laughter that couldn't erase the dull grey film from Keith's eyes — or Marnie's.

Even at my house, where Keith and I spent most of our evenings together, someone else was always present. Mom, Denise, Dr. Burke, Joseph, Amy, Marnie, Stu ….

So many times I wanted to scream for peace, for privacy, but I bit my tongue for Keith's sake. He seemed to need activity and lots of company to keep his mind off Pete. I tried to pretend it didn't matter, but the constant company tired me out. The worst part of it was that Keith and I never had a chance to talk about anything important. Maybe this day would be different.

"Someday, I'm going to build myself a house like this," Keith said. "On a larger piece of land." He pointed to the backyard. "I'd plant a stand of evergreens and border the yard with elms. The ones that resist Dutch elm disease. Or maybe I'll go for oaks. And I'd put a play structure in the shade, close to the patio. You've seen the one Dad built for me, haven't you? Around that big tree in the backyard?"

I nodded. "The elm that's as old as Lower Fort Garry."

"Yeah. But the best part of it is the treehouse overlooking the river. I should take you up there sometime. You'd love the view. I still climb up at night once in a while, just to look at the stars." His shoulders rose and fell easily, and a look of contentment washed over his face.

"Gram and Amy and I used to do that at the lake. Watch the stars, I mean. We'd sit on the dock or the cabin steps and see more stars than you'd ever imagine the sky could hold. Everything is so much clearer without city lights to wash it all away. It's like a little piece of heaven out there."

Keith turned to face me, shadows creeping over his face. "You ever have any ideas about your grandmother, where her ashes should go?"

I shook my head. "No. Not yet. And I guess, even if I did know what she wanted … I'm not sure … I'm not sure if I'm ready."

Keith gently took my hand and swallowed hard. "I know what you mean."

"I can't even bring myself to go to the lake yet. I know everyone else is itching to go, but …" My voiced faded away. A thin cloud passed over the sun and the room cooled.

Keith let go of my hand and pressed his back into the side of the doorframe, balanced on the edge of inside and out. "Do you believe there is a heaven? Life after death?"

Images flashed across my mind: of Gram in the light, and of Pete, whole again, without pain. Isn't that how he would be now — in spite of my dreams? I'd never mentioned the light to anyone but Denise after the reaction I had had from Mom and Dad. But maybe Keith needed to know about it; it might let him feel some peace for Pete. I nodded slowly. "I know there is."

He ran his hands through his hair. "What makes you so sure?"

I leaned against the wall and closed my eyes. "That night, after the accident ... I saw it." I explained what happened after the explosion; the strange sensation of being pulled out of myself, the light and all who lived there, and the feeling of joy it gave me. "That place I saw is real. It has to be. And that's where Gram is. What else could it be but heaven?"

Keith turned his face toward the sky and breathed in deeply. "If there is a heaven," he said slowly, "then there must be a hell." A leathery crease surfaced above his brow and he gave his head a shake, pulling himself upright again. He pointed to the area just beyond the French doors. "Patio there for sure," he said quickly. "On the other side of a multi-level deck. Do you like those slate patios, the ones made with flat slabs of dark grey rock?"

I nodded. "I like slate."

He pulled me in close and pressed his lips to mine. It was a tender, passionate kiss but he held me lightly, as though he were afraid I might break.

A huge lump swelled in my throat. I felt my shoulders stiffen.

Keith pulled away. "What's wrong? Did I hurt you?" Panic flickered across his face.

"No, no. I'm fine. I just ... we need to talk."

"About what?"

"About ... " I closed my eyes and blurted the rest of the sentence. "About everything that's happened."

He pulled me close and held me tight. "There is nothing to talk about." His words were fierce enough to end that discussion and any others that might have followed.

* * *

Keith dropped me off early that afternoon and I spent the rest of the day in Gram's room, searching for answers. When I'd consumed as much as my tired brain could hold, I went back to my own room and wrote in my diary.

Day 75

I feel numb all over. Is it me? Or is he just so sad about Pete that he can't let himself think about what's happened? I miss the way things used to be for Keith and me.

I keep having this dream where we're dancing. As we spin around faster and faster, he slips away — or maybe he isn't slipping away but pulling away. I can't tell.

I find escape in Gram's room and the search for answers. The Robert in Gram's diary is the boy in the photograph. According to Gram's high-school year book, his full name is Robert Carlyle.

Whatever happened to Robert? Maybe when I fall asleep tonight I'll be so busy thinking about the answer to that question that I won't dream about Pete, or worry about Keith sliding into the shadows.

CHAPTER THIRTY-FOUR

Monday, August 25: Day 79

EARLY EVENING SUN shone through the windows, illuminating a row of plaster heads along the sill. One of them was formed from my head and used to cast the clear Uvex face mask I wore as a pressure garment on the right side of my face — except when I was out in public.

Seven of us were gathered around the table in Naomi's office, six of us burn survivors. We were there to share our experiences and a plate of gooey homemade brownies, courtesy of Mrs. Sheffield. At least the others were there to share; I couldn't even bring myself to sample the brownies, as though somehow sinking my teeth into one would be like admitting that I belonged with the group. But just looking at the rich chocolatey treat made my mouth water.

"... people see us different, no matter what we wanna tell ourselves." That was Cynthia, the woman with the thick scarred lips. I studied her mouth as she spoke, curious about how she could have burned only the bottom part of her face. I was far from brave enough to ask her.

Randall, the young man missing an ear, agreed. "It's true. Nobody wants to admit their bias against someone else's physical uh ... limitations."

"Maybe not, but they sure do like askin' questions." Cynthia swirled her cup of milky coffee and stared at it. "People've walked right up to me in the grocery store and said, 'Hey, what happened to your mouth?' Some just gawk at me like I'm a freak, which is even worse. It makes you wanna just stay home."

My face flushed and I smeared a drop of cranberry juice into the plastic wood-grain surface of the table. I knew what she meant about wanting to stay home. I had a meeting with the high-school principal tomorrow morning, to discuss home-study arrangements. I couldn't face the high-school cauldron. Not yet.

Randall nodded. "Yeah. It's okay if kids act that way. They don't know any better. But adults, well —"

"But why wouldn't they be curious?" Gerard, the old man with missing fingers, interrupted. "Most of them never seen people like us before. I got used to being asked what the heck happened to me. I tell 'em I was drunk and fell asleep with a cigarette in my hand. Maybe that'll make them think twice about booze and smokes."

"So, Gerard," Naomi asked, "you don't think their curiosity is rude?"

"Naw." He flicked a gnarled, yellow-stained hand at her. "It's human nature. I did this to myself. It was bad, but it coulda been a whole lot worse. And I got the chance from time to time to turn it into something good."

All things work together for good. Gram's voice surfaced through the echo of Gerard's words. What good could possibly come out of what happened to me? I shifted uncomfortably in my chair and tried to reposition my extended right leg without kicking Gerard in the shin.

Mrs. Sheffield smiled at Gerard. "Mr. Simpson, you have

a wonderful attitude."

A soft, gravelly voice rose from the far corner of the table. It belonged to Esther, a young woman with a badly scarred neck and shoulder, and a pretty face. "That's it, isn't it? Attitude."

"Yeah. But that's not all. You gotta be tough," Cynthia said. "Real tough. And you need tough people around for support."

"My boyfriend wasn't so tough." Esther's voice fell to a whisper. "He broke up with me last weekend."

In the awkward silence that followed, Keith's image flashed through my mind, a broad silhouette against a deep blue sky, caught between light and shadow. I hadn't seen him since that day on Highland Bay. He had phoned a few times, told me he was busy working, but there was a flatness to his voice and a distance that covered more than the length of the telephone line. Maybe his problem *was* me. Maybe in spite of everything he'd said, looking at me was just too much to bear.

A lonely ache rose in my chest and I wanted nothing more than to escape from this place, this horrible discussion. There were too many victims here.

"I'm really sorry that happened, Esther." Naomi said softly.

The others murmured agreement.

"A lot of things change," Cynthia said. "It's like you got a line drawn in your life. Before and after. Your old life, who you were before, is dead, gone ...."

A shiver ran down my spine. Cynthia tended to overre-act. The word *dead* carried too much finality. There was nothing dead about me. Even Gram, who was dead, wasn't. There was that place of light ....

"It *is* like a death." Esther looked at her hands. "It's like grieving. You can't go on until you can find the courage to say goodbye ...."

Why couldn't they leave death out of it? The ache in my chest worked its way to my throat, squeezing. There was too much death already. Gram ... Pete ... I couldn't breathe. I pushed my chair away from the table.

"You have to grieve," Cynthia nodded.

"Makes sense," Randall said, "the idea of grieving, saying goodbye ...."

Grieve, grieve, grieve. Say goodbye. What the hell were they talking about? Why did everything have to be so final? I stood up and slammed my chair back into the table. "You guys are all crazy. I'm not saying goodbye to anyone."

Stunned silence followed me out of the room and drummed against my skull for the entire drive home. Mom, thankfully, absorbed herself in a radio talk show as she drove me, and didn't ask any questions.

* * *

A filmy cobweb dangled from the corner of my freshly painted bedroom ceiling, gently floating back and forth on the evening breeze from the window. One quick whack and it would be gone. Finished. Kaput. *Goodbye.*

Light knuckles rapped on my door. "C'mon in," I growled.

Denise poked her head around the corner. "Keith called while you were out."

I pushed myself up to a sitting position. "Yeah?"

"Guess he forgot you had that meeting tonight. Said to tell you he was thinking about you and he'll call again tomorrow." She smiled and gently closed the door.

I suddenly felt brighter and the weariness in my bones lifted. Keith. I'd been worrying for nothing. He was thinking about me. What more proof did I need?

I fell back on my pillow, elated, and stared at the ceiling again. A tiny black spider made her way along the outer edges of the cobweb, widening the boundaries as she went. I wondered if she realized how precarious her position was, that a huge monster lay below, someone who could destroy her and everything she was working for.

But instead of squashing the spider, I gently scooped her up with a tissue and set her free just outside my bedroom window. She scuttled away, ready to spin a new web — a new life — somewhere else.

Like Gram.

Esther's words came back to me. *You can't go on until you can find the courage to say goodbye ....*

Why did "goodbye" have to be so terrible, so final? Wasn't it just a kind of transition? Life was full of transitions. Changes. Like my room. I couldn't live in it the way it had been, all cold and white, so Denise and Joseph had repainted it for me in a hue of green inspired by *The Tangled Garden*. Amy and I had tie-dyed my curtains and bed cover in varying shades of blue and green to go with the new walls — the new me, whoever that was.

I looked at the urn on my dresser. Images of the lake flooded over me, the woodsy smell of timber and pine, the cool feel of water on my skin — the peace of the place. And I wanted to be there to soak up the space that had meant so much to Gram. To find the courage to look for answers. To do what she had asked me to do. Suddenly, saying goodbye to Gram's ashes didn't seem like such an impossible task.

They were just a symbol of her life anyway; I didn't need them to know that she would always be with me.

Some things changed, others didn't.

An exhilarating lightness filled my chest and I wanted to share my decision with someone. With Keith. Maybe it would help him find a way to deal with his grief for Pete. Then we could get our lives back on track. I swung my legs over the side of the bed. How long ago had he called? I'd forgotten to ask.

I chucked the tissue in my wastebasket and picked up the phone.

Keith was working late, his mother said, at the house on Highland Bay. Did I know where it was? I assured her I would have no trouble finding it, even in the dark.

* * *

Seven of the eight homes on Highland Bay were finished and occupied. Cars and mini-vans lined the street and driveways. Moonlight cast long haunting shadows over the street from several newly installed but unlit street lamps, so in spite of the brightly lit homes around it, the street itself was dark.

Something clattered in the night and childish laughter rang out — kids enjoying the last blast of summer holidays.

Keith's Jeep sat in the middle of the driveway surrounded by mounds of paving stones, leaving no room for my vehicle. I parked on the street behind another minivan, then forced my weary legs to carry me to the house.

Most of what I could see through the dimly lit picture window had been drywalled and taped since my last visit. As I climbed the front steps, the massive bevelled brass and glass doors gradually revealed a narrow view of the kitchen and family room area. Keith stood in the pale yellow light between the two with his back to me, fastening another piece of drywall in place.

I stepped around several empty pails of drywall compound and lumber scraps and watched for a moment, drinking in the sight of him. He looked good in his tight white T-shirt, arms taut, back straight; I couldn't wait to rush in and give him a hug.

A shadow fell over him. He set his power screwdriver on a stepladder and turned to face the darkness. The shadow shortened and narrowed, assuming the unmistakable curves of a young woman as the figure it belonged to approached.

Jade. The back of my neck prickled.

But as the figure came into the light I saw that it wasn't Jade — it was Marnie. I sighed with relief and put my hand on the doorknob. As I was about to turn it, Marnie reached up to wipe drywall dust from Keith's cheek. She burrowed her face in his shoulder, then he gently raised her chin with both of his hands and leaned down to kiss her; a long, slow kiss.

No ....

Keith and Marnie?

But he was just thinking about me — that's what he told Denise.

My hand fell back to my side. Questions — dozens of them — slammed through my head with the horrible weight of betrayal.

Why?

How could they do this?

How could he?

I stepped backwards and stumbled over the empty buckets, sending them down the stairs with a clatter. Both Keith and Marnie looked toward the front door, curiosity written on their faces.

I galloped back to the street in a painful, lopsided gait, just managing to hide behind the van before the huge brass and glass door of Five Highland Bay swung open. Without the illumination of street lights, the van was just another vehicle disguised by the shadow of night.

CHAPTER THIRTY-FIVE

Tuesday, August 26: Day 80

MORE HELL. Heat had stolen the day and turned it into an oven, broiling last night's anguish into a crisp. If the air conditioning hadn't broken down we could have stayed in the kitchen or found refuge in my bedroom. But even the basement had lost its cool.

Instead of staying cooped up inside, I pulled two lawn chairs into a small shady corner of the patio surrounded by the spicy green scent of tall cedars. I motioned for Amy to sit and set the garden hose to a trickle, stretching it across the cement where it made a low cool puddle for our bare feet.

Amy dropped a stack of school books on the patio table and plopped into a chair. She folded open the sheet of paper the high-school principal, Mrs. Campbell, had given me that morning, and studied it.

As soon as I sat down, Bud padded through the water and laid his warm head on my left thigh. He whimpered.

"So." Amy dropped the paper to her lap and slurped cola bubbles from the edge of her can. "What's wrong?"

"Huh?" I massaged Bud's ears. He closed his eyes and whimpered again.

"Something's wrong. You've been grinding your teeth ever since I got here."

"I should have left grade twelve for another year." I motioned to the books on the table and pretended that the prospect of tackling them was far worse than finding Keith with Marnie. "How am I supposed to do all that, go to physiotherapy three times a week, and cope with ... with everything else?"

Amy picked up the paper again. "It's not like everything has to be finished at once." She pointed to one line on a page full of lines. "You've got two weeks to read *Tess of the D'Urbervilles,* then another week to write your report. That should be a piece of cake, seeing as you read the book last year. Plus you've got a week's head start on the rest of us. School doesn't start until after the long weekend."

"A week. Big deal." I snorted to keep the tears from falling and picked up *Tess.*

Amy leaned back in her chair and stretched her legs out. "You said Mrs. Campbell will arrange for extra time if you need it. Don't worry so much. Marnie will help you wherever she can ...."

Heat seared my face.

"... ditto for me. Except math. I love math, but I can't explain it for beans. That's Keith's job, right? He said —"

"Oh stop it! Just stop it!" I shouted.

"What?" Amy looked bewildered.

I slammed *Tess* on the table. "Keith and Marnie. Neither one of them are going to help me now."

"What?" Amy sat up straight and drew her legs under her chair.

"You were right about Keith. He's a jerk."

"What are you talking about?" Amy leaned toward me,

frowning. "Keith is not a jerk. He's proved that, over and over again. Hasn't he?"

Bud whimpered at the sound of Amy's confused voice and began circling between us. Amy plucked a taco chip from the table and tossed it into the yard. She flicked her fingers and pointed at it. "Fetch, Bud."

He took off after the treat.

I stared at the gangly German shepherd. "You made Bud fetch? How did you do that?"

"A book from the library. On training dogs."

I snatched another taco chip and threw it onto the lawn. "Go get it, Bud. Get the chip."

Bud cocked his head to the side.

"You have to say *fetch*," Amy said. She threw Bud another treat. "Fetch, Bud."

Bud snapped up the chip and lay on his stomach in the grass.

"He sits now too." Amy turned to face me again. "Enough of Bud. You're not allowed to change the subject. Tell me what happened."

"You won't believe it. Not in a million years."

I spilled the entire story.

* * *

Amy stared at me thoughtfully, chewing her bottom lip. "There's a reason for this, Dayle. Some simple explanation. You know how crazy Marnie was about Pete. She and Keith are both going through such a hard time right now —"

"They're going through a hard time? What about me?" Tears stung my eyes.

Amy put her drink can on the table and pulled her knees

to her chest. "Keith has been there for you, Dayle, through everything. He's not just some guy you've been going out with, he's a good friend too. I mean, that doesn't make what he did any less lousy, but don't write him off like that. Maybe he and Marnie were just ... just consoling each other."

"You weren't there. You didn't see the way he kissed her, like he wanted to lose himself in her." My voice cracked. Bud crept over and nuzzled my arm.

"That's the whole point," Amy said. "He wanted to lose himself. Lose his misery for a while. And so did Marnie."

"There's more to it than that. There has to be. Just look at Marnie. She's so pretty — you've seen the way guys always watch her — and she's nice too. Too damn nice. And me, well ..." My words were barely a whisper.

"Well what?"

"Maybe I'm Keith's misery," I croaked.

"What do you mean?"

"Look at me. Look what I look like. How can I blame him?"

Amy's voice softened. "Dayle, you're still healing and you haven't had any plastic surgery yet. Give things a chance. If Keith was worried about the way you look, he would have cut loose a long time ago. He cares about you."

"If he cares about me, he wouldn't have been kissing Marnie. And if she was *really* my friend ...."

Amy stared at her toes and wiggled them in the growing puddle of water. "Have you talked to either of them?"

I shook my head. "I don't want to."

"Sure you do. And anyway, you have to."

"I do not."

"You need to know why. You deserve to know why. So what are you going to do when he calls? When Marnie calls?

Ignore them?"

"Maybe."

"That's not fair." Amy picked up her drink can and twirled the straw.

"What they *did* isn't fair." I leaned over and picked up the hose, running the icy water over my feet until they numbed. I dropped it again and a sudden increase in water pressure sent it snaking across the patio. Bud sprang from his spot on the lawn to chase it.

"Bud, leave that hose alone." Amy put her drink can down. "I'd be mad too. But I'd still want to know why."

"Everything's been so different since the accident. We hardly ever spend any time alone together. He won't talk to me about much of anything and he hasn't sent me one of those sticky notes in ages ...."

Amy looked at a mosquito on her knee and squashed it into a red smear. "This isn't easy for any of us, you know."

"What do you mean?"

She looked up, her bottom lip quivering. "I know that you're the one who got burned, but it's hard on the rest of us too."

"Hard on you?"

"Yes. Do you have any idea how tough it is to watch you go through all of this?" Tears rimmed her eyes.

I swallowed the thick dry lump in my throat and ran my fingers over the cover of *Tess*. "I guess I never thought about that."

Amy stood, chewing her bottom lip again. "I wonder ... do you think that maybe seeing you reminds Keith of Pete? I mean, maybe he just has to ... to get it all out of his system. To say goodbye to Pete and get past this."

I laughed bitterly. "Funny. I went over there last night to talk to him about that very subject."

Amy retrieved the snaking hose, then wedged it between a few rocks at the edge of the garden with the nozzle pointed up. The water pressure fell again and water burbled over the lip of the hose.

"You owe it to yourself to find out the truth from Keith." Amy scratched Bud's ears. "Start with Pete and work into Marnie. They're connected. They have to be." She turned to face me. "You have to straighten this stuff out and put the past behind you so you can get on with your life."

There was that miserable dividing line again. Before and after.

I watched the steady dribble of water muddy the soil below the rocks and wash it away.

CHAPTER THIRTY-SIX

Friday, August 29: Day 83

A BLANKET OF FAMILIAR SOUNDS wrapped itself around me
— singing birds, wind-rustled leaves and waves exhaling on
the shore. Tension bled from my shoulders. It was far easier
to avoid Keith and Marnie here at the lake than it had been
at home.

Tell him I'm out, Denise.

Tell her I'm sleeping.

From where I stood at the end of the dock, the island lay
within swimming distance. Amy and I had made that swim
a few times, but we would usually take the canoe. A narrow
break in the island's rocky shore marked the place we used to
moor the *Mockingbird.* From there, a rough path led through
a thicket of brush and rocks to a grassy clearing that rose
from behind the trees. Through small gaps in those trees, I
could see some of the larger rocks bordering Gram's wildflower garden. I could even detect bits of colour that I
imagined to be lady's slippers, yarrow, daisies and tiny yellow
beauties whose name I couldn't recall. But it was the end of
August and I wondered how many of the flowers were still in
bloom, how many weeds had snaked through the garden to
choke them out.

Bud pushed his wet nose into my hand and whined.

"Hungry, eh?"

His ears perked up and he barked.

"Me too. Let's go."

I'd only taken a few steps up the stone path toward the cabin when it hit me — no, punched me — in the stomach. The horrible odour of meat cooking over the bonfire brought bile to my throat.

"Hot dog?" Denise stood in the screen-walled gazebo holding a spear full of wieners over a heap of glowing coals.

I shook my head and flew past the gazebo as fast as I could hobble, then up the stone steps to the verandah.

"Dayle?" Amy touched my elbow as I charged past. "What's wrong?" She followed me into the cabin.

"Oh my goodness ... Dayle?" Mom stopped short, a tray of drink cans and pasta salad in her hands.

I gasped for air, my stomach heaving. "I can't ... the smoke ... the smell ..."

Mom's face paled. "It never even occurred to me —"

"It's okay." I gulped again. "I'm not that hungry anyway. I had a sandwich before we came, remember?"

"You should eat. You're so thin ...." Amy said.

"I'll be okay. I'll get something later. I brought a few of those shakes along. You guys go ahead. Enjoy."

"Are you sure?" Mom asked.

"You want me to stay with you?" Amy studied me, a frown on her face.

I looked out the kitchen window at the fire dancing in the gazebo. A hot sliver of fear scraped against my shoulders with each flicker of the flames. "No. I'm okay. Really. Go ahead. I've got a lot to think about. And I'm tired. Maybe I'll just lie down on the sofa for a while."

They made a reluctant exit through the screen door and

I closed the solid pine door behind it, knowing that I wouldn't feel like eating for quite some time. I shut the west-facing kitchen window too, but it didn't help. The stench stuck to my nostrils. Even though it was different than the horrible odours of those early days in the hospital, it was too strong a reminder.

Through the kitchen window, I watched them walk to the gazebo and join a worried-looking Denise. After several minutes of stiff-postured movements and concerned glances at the cabin, I could see the three of them begin to relax.

I turned my back to the window. The sofa beckoned from its cozy spot in the great room. I *was* tired and I knew I needed to sleep before I could face Gram's room; my search for answers would have to wait.

A thin ribbon of laughter trickled in through the glass panes behind me. I turned around again to see Bud slithering on his belly from Amy to Denise, then Mom, nosing for food. Bits of wieners, pasta salad and crumbs of buns made their way to the ground where he snapped them up, looking for more, until Amy sent him off to the side with a couple of wieners of his own.

Denise leaned in toward Mom and Amy, her hands dancing about, telling a story or maybe a long joke. As laughter escalated and anxious glances at the cabin ebbed away, loneliness washed over me.

Sooner or later, I would have to conquer my fear of fire.

I opened the kitchen window again. The cool evening breeze carried the sound of crackling timber toward me — and the smell of smoke. I fought the gagging sensation and shivered. But I stood there. I made myself stand there, with my hands gripped, white-knuckled, on the counter, staring into the flames.

CHAPTER THIRTY-SEVEN

Saturday, August 30: Day 84

DAYLE ... DAYLE ....

My eyes popped open at two o'clock in the morning, sure I'd heard Gram whispering my name. It only took a moment of staring at the sloped ceiling to remember where I was; a moment longer for me to associate the gloomy weight in my stomach with Keith, not Gram.

I gingerly raised myself up on my left elbow and looked around the moonlit room. Amy and Denise lay in the top and bottom bunks opposite my bed, shoulders rising and falling in the gentle rhythm of sleep. I closed my eyes again but sleep wouldn't come.

Dayle, Dayle.

I groped the bedside table for my glasses, then crept to the next bedroom, ignoring the hard, scratchy-aching pull of burn scars that wanted sleep far more than my mind did. I peeked into Mom's room; soft snores confirmed her status. I made my way down to the main floor, remembering to walk on the side of each step to avoid the loud squeak of aged wood that might rouse the others. What I had to do, I wanted to do alone.

I stopped in the great room overlooking the lake and draped one of Gram's thick, knotty afghans over my shoulders for the cozy feeling it gave me. And then I went to Gram's room. I stood in front of her closed door for a moment, gathering the courage to enter.

The door creaked open and I froze. Even in the moonlight I could see that nothing had changed. Patchwork pillows lined the head of her bed, gingham curtains framed the window beside it and a braided rug of fabric scraps warmed the floor between the two. Gram's favourite drink coaster with hand-painted roses and tea stains sat on the bedside table. I half expected her to march in with a book and a cup of tea, ready for a good read before bed. She'd always been a night owl.

I stepped into the room, closed the door behind me and flicked on a dresser lamp. I stood there for a moment, letting my eyes adjust to the new light, running my fingers over the smooth surface of Gram's pine dresser — the one that had belonged to *her* grandmother. I opened a drawer of neatly folded T-shirts and drew one to my face, breathing in the smell of her, faint but still present. When I replaced the shirt, my fingers felt something cold and hard. A large black key. It was very old; one of those long, thin ones with a sculpted loop at one end and a few rectangular teeth at the other.

What did it belong to? There were no keyholes in the dresser. I glanced at the antique armoire in the corner of the room and noticed a keyhole just below the handle of the right door. I slipped the key into the opening, wiggling it a bit before something clicked and the door popped open.

The armoire was empty except for a small suitcase on the bottom shelf. I lifted it out and blew a cloud of dust from its surface. Canvas straps bound its cracked leather shell. It took some work to loosen the rusty buckles fastening them, and when I finally raised the lid, stale mothball air swelled from the case and stuck to my throat.

I sifted through the contents — an ancient box-shaped camera, diaries, a large manila envelope, brown-tinged photos, stacks of letters tied up with yellow ribbon.

Excitement rippled through me as I flipped through photographs of Gram's grandparents, pictures of Gram and Uncle John as babies — some taken at their home in Kenora, others at the cabin. One picture captured a picnic on the island with Gram's wildflower garden — the one her mother had started — as a backdrop. A familiar gingham cloth was spread over the ground beside a picnic basket overflowing with sandwiches and fruit.

The largest photo was a formal black and white family portrait. Gram's older brother, John, looked to be in his early teens. He stood with one hand behind his back, obviously struggling to contain his laughter. Gram, several years younger, clutched his free hand. My great-grandmother stood just behind them both, tall and slim like Denise and me, but with fuller cheeks and a smile like Gram's. My great-grandfather towered over them all, as rigid as a fencepost.

Gram's diaries were packed with entries from her child-hood. I skimmed through them hungrily. Although her father appeared to be strict, he clearly had a sense of fun that I hadn't seen in the other diaries I'd read. Entries told of him taking Gram beachcombing along the lakeshore and teach-ing her how to play ice hockey. One summer evening he had kept Gram and Uncle John up until two in the morning to show them how the stars moved across the sky.

Gram's family came to life in the pages of her diary. I could feel the loving devotion of her mother, Mama, and the kind but mischievous adoration of her older brother, John.

I untied the smallest bundle of letters, all from Uncle John, and skimmed through the addresses. They came from a variety of places like Toronto, New York City, Chicago, Vancouver — places where he apparently travelled on business.

Most of the letters in the other bundle were from my great-grandmother to Gram.

My dearest Olivia,

Papa does not know I am writing to you and for now, we must keep it our secret.

I wanted you to know that John was married last week, to a charming young lady ....

Dear Olivia,

John Junior did not survive. He was born far too early ....

Darling Olivia,

I must go in for surgery tomorrow. The doctors tell me that the operation is relatively safe, but still, I worry. Please know that if anything should go wrong, I will watch over you from above.

And please, try and find it in your heart to forgive Papa. He is a stubborn old mule, but he loves you so. What a shame he does not know how to show it ....

That was the last letter I found from my great-grandmother.

Gram's father wrote only one letter. The envelope was

dated just a year after the last letter from Mama. I looked at the family portrait again, wondering how to connect the strict, unsmiling Papa with his playful side.

Dear Olivia,

In the time since your mother passed, guilt has paralyzed me. I know that both she and John wrote to you many times, and I am grateful for that.

By the time you receive my letter, it will be too late for us to make amends face to face. I confess, I am not a courageous man. My stubborn, foolish pride kept me from telling you that I love you. So I tell this you now and ask for your forgiveness.

I want you to have the cabin in remembrance of the good times we shared there, of how close we used to be. John knows of my wishes and is in full agreement.

If you can find it in your heart to forgive me and grant me one request, I would ask that you spread my ashes over the wildflower garden on the island, so that I may rest with your mother. John and I laid your mother's ashes there in the spring, to symbolize our faith in life's renewal. Perhaps a similar gesture from you will serve as a way for you and me to say goodbye.

You should be proud, Olivia, of the fine young daughter you're raising, and the way you managed to cope with adversity.

With love and respect,
Papa

The wildflower garden ... a way to say goodbye.
Denise had been right about Gram's last request. And

now I knew what Gram had been trying to tell me just before she passed away — that she wanted to have her ashes placed on the island with those of her parents.

The last envelope had no return address on it. I slipped out a single crisp sheet of yellowed linen paper and unfolded it.

Olivia,

I know I am not behaving in the manner suited to a gentleman, but you must understand the pressures I face.

As the oldest child and only son of the Carlyle family, it has long been assumed by my parents that I will attend university and obtain a commerce degree. Father expects me to take over Carlyle Hardware when I graduate and expand the family business to include several outlets in Toronto.

I cannot bear the thought of letting my family down.

I will think of you often, Olivia, and I wish you the very best as you face your own personal challenges.

Robert

Your own personal challenges? What did Robert mean by that? It didn't matter. It was an awful way to cut someone off — almost as bad as sneaking around with someone else behind their back. Wasn't that what Keith was doing — cutting out to let *me* face *my* own personal challenges? Rage shook my limbs — for Gram and for me. Gram didn't deserve to be treated that way any more than I did.

When I stopped shaking, I picked up the manila envelope. Something was stuck to the bottom of it. I flipped the envelope over and freed a photograph — a close-up colour snapshot of Robert and Gram. Although the picture was slightly blurred, Gram's infatuation with Robert was obvious in the way she smiled up at him. He, on the other hand, looked straight into the camera with a smile that creased only one side of his face. But the thing that struck me most about the photograph was the robin's-egg blue of Robert's eyes. *Arrogant eyes*, Gram had called them. That thought obviously had not occurred to her at the time the photograph was taken. Those eyes looked so familiar ....

I thought of a photo in my scrapbook — one of Keith and me, the picture Joseph had taken before we left the house on my birthday. The night of the accident. Pale blue eyes smiled out from that picture too. *My* eyes. An unsettled feeling rose in my stomach.

I dropped the picture to the bed and slipped my hand inside the envelope to feel a wad of pages with rough edges. My fingers trembled as I pulled them out. Torn and yellowed, marked with Gram's unmistakable fountain pen script, they had to be the missing pages from her journal.

As I dropped the envelope on the bed to begin reading those pages, another larger sheet of paper slipped out of it. A birth certificate. I read it once, then again.

Aileen Roberta Carlyle.

Carlyle?

Robert Carlyle was my mother's father. *My* grandfather.

I didn't have my *mother's* eyes; I had my *grandfather's* eyes.

The door creaked and I jerked my head up from Mom's birth certificate to see her standing in the doorway. My heart leaped into a wild erratic rhythm.

Mom rubbed her eyes and yawned. "Came down for a drink of water and saw the light under the door. You couldn't sleep either?"

"No." Mom's birth certificate fluttered in my hands.

"Itchy? Need some aloe cream?"

"No."

Mom stretched her arms and lazily surveyed the room. Her eyes came to rest on the old leather suitcase, the papers cluttering Gram's bed. She lost her sleepy stupor. "What's all this?" She looked at the paper in my hands. "What are you looking at?"

I swallowed hard and handed the birth certificate to Mom.

A small "o" formed on her lips, and she sat on the bed beside me. Another "o" escaped her lips in a long whispery sigh.

Eventually she put the paper down and sifted through the other papers and photographs scattered over the bed. I sat there wishing I could quietly escape, but not knowing how. Questions, loads of them, tumbled through my mind, but I didn't know which one to ask first, or if I should ask at all.

"I always wondered how I'd tell you girls." Mom picked up her birth certificate again.

I still wasn't sure what to say, so I let her speak.

"All of this ..." She motioned to the clutter of papers and photographs around her. "It brings back so many memories." She smiled ruefully. "I suppose I should have gotten over it by now. I was twelve when I learned the truth. Just after your Grandpa died. I felt as though I'd been cheated, loving your Grandpa the way I did when he wasn't my real father."

"But he *was* your real father. He raised you, didn't he?"

Mom nodded. "I understand that now. I must have known it on some level even then. I suppose I chose anger over grief. Anger is easier."

"That's when things went wrong between you and Gram."

"I guess it was." There was a note of surprise in her voice. "You and Denise pointed that out a while back, but it didn't register then. I guess I didn't let it. I wasn't ready to think about any of this."

She picked up the family portrait, her fingers gently touching Gram's young face. "I took everything out on her. That must have made it as difficult for her to talk about all of this as it was for me." Mom blinked and wiped the corners of her eyes. "She did her best, you know. She only kept the truth from me because she was afraid I might be as hurt by it as she was."

"Didn't you ever want to know about your — about Robert?"

"I *was* curious. I did try to find him once, not to meet him, but just to see what I could find out about him."

"And?"

Mom shrugged. "I couldn't find him." She picked up the journal pages and sifted through them, reading portions here and there. She handed them to me. "These pages tell the story in detail. You really should read them if you haven't already. Denise too. I'm so glad you found this, Dayle. It's an important part of my history. Our history. All those years ago ... I thought she might have destroyed it."

I smiled. "Are we speaking of the same Gram? The woman who saved old shoes and hair ribbons?"

Mom laughed. "Guess I didn't consider that."

"Oh. I found something else too — something impor-tant — what I came in here looking for in the first place. I know what to do with Gram's ashes." I sorted through the letters, looking for the one from Papa, then handed it to Mom.

She read it slowly, nodding as she went. A smile softened her face.

"But I should wait until spring."

"Spring will come soon enough." Mom wiped her eyes again. "Let's go make some tea and take it out on the verandah to watch the sunrise."

"I'd like that, Mom."

We left the room with Gram's memories scattered over her bed, no secrets left to hide.

CHAPTER THIRTY-EIGHT

Monday, September 1: Day 86

IT SEEMED that in only two days, vibrant summer green had begun to wane and a cool whisper of fall had slipped into the air moving off the lake. The sound of water gently lapping against the dock was so inviting that I couldn't resist dangling my legs into the lake, even though I hadn't asked Dr. Burke or anyone else if it was safe. I didn't care. The water might have been less than pure and it was cold, but it felt good swooshing against my skin.

Amy plopped down beside me cross-legged, and Bud weaselled in between us. He wagged his tail with a fury that sent his behind bumping into Amy's shoulder, then mine. I tried one of Amy's new tricks; flicking my thumb and middle finger together and pointing to the ground. Bud dropped into a sitting position between Amy and me, his tongue lolling.

Amy scratched Bud's ears. "It feels strange being here alone, just the two of us."

"Don't you mean the *three* of us?" I patted Bud's back.

Amy grinned and pulled off her runners, then slipped her legs into the water. "Glad I brought my truck so we didn't have to go back with your mom and Denise." She threw her head back and sniffed in a noisy draft of air before she spoke again. "You decide what you're going to do?"

"About what?" I picked a splinter from the edge of the dock.

"About Keith and Marnie."

"No. Not really." I flicked the splinter into the water. "Maybe I should just write Keith a 'Dear John' letter like the one Robert sent Gram and beat him to the punch."

"I know what you're thinking and you're wrong," Amy said. "Robert and Keith are *nothing* alike. Robert cut out at the first sign of trouble. Keith didn't. And you still haven't spoken to him about it to find out what really happened." Amy sighed and rumpled Bud's fur. "Sooner or later you're going to have to face him — and Marnie."

"I know this sounds strange, but facing Marnie won't be so bad. I can forgive her. I know how broken up she's been and how much Pete meant to her."

"Too bad you can't give Keith the same kind of break."

"*He* kissed *her*." I shook my head, trying to loosen the image that had been haunting me for a week.

Amy didn't say anything. She pulled her legs out of the water and drew her knees to her chin.

"I guess I just have to ... to sort everything out in my own mind before I talk to him. Can't we just *be* here for a while, without worrying about anything?" I swirled my legs in the water and watched the ripples spread out and away, fading into oblivion.

* * *

Tires crunched over gravel, breaking the pleasant stillness of the afternoon.

I quickly swallowed a mouthful of peanut butter sandwich and put the rest down on a paper plate. "Who's that?"

Amy looked up from her magazine and pushed herself away from the kitchen table. "Do you suppose your mom and Denise decided to ...." She looked out the kitchen window, then whirled around to face me. "You won't believe this."

"Believe what?"

"Hi."

His deep familiar voice floated into the cabin. I didn't know whether to be relieved or angry. I gulped, trying to push sticky peanut butter residue down my throat, and turned to meet his eyes through the screen. "Keith."

His face twisted into a wry grin that made my heart ache and my knees go numb.

"You have any idea how tough it is to find this place?" he asked. "I must have made ten wrong turns before I finally got here."

I forced my wobbly legs to stand, my stiff lips to move. "I guess that's part of what makes it so private."

"Are you going to stay out there or are you coming in?" Amy pulled the door open. "What are you hiding behind your back?"

"Oh." Keith stepped in through the door and presented me with a beautiful bouquet of forget-me-nots and daisies. "Thought these looked like the right kind of flowers for a cabin." His eyes swept the interior and he gave a low whistle. "If you can call this place a cabin."

I took the flowers and stared at them. A polite *thank you* stayed lodged in my throat.

Keith put his hands on his hips. "You said your great-grandfather built this?"

"With his bare hands," I said. "Log by log." I ignored the hand-painted vase on the counter by the sink and dropped the flowers into an empty plastic cup.

* * *

Keith wanted the grand tour, so I led him through the cabin as quickly as I could, to get it over with. But Keith wouldn't be rushed. He marvelled at the upstairs, which was actually a two-bedroom loft overlooking the great room below. "This whole layout looks so modern. And it was built when?"

The 1930s. But what do you care? I shrugged.

"In 1932," Amy piped up. "It was her grandfather's wedding gift to her grandmother. And the only renovations since then were for indoor plumbing."

History saturated every inch of the place, from the stones of the fireplace — hand-picked and hand-laid by my great-grandfather — to the green brocade sofa in front of it. That sofa had been the first piece of furniture Gram and Grandpa had chosen together. The oval braid rugs warming the floor grew from my great-grandmother's basket of fabric scraps. Uncle John's hands had crafted wooden lamp bases, the coffee table, even the clock on the fireplace mantle. Paint-by-number pictures — some Gram's, some Mom's — hung on several walls.

It seemed almost sacrilegious to share this with Keith, after what he'd done. But Amy told him everything. "... and that's where Gram's dad carved her name when she was born." Amy pointed to a smooth dark stone in the fireplace. "Dayle's name is there too."

"Your family's roots are wound around every log of this place," Keith said. "It's kind of fitting. There's something timeless about a log cabin. I've always wanted to build one."

Go ahead. Try. But timelessness means staying in one place.

"There's lots of neat stuff outside too," Amy said. She turned to face me, hands on her hips. "Why don't you show him the birdhouses, Dayle?" She spoke a little too loudly, removing the question from her words.

"Birdhouses?" Keith put down the lamp he was examining and smiled at me. But his smile didn't ease the tight feeling in my chest.

* * *

A half-dozen birdhouse of different shapes and sizes were scattered around the cabin, all made by Gram — with a little help from Grandpa.

"She was a real nature lover, your Gram." Keith shoved his hands in his jeans pockets and watched a flock of sparrows peck seeds from a birdhouse-shaped feeder. He looked at me. "Did you ever find out where she wanted you to ... say goodbye?"

I nodded half-heartedly.

"So? Where?"

I pointed down the path to the lake. "There's a wild-flower garden out on the island. That's where Gram's parents are."

"So when are you —"

"In the spring."

"Oh. A time for starting over. Symbolic." Keith nodded approvingly. "You're awfully quiet today. Anything wrong?"

Before I could answer, a noisy scolding crow swooped

overhead. Keith followed its flight and watched it land on the roof of the screen and stone gazebo, casting long grey shadows over the sooty fire pit within. "Let's go down to the lake," he said.

We made a wide circle around the gazebo and followed the stone path to the waterfront with Bud on our heels. I stopped at the foot of the dock.

Keith shoved his hands into his jeans pockets. "Your canoe here?"

"No. No one got around to bringing it this year."

"Oh. That's too bad. I thought it might be neat to paddle out to the island so you could show me the wildflower garden."

"Don't feel much like it today, anyway."

Keith cleared his throat. "You want to sit on the dock?"

I shook my head.

He jingled his keys. "What ... uh, what do you want to do?"

I rubbed my rubber-soled toe on the smooth deck. "What made you decide to come out here today?"

Keith looked at his runners. His voice fell to a whisper, his words became halting. "I've been waiting all week to see you. There's something I need to tell you about. Something I need to say."

"Let's go back to the cabin." I forced my legs to follow the path one stone at a time with a numb ache bleeding through my arms and chest, sure that I was about to be ditched.

* * *

Amy suddenly decided to take Bud to the shore for a game

of fetch. Keith and I sat on the porch swing, gently creaking back and forth as we watched the two of them shrink into the distance.

"So?" I looked down at my hands — the left one, smooth and pale, the right one, leathery, mottled and red.

Keith cleared his throat. "This isn't easy ... I mean, I don't know exactly how to say this ...."

I looked up, determined to take the bad news without blinking. "Then cut to the chase. I can take it."

Keith studied me for a moment, then rested his forearms on his legs and pressed his fingertips together. "First of all, I want you to know how important you are to me."

I didn't say anything.

"And you have to understand that I didn't plan for this to ... it just shouldn't have happened."

My jaw tightened.

Keith drew in a long deep breath. "I was with Marnie last week. Last Monday night. I mean, nothing much happened except that ... except that I kissed her. It was a dumb thing for me to do. She was feeling lonely and sad and missing Pete ... Anyway, I wanted to tell you about it before you heard it from someone else. I was afraid ... when I didn't see you all week ... you're so quiet today." He took another deep breath. "There were kids horsing around outside when it happened and I thought maybe ... well, you know how rumours spread ...."

My mouth opened but no words came. It had never occurred to me that Keith would confess. Gratitude and relief diluted my anger, but it didn't soothe the wound.

Keith reached over and took my hands. "I'm sorry. Really sorry. I can't believe I did something so stupid ...."

I met his eyes and forced my stiff lips to move. "I can't either. But I'm glad you told me." It was my turn to take a deep breath. "I saw you."

He looked puzzled. "You what?"

"I saw you Monday night. On Highland Bay."

"But you were at your meeting —"

"I got home early and phoned your place. Your mom told me where you were. Remember the lumber scraps and empty pails?"

"That was you? Oh, god." He ran his hands through his hair. "We thought it was some neighbourhood kids ... you know ... a prank. Look. Marnie is ... well, she's a friend, Dayle. That's it. You can ask her. She'll tell you the same thing. She feels as awful about this as I do. Don't be mad at her. It was my fault and it didn't mean anything." His voice cracked.

"It meant something to me," I said.

His eyes met mine, then fell on the pendant dangling from my neck. He reached over and touched it lightly, and the heat of his hand rushed through my chest.

"You remember what I told you, when I gave you that?"

"You said a lot of things. And you'd been drinking."

"I told you that you were special. And I meant it. I still do and I won't let anything like this happen again. I owe you more than that."

"You don't owe me anything. But why did you do it?"

"Why?"

"There has to be a reason."

Keith leaned forward, his hands clasped loosely over his knees. He shook his head and stared at his hands. "I don't think there really *is* a reason ...."

"Does it have anything to do with Pete?"

"With Pete?" Keith looked up. "Well, we both miss him. And since the ... the explosion ... there's just been so much ...

I mean Marnie's the only one who knows how I ...." His voice faltered. "Does it really matter why?"

"Yes. It does. And I think it has something to do with how you feel about Pete's death."

Keith's face paled. "What do you mean?"

"You've been different somehow, since the accident. Sometimes I think it's because of the way I look —"

Keith grabbed my hand. "I told you. That *doesn't* matter to me. It used to, when we first started going out, but that changed pretty quickly. There's something inside of you that's strong and steady, and you have this ... this presence that has nothing to do with how you look. You know what I think of when I think of you?"

I shook my head slowly.

"You'll think I'm nuts." He folded his hands together, and a smile touched his lips.

"Try me."

"I think of Palladian windows with lots of sunlight streaming through them."

I raised an eyebrow.

"Told you." He grew serious again. "See, windows let light shine through. And they're fragile, but they're strong too, strong enough to take cold and heat."

"I've never been compared to a window before."

"You'll notice I chose a classic, elegant style for the comparison."

I laughed in spite of myself. Keith grinned.

"We really shouldn't joke about this," I said. "And you're changing the subject. I was trying to say that you've changed even more since Pete died. It's almost like you're lost or something."

Keith put his elbows on his knees and buried his forehead

in his hands. "I don't know what to say."

"I have trouble dealing with his death too." I sucked in a long deep breath, deliberating on how much I *should* say. "When I first realized that all of this was Pete's fault, I wanted him to pay for it, to suffer —"

Keith's head shot up, his brows furrowed in pain. "Don't say that. Please, don't say that."

"Well, that's how I felt. But I don't feel way that any more. I guess at the time I needed someone or something to be mad at. Now I just miss him. He was my friend too." I took Keith's hand. "Does looking at me remind you that Pete's gone?"

"He shouldn't be gone." Keith pulled his hand away.

"But he is gone, and you have to find a way to accept that. You have to let go and move on. That doesn't mean you have to forget about him. It just means you have to ... to think of him differently." I put my hand on his knee. "I know how hard it can be —"

Keith sprang to his feet and twirled around to face me. "No, you don't know. You don't know at all."

"What are you talking about?"

Keith paced in a small, tight circle. His words splattered out between gasps. "It shouldn't have happened. I'm sorry. I didn't mean for any of this ... for you ... or Pete ...."

"You don't have anything to apologize for." I rubbed my temples and closed my eyes, wishing I could find a way to get through to Keith and dig out what really mattered.

I heard the verandah floorboards creak, then heavy footsteps rushing across the dry fall grass. At the sound of loud agonized cries, I opened my eyes to see Keith slamming his right fist into a nearby tree over and over again, his shoulders heaving, a huge man — no, boy — crumbling. It terrified me. I slowly rose from the swing and stood, tempted to run but unable; unsure of what to do next.

Keith suddenly stopped and gasped for air. When his breathing steadied again, he turned to face me. He leaned back into the tree with his arms dangling at his side, blood dripping from his knuckles, and he closed his eyes. "It wasn't Pete's fault. It was mine."

An icy chill flushed through my veins. "I don't understand."

"Remember how wet everything was?" His eyes opened. I nodded.

"Little bits of paper would light, but they'd burn up before the wood had time to catch fire. I asked him to ...." He gulped. "It was *me* who brought the gasoline over. I was the one who told him to throw it on the lit paper. And he did." Keith laughed shortly. "Good old Pete. Never did anything I told him to before ...." He shook his head. "I was just out of range just as he threw it. It should have been me. Not you and Pete. It should have been *me*."

Images of that night flooded back. The red gasoline can in the back of the Windstar. The taste of Keith's kiss, bitter with the residue of beer. Keith, heading for the van while I showed off my new necklace to Marnie and Jade — heading for the van to pick up the can of gasoline ....

Anger ripped in and out of my gut with the swiftness of lightning — there, then gone. How could I condemn someone in so much pain? My legs wouldn't hold me, so I dropped to the step. "Why didn't you — why didn't *someone* — tell me?"

Keith wiped his eyes. "Pete and Marnie and I were the only ones who knew. Everyone else was just too drunk to notice. Guess Pete and Marnie didn't think it was their place to say ...."

Keith's a good guy, you know. Even if he does dumb things sometimes. Pete's words tumbled back, suddenly making sense. Pete must have told his mother about it too; she had mentioned it at the funeral. *He feels terrible about his part in what happened ....*

"And Marnie ... she *knew* ... she understood ... about everything. So we spent a lot of time together. But she's just a friend. A really good friend, but I swear to you, that's all she is."

I grabbed the railing and pulled myself to my feet. I walked over to Keith and took both of his hands in mine. "It'll be okay." I couldn't feel my tongue or my lips move, but words kept tumbling out of my mouth. "It doesn't matter who did what. Let's just agree to forget it and —"

"Forget? How can I forget?" Keith pulled his hands away, smearing blood over the top of his hand, the palm of mine. "Every time I look at you, I remember what I did. How stupid I was. My God, I killed my best friend and —"

"Pete never blamed you, Keith. I know it. And I don't blame you either."

"But I blame myself." He reached out and touched my cheek, the right one. "I blame myself."

* * *

Gram's afghan kept us warm as we watched the sun set from the end of the dock. The cool smell of autumn unleashed a feeling of decay in the pit of my stomach. Neither of us had spoken much since Keith told me about the explosion, and the pain in his eyes twisted my heart.

Every time I look at you, I remember what I did.

Nothing I could do or say would erase his feeling of guilt

and as long as I was around, he'd keep on punishing himself for something that couldn't be undone. But how could I hide from him? Where could I go? I could tell him I didn't want to see him any more, but that would be a lie and a condemnation all rolled into one and he'd probably feel worse than ever.

Maybe *he* could go ....

I reached for his hand. "When do classes start at the University of Waterloo?"

"Waterloo? Tomorrow, I think."

"Is it too late to register?"

"Why?"

"Maybe you should go. Forget U of M. You and Pete spent two years planning for Waterloo."

"But how can I be so far away while you're going through all this stuff?" An astounded expression washed over his face.

"You can't do any of it for me. You should go. Wouldn't you still like to go?"

Keith shook his head. "Not really. I —"

"Go. For Pete. Think of it as a kind of tribute to him. Finishing something that he couldn't. Look. Whose idea was it?"

"Pete's."

"So it was important to him."

"I guess. But it's not as important to me. Not as important as —"

"You need to go." I took both of his hands in mine and looked directly into his eyes, willing myself to keep a level tone of voice, willing the tears away.

You can do it. You're an actor.

Keith was silent for a moment, then the puzzled look on his face dissolved. "You're breaking up with me." His words sounded as numb as I felt.

I drew in a long breath of cool air. "Not in a bad way."

"I can't just walk away —"

"Yes. Yes you can. I'm telling you to. I can't stand knowing that every time you look at me, you think about what happened and beat yourself up over it. You can't live like that and I can't *watch* you live like that." Even as I spoke with all the determination I could muster, another voice screamed inside my head. *Don't go.*

Keith shook his head. "I care about you too much to walk away. Way too much. Don't you know how I feel about you? I —"

I quickly touched his lips with my fingertips. "Not now."
I feel the same way! Don't go.

"I'll find a way to get past all this." His voice faltered.

"Will you? I mean, don't you think it's always going to be there, somewhere in the back of your mind? You'll never be able to look at me without seeing Pete's ghost, and I'll never be able to look at you without feeling as though you think you owe me something. And you don't, Keith. You don't owe me anything. Sometimes things just happen."

"I won't go," he said fiercely.
Don't go.

The torment in his eyes ripped my heart wide open. Leaving would hurt him; staying would kill him. Tears stung my eyes and what I really wanted to do was hold him and never let him go, but I couldn't let myself cave in like that, so I shouted to hammer my selfish thoughts into oblivion. "Yes. You will. You'll go. You *have* to go ..." I fumbled with the clasp on the chain around my neck.
Don't go.

Keith pressed his hand over the gold heart drop. "Don't."

My hands froze.

He choked over his next few words. "If you really
me to, I'll go. But don't give the necklace back. It means too
much. To both of us."

We sat there for a few minutes, looking at each other,
absorbing everything that had just happened. Then he kissed
me one last time and slipped out from under Gram's afghan.
With a look on his face that said more than any words, he
helped me to my feet and we followed the stone path back to
the cabin.

Don't go!

"Well, then." He stopped by the cabin steps. "I guess this
is it."

I smiled bravely. "It'll be great in Waterloo. Winter's a lot
milder there."

He nodded and shoved his hands into his pockets. "But
I'll miss the cold. Guess I'm used to it." He threw his head
back and studied the sky for a moment. "Clear night. You're
right about the stars out here." His eyes met mine and he
took my hand and squeezed it. "A little piece of heaven." He
gave me a quick smile and straightened his shoulders, then
headed toward his vehicle with steady, mechanical steps.

Don't go, don't go, please don't go!

I pulled Gram's afghan tighter over my shoulders. With
a hole in my heart and that voice in my head silently screaming, I watched the tail lights of Keith's Jeep disappear
through the trees.

ΛPTER THIRTY-NINE

Monday, September 15: Day 100

COME BACK, *come back, please come back.*

I laid the small cluster of soft, creamy suede-petaled roses on Pete's grave, flowers like the ones he'd missed at his graduation ceremony, and turned away. What more could I do?

"You ready to go?" Denise stood behind me, shivering, her hands shoved into the pockets of her coat.

September was cold and hard.

Come back, come back, please come back.

The words followed me all the way home, but it wasn't Pete I was thinking of.

* * *

Day 100

One hundred days ago I was normal and had a life. So did Pete. It's just not fair.

That's what Stu said when I told him what had happened, and that's what Marnie said when Amy told her.

Marnie showed up at my door after that, red-eyed and sad, apologizing over and over again. She asked if there was any way we could still be friends and I told her of course we could, that what happened had nothing to do with her. It was no one's fault. I meant every word.

No one's fault.

Keith starts classes today at the University of Waterloo. He called last week to tell me that he'd been able to register for all of the courses he wanted, and that even though he'd started late, he wouldn't have any trouble catching up. He found accommodation with several other students in an old house near the campus.

"It's weird sharing space with people I don't really know," he told me, "The rent is good, though, and everyone seems pretty friendly. But it's not like home."

He didn't say missed me or that he'd call again and I didn't offer any sentiments like that of my own — even though they were still there, pounding the walls of my brain. They're always there.

But I know I've done the right thing. I keep telling myself I've done the right thing. It doesn't make any difference. It doesn't make any difference at all.

I closed my journal and opened my scrapbook, the one with the folk-art angels on the front, full of messages from Keith. A photograph lay inside the front cover. Keith and me. A nice, tight head-and-shoulders shot, the one Joseph had taken on the front step the night of the party at the Meadow.

Before.

I held the gold heart resting against the base of my throat for a moment, warming it in my hand.

Come back, come back, please come back.

The lump in my throat thickened as I flipped through

the book. A small bouquet of dried forget-me-nots and daisies lay inside the back cover, just across from the last sticky note he'd given me, the one I'd found on the door when I got back from the lake after we'd said our goodbyes.

I ran my fingers over the familiar handwriting and told myself that his note made everything worthwhile, even though I knew it meant he'd never come back — no matter how badly either one of us wanted him to.

Thank you, it said.

He didn't sign his name. He didn't have to.

EPILOGUE

May 31: One Year Later

DIP AND PULL, *dip and pull.*

The canoe slipped through the lake with ease and lightness, guided by the sure steady strength in my arms. Sunlight glinted on droplets of water dripping from the paddle with each stroke and spread across the rippled surface of muddy green.

I peered into the water at my reflection. The burns on my face and neck had faded but they were still there. Although I'd had several surgeries and lots of therapy to restore use of my right arm and leg, most of the procedures that would help make me *look* better wouldn't happen until the end of the year. But Dr. Burke was confident that when everything was finished, the scarring wouldn't be terribly noticeable unless I pulled my hair back.

That was easy for *him* to say. He wasn't the one who had to live with those scars. Still, it sounded hopeful. And as Stu pointed out, scars were a mark of experience. How could I argue with that?

Distant music and laughter trickled across the

water from Joseph's guitar and Denise's flute and a medley of voices — Amy, Marnie, Dr. Burke, Stu. It reminded me that I had somewhere to go when I was done, a place where friends waited and no one worried about my scars.

A family of loons swam just beyond the *Mockingbird;* the proud father escorting a mother with two babies nestled in her back feathers. Spring, the season of renewal, just as my great-grandfather had said in his letter to Gram — the perfect time for the quiet tribute I was about to make.

* * *

I chose to do it just before sunset while the birds still sang and the sky cast a warm glow over the wild-flower garden. A breeze took the ashes from the canister and sent them dancing over the garden and beyond. Gram lived on in memory and spirit, and now she would replenish the soil, giving rise to new life.

As I watched her ashes scatter, I thought about how life's experiences and relationships lived on in memory, shaping the person they belonged to. Like the accident. Like my time with Pete and Gram. Like my family and friends — people who'd been with me all the way. People who would be with me for a long time to come, through university or college — eventually — and everything that lay beyond.

And then there was Keith. Thoughts of him still brought a bittersweet pang and made me wonder *what if* ... No matter how far behind we left each other, he was always there, a part of me, a strong thread in the fabric of my life.

In spite of everything else that had happened between us, I would remember him first and foremost as a friend. That's what I told myself whenever I looked at my scrapbook and fingered the heart-shaped pendant inside. It was easier that way.

Gram was right; friendship *did* outlast romance.

Humming the familiar melody that had cradled us all when we were young, I left the wildflower garden knowing that it was done and it was good. I carried the song with me over the meadow, down the trail through rocks and brush, breathing in the freshness of spring, the scent of new green and hope.

Near the end of the trail, I stopped to look through leaves and branches at the *Mockingbird*, waiting in the sand for the journey back.

I took another step forward. Something crackled.

My heart leaped. Visions of flames exploded in my head and heat washed over my body.

Smoke. Did I smell smoke? I twirled around in a panic, looking for the source of the noise, and a flash of red caught my eye. I twirled around again and stopped short. My shoulders slumped with relief. A wide band of sunset red reflected off the surface of the lake. I looked down; broken twigs lay under my feet.

I laughed softly and looked up again, following the fiery reflection to the dock where Amy sat beside Bud, waiting for me. Smoke rose from somewhere in the trees behind them. Although I couldn't see where it came from, I knew. There was a fire burning in the gazebo, a welcoming, cozy fire — the kind to be shared with friends.

I stepped into the canoe and paddled toward the flames.

OTHER BOOKS FOR YOUNG ADULTS
FROM SUMACH PRESS

The Secret Wish of Nannerl Mozart
by Barbara Kathleen Nickel

The Shacklands
by Judi Coburn

Miracle at Willowcreek
by Annette LeBox

Sweet Secrets: Stories of Menstruation
Edited by Kathleen O'Grady & Paula Wansbrough

www.sumachpress.com